Heir Today . . .

Other Five Star Titles
by J. J. Lamb & Bette Golden Lamb

Bone Dry

Heir Today . . .

J. J. Lamb & Bette Golden Lamb

Five Star • Waterville, Maine

First Edition
First Printing: August 2005

Published in 2005 in conjunction with
Tekno Books and Ed Gorman.

Set in 11 pt. Plantin by Carleen Stearns.

Printed in the United States on permanent paper.

Library of Congress Cataloging-in-Publication Data

Lamb, J. J.
    Heir today— / by J.J. Lamb & Bette Golden Lamb.—
1st ed.
        p. cm.
    ISBN 1-59414-356-0 (hc : alk. paper)
    1. Inheritance and succession—Fiction. 2. Murder
victims' families—Fiction. 3. Americans—China—
Fiction. 4. Hong Kong (China)—Fiction. 5. Uncles—
Death—Fiction. 6. Journalists—Fiction. I. Lamb, Bette
Golden. II. Title.
PS3562.A423H45 2005
    813'.54—dc22   2005007911

Dedication

For Chelsea, Brianna, and Alexandra—the brightest stars of a new generation—with love.

Acknowledgements

This book would not be complete without mentioning Aunt Olga, whose idiosyncratic approach to money dropped us into the world of heir tracers. We must also thank the keen critical eyes and minds of "The Group"—Margaret Lucke, Mary Alexander Walker, and Judith Yamamoto—and our editors, Pat Estrada and John Helfers. And, finally, our gratitude goes to Marcia Muller and Bill Pronzini, who aided and abetted in so many crucial ways.

No one has lived longer than a dead child, and P'eng Tsu died young. Heaven and Earth are as old as I, and the ten thousand things are one.

Chuang Tzu, 4th Century B.C.

Prologue

It would soon be dark.

He watched the staff carefully, surreptitiously—both individually and in relationship to one another.

He tugged an ear and tried to remember how long he'd been studying and memorizing their routines and habits. His mind drew a blank.

He tightened the drawstrings of his pajama bottoms and absently scratched at his crotch, all the time trying not to lose the journal stuffed into his waistband.

Damn his memory for playing tricks on him. Had *she* caused it, or was the goddamn bug finally winning?

But what difference did it make if details drifted in and out, misplaced temporarily? Nothing had been totally lost, at least not yet. He dismissed their harping on his forgetfulness with a shrug, taking perverse pleasure in seeing how upset they became when he didn't show up for a meal, or wandered around half the day with his fly unzipped.

After seventy-one years, he was damn well entitled to a few eccentricities. Besides, the routine of his daily existence had become a bore, as it always did after a couple of weeks at Lester's goddamn convalescent facility.

He smiled grimly.

Even though it took longer each time he was forced to sign himself into Ocean Shores, he always got better.

He glanced over his shoulder. Was anyone watching him

watching them? He snickered. They treated him as though he was senile, even discussed it in front of him. To hell with them. Let them think what the fuck they wanted. It was still his show . . . barely.

He continued to observe, concentrating on the young, dumpy one. She was his favorite—her stringy, greasy hair; the perpetually food-stained uniform; her stale body odors; her disdain for the rules. She fit his plan perfectly. Still, wouldn't the patients' relatives have a fit, if they could see the second-rate staff that ran Lester's posh convalescent home after dark?

Partially hidden behind the end of a heavy walnut bookcase, he watched the flickering television images dimly illuminate those who had gathered in the carpeted recreation room, many wheeled in by the orderlies.

Their solemn faces depressed him. *Storage—storage for the old and the sick and the feeble.*

He shook his head. He wouldn't dwell on that now. He'd made that mistake in the past. Each time, it had almost been his undoing.

No, Jocko Boylan, you've got to stay sharp. They're not going to just let you check out of here this time.

He tugged at his perspiration-soaked sleeves, caressed the stubble on his chin.

She's trying to make you one of the permanent zombies with her drugs. She's getting pissed. Got lucky yesterday, but can't count on fooling her again. She'll catch you the next time, Jocko. If not then, the time after that, or time after that. Sooner or later she'll make you tell. Can't let that happen. Can't let the bastards get off.

Damn, he'd failed to keep track of time. His chest constricted, his heart pounded in his ears. He raised his wrist quickly in front of his face to look at his watch. No, it was okay . . . still a couple of minutes before most of the skimpy night staff took its break.

Gotta get the hell out of here, before Lester lets her into my room again. How could that bastard betray me after all these years? Christ, the money I've paid him!

Boylan's eyes followed the night supervisor and single on-duty male attendant as they drifted toward the staff lunchroom at the far end of the corridor. The dumpy LVN, as usual, moved into the nurse's station to keep an eye on the patients for the next half-hour or so. But he knew she wouldn't stay any longer than it took the other two to move out of sight.

Right on cue.

She moved out from behind the counter and walked rapidly on her white, squeaky shoes toward the front door. He didn't have to watch her after that. The sound of her movements was enough. When he heard the telltale clicks of the double locks on the front door, he counted slowly to twenty. He visualized her grubby motorcycle jockey waiting outside. He had at least ten minutes, maybe fifteen, while the pair groped one another.

Boylan silently left his observation nook, tipped an imaginary hat to his companions, and walked quickly out of the recreation room into the corridor. At the room of one of the wheelchair-bound television viewers, he opened the door and slipped inside. He leaned against the wall for a moment to allow his heart to stop pounding, then crossed the darkened room, one hand gripping the journal to make sure he didn't lose it. A sliding glass door opened onto a tiny landscaped patio.

Outside, he took a deep breath of fresh air and listened to the roar of the ocean. He missed the sea, wished he were there right now, studying the star-filled sky. He looked up, sighted Polaris, then picked out a number of other old friends: the eye of the lion, Orion's belt, and the seven sisters. They wouldn't guide him now, but it gave him comfort to know they were still there.

He exited through a gate in the high wooden fence surrounding the patio and eased his way along the side of the building until he reached the floodlighted rear parking area. He had to cross it . . . in full view of the staff lunchroom.

Need a bit of the old Irish luck here, Jocko.

He peered around the corner of a window and looked inside: the supervisor and the orderly were deep in conversation. But for how long?

If they see me, they'll make me go back.

He was torn between the risk of going and the risk of staying.

Sweating, his knees wobbly, he stepped out and walked with determination along the edge of the parking lot pavement, intent on not looking back at the nursing home. When he reached the street, he gritted his teeth before moving onto the sidewalk.

He paused, listened, but there was no shout, no sound of pursuing feet. Now there was a jounce in his step as he strode toward the nearby intersection.

For years, whenever the fever had struck, he signed himself into Lester's convalescent home, and then checked himself out when the bug was squashed. This was the first time he'd had to sneak out.

By God, it's going to work!

As he started across the street, the traffic light turned red. Even though there was no traffic, he waited patiently for the WALK signal, the sense of urgency all but gone.

When the green light blinked on, he pulled the ties of his robe tighter and started across the street. Halfway, he lost one slipper. As he paused to flip it upright, he saw a car, lights out, pulling away from the curb. It accelerated toward him.

What's that bilge rat up to?

A chirp of tires and the roaring engine gave an answer that surprised him. He abandoned the slipper and scrambled toward the far curb, sensing that his stiffened joints and fever-debilitated muscles weren't going to save him.

The car slammed into him without slowing. His right leg and hip shattered with a crack that echoed sickeningly in his head. Airborne for an instant, he dropped heavily onto the top of the car, slid off the back, and bounced to a rolling stop on the asphalt.

Unable to move, he squinted at the departing taillights; saw the brake lights flash on. Somewhere, far off, he heard a grinding of gears. The car lurched back toward him.

"Not fucking fair," he groaned, the pain engulfing him. "*I* wanted to finish it, nail your hides to the bulkhead."

The heavy sedan backed over him with both rear and front wheels, and then stopped. Someone snatched the journal from his waistband.

You're . . . still not . . . off the hook, Tan . . . got . . .

The car drove forward across him again, taking his last breath with it.

Chapter 1

Paige Alper studied the envelope with its return address in glistening, black, raised letters, hefting it in the palm of one hand. The parchment-like paper would have been impressive, even if it hadn't been the only first-class letter among the collection of junk mail she'd just taken from the mailbox.

She continued to ponder the envelope as she walked back through the two-car garage, stopping briefly to see if Max had washed their Porsche in preparation for the weekend regional Solo I event. The car was immaculate, and he'd already placed their driving gear on the car seats.

She was proud of her husband's restraint—running against the clock was the one auto sport he allowed himself, after almost getting killed in a multi-car pile-up at Daytona the first year of their marriage.

She never asked him to stop racing. He'd simply sold what was left of his race-prepared 911S and bought the Meissen blue 914-6 that now occupied one-half of their garage. He'd set up the mid-engine car for autocrossing and Solo I events, then brought her into the sport by teaching her the finer points of high-speed driving.

She shook out her long black hair, looked in the hallway mirror, and smiled. She always looked like a drowned rat after removing her helmet at the end of a day's competition, but she didn't care. She'd come to love the speed and excitement almost as much as Max.

After closing the garage door to shut out the chill of the late-summer San Francisco fog, she entered the two-story townhouse.

While she wanted to toss all the other mail into the trash, she piled it neatly on the hall table instead. Max would open and scan it all, regardless of content: solicitations for contributions, invitations from visiting Hong Kong tailors, sweepstake ploys, whatever. It was a treasured part of his routine when he came home from work, regardless of the hour.

"To think some poor tree gave up its life for all that crap," she muttered, looking back at the hall table. She opened the mini-blinds in the living room, standing on tiptoe to catch the townhouse's one slim view of the Golden Gate Bridge.

She carried her letter into the kitchen and poured herself a glass of orange juice as she reread the return address:

Heirs Apparent, Inc.
527 Lexington Avenue
New York, NY 10017

"Intriguing," she said, perching on a stool at the snack counter while she contemplated how the letter was addressed:

Paige Boylan Alper

"Where did they get that?" she asked the bulletin board. She never used Boylan, which had been her mother's maiden name. It, together with "Paige," had always sounded like a person she wouldn't want to know.

Unable to prolong the suspense any longer, she slit open

15

the envelope and removed three sheets of paper—a typed letter and what appeared to be a printed contract of some kind. She read the cover letter, also on parchment-style paper:

August 26, 2003
Mrs. Paige Boylan Alper
6666 Oro del Pacifico
San Francisco, CA 94117
Re: JOCK IAN BOYLAN, DECEASED

Dear Mrs. Alper:

It is with great pleasure that I am able to advise you that as a result of investigations conducted by this organization, we have been able to locate you and your twin sister, Sheryl Boylan Fenster, who are the only known heirs of Jock Ian Boylan.

We have ascertained that Jock Ian Boylan, born in New York City, June 12, 1927, was one of two children of Terrance and Mary Boylan; and that on March 4, 1998, he died in the city of San Diego, California.

This letter will advise you and your sister that you both are in line to share in an inheritance. To that end, please find enclosed a retainer agreement between you and Heirs Apparent, Inc.

Upon receipt of the signed retainer agreements from you and your sister, you will be advised in detail by Heirs Apparent, Inc. how this inheritance can be collected, and the terms of its distribution.

Please understand that at the present time, Heirs Apparent, Inc. cannot furnish any additional informa-

16

tion until such time as this organization has been retained in this matter. It should be of paramount interest, however, that you and your sister stand to inherit, *each,* an amount in excess of $62,500 net, which is not subject to federal income tax.

Time is of the essence in this matter, since the Statute of Limitations could negate the collection and distribution of the funds involved in this inheritance.

I look forward to your prompt reply.

Sincerely,
Russell D. Kerwin
President

RDK:bdl
Encl.
cc: Mrs. Sheryl Boylan Fenster

"My God!"

She gulped down the rest of the juice and read the letter a second time. Her hands trembled as she held the retainer agreement out to one side and twice more read the paragraph about the sixty-two thousand dollars.

"Uncle Jock!" She'd rarely seen the man, but he was always her most fascinating relative. His accidental death five years earlier had robbed her of ever getting to really know the black sheep of the family. As for this unexpected inheritance, it was virtually unbelievable—there'd been barely enough money to cover the cost of having his ashes scattered at sea.

She stretched across the counter, grabbed the cordless phone, and punched in Max's direct office number. After several rings, his secretary answered: "Max Alper's office."

"Is he in?"

"Sorry, Paige, he's out with a client."

"Damn!"

"Any message?"

"Would you please ask him to call me as soon as he has a chance, Joannie? I'll also leave a message on his cell phone."

Chances were she wouldn't be able to reach him before she had to leave for work at eleven. It was one of several disadvantages in working for a morning newspaper—her and Max's schedules were almost never in sync.

Originally, they'd both worked for the same newspaper, but getting married changed all of that. Rather than buck the publisher's policy of not allowing both husband and wife to work on the editorial staff, they'd tossed a coin. Max lost and went to work for a public relations firm that had been courting him for a long time.

Without hanging up, she tapped out her sister's number in Albuquerque, and then quickly hung up. She wanted to read the retainer agreement one more time before discussing it with her twin. Experience had taught her to be fully prepared, before consulting on anything with Sheryl.

She grabbed a bowl of leftover pesto spaghetti from the refrigerator, stuffed a forkful into her mouth, and dived into unraveling the legalese of the document. Essentially, she learned that by signing, Heirs Apparent would be their legal representative with respect to obtaining the inheritance. While that seemed reasonable, the section on compensation made her bristle. She went through that section again, line-by-line, word-by-word.

"One-half!" she shouted, tossing the document onto the counter. "Who the hell do they think they are?"

She grabbed the telephone again and stabbed out her sister's number, more incensed each time she glanced at the offending piece of paper. Finally, on the fifth ring, her sister answered.

"Sheryl! Paige!" She'd long ago given up any attempt at making small talk with her twin, who invariably put her own twist on anything Paige said.

"I've been expecting your call," Sheryl said.

"Then you got the letter about Uncle Jock."

"Yesterday."

"Yesterday? Why didn't you call me?"

"George and I wanted to check on a couple of things first. Besides, I knew you'd call."

Cheap as ever.

She envisioned her sister fingering permed little-girl black curls and affecting an air of innocence with her sea green eyes. For the umpteenth time, she wondered how they could be so alike physically and so unalike emotionally and intellectually. Their personalities had never fit the prototype for identical twins—Sheryl had no interest in athletics, was a social climber, obsessed about money, and didn't give a rat's ass about anything that didn't affect her directly.

"I assume," Paige said, "you were as incensed as I was about handing over half of Uncle Jock's estate to those parasites."

"George says it's common practice."

"For whom? Are we supposed to agree to anything because someone waves impressive dollar figures at us? We at least should try to dicker with them."

"Hey, it's found money, isn't it? Who would have thought the old geezer had that kind of money? Mom always said he was just an itinerant sailor."

"He was a ship's captain."

"I'm not going to fight with you about this, Paige. The

point is, *we* sure as hell could use a tax-free sixty-two thousand dollars. And if this Heirs Apparent bunch can get it without a fuss, let them."

"Hey, Max and I could use the money, too. But that *isn't* the point. I simply don't see why these guys, whoever they are, should collect that kind of fee."

"Apparently you weren't listening," Sheryl snipped. "George says that's the way it's done; it's all perfectly legal."

"But do we have to accept their first offer?" She avoided saying anything about George's less-than-stellar legal career.

"George doubts it would even be worth the effort to try to negotiate with them. After all, they know where the money is . . . we don't."

Paige rolled her eyes. She'd never liked her brother-in-law, nor trusted his advice. "Look, Sheryl, it wouldn't hurt to get a legal opinion other than George's."

"George is a damn good attorney."

"And attorneys are accustomed to taking up to one-half of what their clients are awarded, so why wouldn't he think this is business as usual?"

"Knock it off, Paige! I have no intention of losing out on that money just because you think you're smarter than everyone else."

"Not smarter, Sheryl, more suspicious. I just don't gallop after any carrot that's dangled in front of me."

"You're a bitch!" Sheryl's voice quavered.

"But a cautious bitch."

"Look, not everything's a potential Pulitzer Prize for you and that goddamn newspaper you work for."

"Sheryl, my only concern at this point is that we're not getting shafted by Heirs Apparent. And for all I know, there may even be a way to collect the entire two hundred and fifty thousand dollars. That's a hundred and twenty-five thousand dollars each!"

There was a prolonged silence before Sheryl spoke, slowly and evenly: "Are you going to sign the retainer agreement or not?"

Paige sighed into the receiver. "No, Sheryl, I'm not going to sign it . . . at least not until I've looked into it a lot more closely."

Chapter 2

Journal—1983
Jock Ian Boylan

November 2—Port of Los Angeles

San Pedro Harbor filled with ships again. Last-minute goodies for L.A. Christmas shoppers. I should talk. Haven't bought one thing yet for Nolla and Sallee.

Harbor gets more congested every year, but we still managed to dock on time. Off-loaded without a hitch.

These new containerships are efficient, too much so. Crews unhappy with the quick turnarounds. Not enough time in port. Might help keep them out of trouble. Ha!

Less than a week until I'm back in Sri Lanka with Nolla and Sallee.

Worried about them. Damned Tamil terrorists don't care who they kill. Got to get the two of them out of there.

Can I convince Nolla to move to Hong Kong, where it's safer? Would get to see them more often. Difficult to believe Sallee is already eleven.

These six-month tours seem longer and longer every year.

Turned command over to Ellis. He wouldn't stop bitching about being at sea over the holidays. He should plan better. Having a family can be a problem. Six months on, six off, is hard on a marriage.

Confirmed my flight reservation with Pan Am.

Get the jitters thinking about all those hours cramped in an airplane. Only way. Sea travel takes too long.

Besides, can't seem to stay out of trouble aboard other people's ships. Ellis is still pissed about the time I got permission to use the owner's suite on his vessel and began giving orders to his crew. Ha!

Have to get something nice for Sallee. What does a girl that age want?

Should have called Nolla and asked. Too late now.

Antsy to be there, antsy to leave again. That's me, all right. No wonder that woman won't marry me. Been asking for ten years. Keeps giving me that nonsense about not wanting to tie me down. Damn!

She knows I love her. Why won't she say yes?

Reminder: Stay well this time, Jocko. Don't want to spend the holidays in bed with that goddamn Lassa fever!

Stupid disease!

Damn! One voyage to West Africa. That's all it took. Should have stayed in the Pacific, where I belonged.

Chapter 3

By the time Max caught up with Paige, it was late in the day and she was on deadline for the first edition. Staring at a blank screen, she was trying to compose the lead for a page one story. The seemingly impatient blinking cursor on the monitor made her wonder if the next step in the progression from quill to typewriter to computer would be direct brain interface—she visualized a maze of multicolored wires sprouting out of her head as she answered her buzzing telephone: "Alper!"

"Likewise!"

"Max! Where are you?"

"Home. It was closer than going back to the office after my meeting. I'm about to hop into the shower. Got your messages. What's up?"

She quickly told him about the letter and her conversation with Sheryl.

"So, old Jocko had a quarter-million bucks stashed away someplace. That's a surprise, isn't it?"

"Yes, in more ways than one. Like, I'd love to know where he got that kind of money. And why didn't anybody know about it when he died?"

"The letter doesn't give you any clues?"

"They took two pages to say practically nothing. Typical lawyerese. Anyway, it's on the dining room table for you to read." She sighed. "Mainly, I'm pissed at Sheryl."

"What this time?"

"Just being Sheryl is enough. But I won't bug you with that part now. I've got just twenty minutes to deadline. Trying to nail a minor city bureaucrat who's had his hand in the public till."

"Sounds like fun . . ."

"I know how you miss it, Max."

"Yeah, but what the hell—" It was a moment before he could continue, "—just give me a call when you get a chance. I want to hear more about how I'm going to be married to a rich woman."

"Not rich. But the money will be nice, maybe enough for you to take a year off and write that book you're always talking about."

"We can talk about that when the money's actually in our bank account."

"No, let's talk about it when I get home, which should be soon. Once I finish this piece, I intend to take off immediately."

"Good! I'll be showered, cologned, and waiting for you in my black satin pj's."

"Now I *know* I'm getting away early."

After a couple of false starts, Paige found the lead she'd been looking for. The rest of the story fell neatly into place. She turned it in with time to spare, even though she was distracted by thoughts of Uncle Jock's secret treasure:

Where did the money come from? Where had he stashed it? Why hadn't there been some evidence of the money in his belongings when she'd gone to San Diego five years ago to claim his body?

For as long as she could remember, Uncle Jock had been one of her heroes. A frequent childhood fantasy flashed through her mind—Uncle Jock standing at the helm on a storm-tossed deck, one arm around a beautiful woman, a Jolly Roger flapping in the wind atop the main mast—her Sinbad, sailing the Seven Seas, from one adventure to another.

Her reverie was interrupted by the managing editor, who, fortunately, liked the first draft of her story. At least she wouldn't have to waste time doing a rewrite. While they waited for the piece to be cleared by the legal department, she logged onto the newspaper's morgue to check for any background data on heir tracers.

Max handed Paige a glass of chilled wine as she walked through the door a few minutes past eight thirty. He then dangled the laciest of her negligees in front of her.

"Am I being propositioned?" She tossed her keys onto the hallway table. The junk mail was still there, unopened.

He nuzzled her neck. "Ah, you *smell* like a rich woman."

"You nut!" She put down the wine, took his face between both hands, and kissed him. "Do you want the details before or after my shower?"

"After." He took her by the hand and led her down the hall toward their bedroom. "I'm much more attentive after you've slipped into something comfortable."

They were propped up in their king-size bed, munching from a huge bag of tostados and sipping more wine. "I downloaded some stories from the morgue before I left," Paige said.

"I had a hunch you'd do that," he said, feeding her an oversized chip that crumbled before he could get it all into her mouth. "No doubt looking for any dirt on Heirs Apparent."

"Good guess," she said, picking crumbs out of her belly button.

"Not really. I know you, Paige Alper."

"In the biblical sense?"

"Especially in the biblical sense," he said, crumbling another tostado on her midsection. He bent over and began picking up the pieces with a sweep of his tongue.

"Do you want to hear what I found out or not?" she laughed.

"Yep!"

"Then behave yourself."

"Okay," he sighed. "I'll clean up the rest later."

She nudged him back onto his pillow. "The best of the lot was a feature story about another heir-tracing firm. It ran not too long ago in the Sunday magazine section; a *Washington Post Syndicate* piece."

"Any mention of Heirs Apparent?"

"Only briefly, in connection with how highly competitive the business is. Apparently most of these missing heirs searches are conducted with great secrecy. Some of these characters aren't above stealing each other's clients."

"What did they say about fees?"

"This one charged one-third of recovered monies, plus expenses."

"That sounds a little better than what Heirs wants," Max said. "One-half seems like a helluva cut . . . let's dicker."

"My thinking exactly. I plan to call this Russell Kerwin guy first thing in the morning. We'll find out exactly where he stands on negotiation."

"Of course," Max said, "he does have the advantage of knowing where the money's stashed."

"Worst-case scenario is a Mexican standoff."

"We should be prepared, though." He ran his fingers through his carrot-colored hair and pointed the last tostado at her. "We need to decide what our next move is going to be, if he won't negotiate."

"Any ideas?" She fitfully began shredding the empty tostado bag into smaller and smaller pieces. "I mean, Sheryl thinks we should sign and be done with it."

"So, is it Sheryl or Heirs Apparent that has you so worked up?"

"Both. But I know I'm never going to be able to change my sister. Getting a chance to pull the rug out from under some con man, though . . ."

"That's a very devilish look you have on your face, Paige Alper."

"Are we or are we not the world's greatest investigative journalists?"

"Absolutely!" He slammed his hand down onto the bed. "If Heirs won't budge, we'll go after the money ourselves."

"Yes!" she shouted. "If they found it, why can't we?"

"Food!" Max yelled and bounced out of bed. "I need to fuel my decrepit brain!" He darted out to the kitchen.

"Wait for me," Paige yelped, scampering after him.

As they nibbled leftovers, Paige flipped through an old notepad, looking for a blank page. "First move in the Alper treasure hunt caper is to call Russell D. Kerwin."

"Maybe we should just forget all about him and go directly for the loot ourselves," Max said. "What about that?" He dipped a cold Brussels sprout into a container of yogurt and dribbled it across the table.

"I figure a little dickering can't hurt; let the guy know he's up against a couple of relentless journalists who can't be conned. If I can convince him he's looking at a no-win situation, who knows, he might go for a quick and easy ten percent."

"Worth a try. It could cost us that much money doing it on our own."

Paige pondered a half-eaten chicken leg, then pointed it at Max. "Sheryl's going to scream bloody murder, you know. I got the distinct impression they're overextended again. She and George want the sixty-two grand now, not some cockamamie story about getting twice that amount sometime in the indefinite future."

"But if you don't sign, what can she and George do?"

"George is a lawyer, remember?"

"So we don't tell them anything until it's too late. Let him sue our answering machine."

"You're a very intelligent, devious, and sexy man, Max Alper." She dropped the chicken leg on the table and threw her arms around his neck.

Chapter 4

December 10—Colombo

My Nolla is dying!

So much we were going to do together. So many places I promised to take her. The trip to the States, the tour of Europe.

Too busy. Always too busy.

Now it's too late.

Should never have come back here, when I had that first bout of Lassa. Didn't know she could catch it. Only wanted to be with her and Sallee.

Stupid, stupid, stupid!

What am I going to do? She's so weak. Still fights like hell to keep me from taking her to the hospital.

Her friends did their best, but she wouldn't leave our home.

Too far gone when I got here.

December 12

Tried to tell the doctors about Lassa. They won't listen, won't believe it's contagious. They keep insisting it's malaria and feeding her quinine.

Assholes!

Nolla knew from the beginning. She sent Sallee to

Kandy in the mountains as soon as the fever struck. She tried to protect our baby.

I pray for both of them.

December 18

She died in my arms today.

The thought of never seeing Nolla again is more than I can bear.

Unfair. So goddamn unfair.

My disease killed her.

Can still see her in that sterile bed. Her soft eyes filled with pain. Watched me every waking moment. Nothing to do but be there.

So helpless.

She pleaded with me not to blame myself. I promised I wouldn't. Can't help it. I loved her and I brought her death.

Idiot doctors just stood there.

Watched her vomit her life away.

Wanted to grab them, shake them, strangle them.

I couldn't save her.

Nolla! Nolla! An empty world without you.

December 29—Kandy

Thank God! Sallee escaped the infection.

Hardest thing I've ever had to do. Think she knew her mother was dead before I said a word.

We cried for a long time, wrapped in each other's arms. Couldn't cry until that moment.

Celebrated Christmas four days late. The old Sinhalese capital's ancient Buddhist temples were the backdrop for our sad little holiday.

Nolla first brought me to Kandy years ago. Showed me where she'd been raised. So proud that it was the home of the Dalada Malagawa, the most sacred of all Buddhist temples.

Here, she brought me closer to the spirit of the Tao.

High in the mountains, near the stars, she taught me to empty myself, allow my restless mind to find peace.

Sallee was surprised I'd brought presents for her.

Gave her something pleasant to think about, something to take her mind off Nolla. It helped ease the pain of her loss, our loss.

Our daughter is so lovely. Slender and willowy, with lustrous eyes that make me want to weep with happiness.

She is her mother's child. An exact reproduction of that Eurasian beauty who captured my soul more than a dozen years ago. Not a sign of my black Irish blood.

What to do now? How am I going to raise her?

Nolla has no family in Sri Lanka, or anywhere else, as far as I know.

If only I could take Sallee to sea with me.

I'll call Moira in San Diego when we reach the Port of Colombo tomorrow. She has the twins, only a year younger than Sallee, maybe—

Chapter 5

"Where are *you* going?" Max asked from the bed, squinting at Paige with one blurry blue eye.

"Running, of course."

"Running? I thought we were going to call Heirs Apparent first thing this morning."

"Hey, the bod still comes first." She rose up on her toes and patted her flat stomach. "Get out of that bed and get moving!"

"But it's already nine in New York." He stretched lazily. "Besides, there's nothing wrong with that body that I can see."

She did a nude curtsy, allowing her long black hair to sweep across her face. "Another hour will simply give Mr. Russell D. Kerwin time to get settled in his office before we ruin the rest of his day." She stepped into her shorts, then pulled the covers off the bed. "Up, you lazy bum. You'll do anything to get out of exercise."

Ten minutes later, they were in Golden Gate Park, jogging toward the botanical gardens.

"If we have to go after your Uncle Jock's money ourselves, it could take a lot of time," Max said.

"You still have a week's vacation coming," Paige said. "Too bad we used up the other two weeks goofing off in Mexico."

"Really? I like goofing off with you. Besides, we earned

every minute of that time away."

Paige smiled and motioned for him to pick up the pace.

"Okay, okay! We won't worry about the time thing until after you talk to Heirs Apparent." He began to jog faster. Paige, a couple of inches shy of his lean six-foot frame, effortlessly matched his stride.

"Hey, we might be a team again." She raced ahead and turned around to face him while she jogged backwards. "Long time since we did that. Have you forgotten how much fun it was?"

"You're hoping Kerwin says no, aren't you?"

"It's just that I've got this creepy, crawly itch that says everything isn't quite kosher with that man."

"You could be right. In fact, in some perverse way, I hope he really *is* a lowlife."

"Like I said, we were a great team."

"The best!"

Paige pivoted around to jog alongside Max again. "Remember the Kemtek toxic dump story? You picked up on what those nurses were saying, when you were researching that feature on urgent care facilities."

"But it was *you* who caught their comments about unexplainable rashes and headaches. Tied them in with something your teacher friend Joan mentioned about similar outbreaks among her fifth-graders."

"Yeah! Then we found out they'd built that neighborhood park on land Kemtek gave to the city."

"Just kept mushrooming," he said. "How many sites in how many cities did we finally uncover?"

"Five. Five lovely parks built on top of buried poison. It was a great PR ploy on their part, but one that backfired on them because of you and me."

Max beat on his chest. "Invincible!"

Paige took Max's hand and they jogged in silence, smiling idiotically at passersby who kept looking at them as if they were a little crazy.

"Damn!" Max finally said, shaking his head. "I didn't realize how much I missed journalism, missed our working together."

Paige squeezed his hand and brought them to a halt. "Now's the time, Max, our time."

Still in her damp shorts and T-shirt, Paige mopped her sweat-covered face with a towel while she tapped out the phone number of Heirs Apparent in New York.

"It's ringing," she yelled to Max, who was in the kitchen on the extension. While she waited, she centered Heirs' come-on letter and irritating retainer agreement in front of her. When someone answered, she identified herself and asked to speak to Kerwin.

"Mrs. Alper?" said a friendly male voice.

"Is this Russell Kerwin?"

"It is, and thank you *so* much for calling. I just *knew* I would hear from you today. Mrs. Fenster called not more than an hour ago."

"I see," Paige said. *Should have listened to Max and called before our run.*

"Does that create a problem?" Kerwin asked.

"Not particularly."

"I take it then that you, too, are ready to proceed with the collection of the substantial estate left by your uncle."

"Not quite." She let him hang for a few seconds while she rearranged the papers in front of her. "First, I have a few questions about some of the specifics in your correspondence."

"I think you will find, Mrs. Alper, everything is spelled

out quite explicitly, both in my letter and the retainer agreement I sent you." He was noticeably less cordial. "I assumed you and your sister had already agreed to our terms."

"Not necessarily."

There was a short pause before Kerwin continued: "Perhaps you're also curious as to how long it will take to collect the money once Heirs Apparent has been retained. That's what concerns most people in the beginning."

"*If* you're retained, you mean."

"I informed your sister," he continued, ignoring her remark, "that it would take a minimum of ninety days. How much longer would depend upon the cooperation we get from the various entities involved. I should note, though, that our reputation is such that we're able to move these matters along quite rapidly."

Paige laughed. "My guess is that my sister Sheryl wasn't too happy about the ninety days."

"I have no way of knowing that," he said. "She only said she was signing the agreement and returning it by overnight courier."

"Why does it take ninety days to clear funds from New York banks, when you're right there?" she probed.

"I'm sure you can understand that I cannot answer *any* questions of that nature without your signed letter of agreement."

Paige shoved the agreement to the far side of the desk. She wished Sheryl hadn't made a commitment. They could have shown at least a semblance of unity.

"Mrs. Alper?" Kerwin queried after several seconds.

"I'm still here."

"Well?"

"On the face of it, I find your fifty-fifty proposition unacceptable."

"Ah, I see." He paused. "That's not unusual, Mrs. Alper. Many people have that first reaction. However, let me explain: Heirs Apparent possesses the expertise to extricate the funds in the shortest possible time. And I should emphasize, if we do not proceed with this matter expeditiously, the statute of limitations will expire—"

"What statute of limitations?" Paige interrupted.

"Being aware of such legal subtleties is part of the expertise I mentioned." When she didn't immediately respond, he continued: "You also must appreciate that we have already expended considerable time and money to establish the nature and whereabouts of your uncle's estate, and to locate you and your sister."

"What you've invested on speculation is your problem. Besides, isn't it true that some of your competitors charge one-third rather than one-half of the estate's value?"

"You certainly are free to deal with whomever you please." After a couple of beats, he added, "But it strikes me that since you've taken the time to make this call, you obviously have something in mind."

"Mr. Kerwin, I'm prepared to offer Heirs Apparent ten percent of the estate, plus reimbursement for all out-of-pocket expenses."

He snorted a humorless laugh. "I'm sure you are, but there is no way I could agree to such an offer."

"Then make a counter-offer."

"Mrs. Alper, you haven't been paying attention: The fee is fifty percent. Period!"

"Apparently the people you usually deal with are more acquisitive than inquisitive," she snapped. "Ten percent of something is a whole lot better than fifty percent of nothing."

"If fifty percent of nothing is necessary to preserve the

integrity of Heirs Apparent, then that's the way it will have to be. However, having talked at length with your sister, I doubt if she is going to appreciate your stance in this matter."

"What my sister appreciates or doesn't appreciate is of little consequence to me."

"Mrs. Alper, sixty-two thousand dollars is a lot of money. Think about it!"

"I have thought about it. My conclusion is that a hundred and twenty-five thousand dollars is twice the money, and obviously a much better deal."

It was several seconds before Kerwin responded. "Look, there's no reason for both of us to go away empty-handed."

"Agreed," Paige said. "I'm still willing to dicker over your fee. Are you?" She heard him take a couple of deep breaths before responding.

"No," he said softly.

"Then we have nothing further to discuss."

"I wouldn't be so sure about that. After all, I *do* know where the money is."

"And I would venture that if *you* found it, then it's possible for others to find it, too." She hung up without waiting for a response and smiled wryly at the telephone. Before she could push herself away from the desk, Max came in from the kitchen.

"So, how much time off are you going to ask for?" he said with a laugh. His soft blue eyes danced with mischief.

"Did I handle it okay?"

He wrapped his arms around her and pressed his forehead against hers. "Didn't you hear me applauding in the background?"

"Sheryl's going to be mad as hell. No, make that furious."

"Won't be the first time. She's gotten over it before; she'll get over it this time."

"I know, but she still irritates me. Always comes on like she's my mother. She's even worse since our parents died."

"She is older than you," he said and kissed the top of her head.

"One minute!" She was quiet a moment, then mumbled into his shoulder, "Suppose they really *do* need the money right now?"

"Paige, it's up to you. But we both know you're never going to make a fifty-percent gift to that shark in New York."

She nodded.

"Poor Sheryl and George, they'll just have to settle for twice as much as they thought they were going to get," he said.

"Do you *really* think we can find it?"

"Hell, yes!"

Chapter 6

Journal—1983
Jock Ian Boylan

December—Colombo

Terrorists swept through the capitol again, killing, burning, looting.

Nolla's cabaret and home are in ashes.

Sallee has nothing left other than what I brought her for Christmas.

The call to Moira was a disaster. Shouldn't have lost my temper. She didn't need to make snide comments about Nolla being Eurasian, about our never getting married.

Why should any of that make a difference?

If only I could have convinced Moira. She could have provided a home. I would have taken care of the schooling, for hers and mine.

Seemed so right that the three girls should grow up together.

Moira wouldn't even discuss it.

Still a brat.

But shouldn't have lost it. Bad failing of yours, Jocko.

Never learned to keep my thoughts to myself, especially when asking favors of my one and only sister. Those thirteen years separating us are still damned difficult to bridge.

She's right about one thing—it wouldn't have killed me

to call her more often than every three or four years.

How long since I've seen her? Paige and Sheryl weren't quite one, and Sallee was in her terrible twos.

Nolla, Nolla! What am I going to do with our lovely daughter? She needs care. An education.

Don't have many choices.

Must get Sallee out of Sri Lanka. Need to take her someplace less violent.

Doubt they'll settle this separatist thing anytime soon. Hate to see it turn into another Vietnam.

Don't know why people would rather kill each other than work together peacefully.

January 5

Sallee and I have agreed on Hong Kong.

My sailing schedule will get me there about once a month. I'll have the off-duty months with her like before.

Friends are going to help us find an apartment and pick out a good nanny.

Sallee refused to be stuck away in a boarding school. Don't blame her for that.

I fear she will be lonely all by herself. She says no.

Almost as independent as I am.

God, I miss you, Nolla.

Chapter 7

Russell Kerwin sat at his desk, tapped his index finger on the Jock Ian Boylan file. He wasn't pleased with the way his conversation had gone with Paige Boylan Alper. He had assumed she would be a carbon copy of her twin sister. Serious mistake. He whistled an exasperated breath from between pursed lips and pressed the intercom button.

"We have a shit-disturber," Kerwin said to Alex Pickerel, his partner.

"Which estate?"

"Boylan."

"I'll be right in."

Pickerel entered the office and slouched into one of the overstuffed, brown leather chairs opposite Kerwin's antique oak desk. His long, lanky frame was almost too big for the chair.

"Boylan?" Pickerel wiped the thin features of his face with a bony hand, turned his pale eyes to the ceiling. "That's a fat one. Are we at risk?"

"Only in losing the deal."

"We couldn't be out-of-pocket more than a couple hundred bucks at this stage."

"That's not the point and you know it," Kerwin said.

"So what's the problem?"

"One of the heirs says it's the fee. I think there's more to it than that." Kerwin reached up with both hands and adjusted the slim knot of his silk rep tie, then tugged gently at the lower tips of a pale gray moleskin vest that covered his substantial stomach.

"Which of the twins were you talking to?"

"Paige Boylan Alper."

"Oh, the *California* one," Pickerel said. "Those left coast people are never predictable." He readjusted himself in the chair. "Was it something she said, or another of your infamous hunches?"

"You know the type as well as I do—pushy broad, picked up a few facts before calling. Thinks she knows it all."

"What do you think it's going to take to nail her?"

"I don't know. We need more background on her. On both sisters, actually."

"The Fenster woman a problem, too?"

"Fortunately, no," Kerwin mused. He leaned back to look around the large room. He'd started the business some thirty years earlier with a part-time secretary. Now, a dozen employees occupied the entire floor of the building, but he'd kept the original office for himself. "I don't need any more surprises," he added.

"Want me to handle the snoop work?" Pickerel asked, already knowing the answer. He'd been with Kerwin almost from the beginning, primarily responsible for building the agency's extensive three-room research library and network of informants. "We have reliable contacts in both San Francisco and Albuquerque."

Kerwin opened the bottom desk drawer and lifted the tape from a voice-activated recorder that was connected to his telephone line. "Have a listen to my conversation with Alper. Maybe you'll pick up something I missed." He handed the tape to Pickerel. "If she's one of those irritating people who put principles before money, this could be difficult."

"Might as well get to it," Pickerel said, levering his lean frame out of the overstuffed chair.

After Pickerel quietly closed the door behind him, Kerwin swiveled around to gaze out the window at his limited view of midtown Manhattan.

It's all become so goddamn complicated.

He recalled how he'd been employed as a junior clerk in the estate administration department of a New York City savings bank. He'd known that his lack of connections and City College education were not going to carry him very far in the banking business, but he had no intention of going through life living from paycheck to paycheck.

He'd always been fascinated with the minutiae of banking. He'd probed every facet of the process for a way to line his own pockets. And it had come.

He laughed aloud, unmindful of the bleat of traffic sounds coming through the open window: *So much idle money looking for a home!*

The bank had given him responsibility for placing the legal advertising for the annual list of inactive and/or abandoned accounts. One reading told him this was exactly what he'd been looking for. After that, every spare minute went into researching the paper trail of these forsaken funds.

His enthusiasm soared when he discovered the legal resolution applied not only to savings accounts, but to checking accounts, trust accounts, safe deposit boxes, real estate, and virtually every other asset entrusted to a financial institution.

God, what a struggle to find a way to capitalize on all that wonderful, arcane shit.

The exhaustive hunt had ended when he found out he could earn lucrative fees by rooting out the rightful heirs to abandoned accounts. That there were others already doing this didn't deter him. He was in the catbird seat.

Armed with inside information, he'd launched his own heir-search operation while still working at the bank. Within six months, he'd more than doubled his entry-level salary by taking only a ten percent finder's fee.

Trying to juggle both his job and the rapidly growing heir-tracing business from his bank desk became too risky. He leased a one-room office and hired a part-time secretary to run it. He waited to quit his job, because he was still dependent on the bank as his primary data source. It took another long year before he was able to cut the umbilical.

The door to Kerwin's office eased open, interrupting his reverie.

"Bad news," Pickerel announced as he entered the room. "The California chickee is a hot-shot reporter."

"So?"

"So, you drive me nuts sometimes, Russ. Hunches don't handle everything."

Kerwin wiggled his fingers at his partner. "Get on with it. What are you trying to tell me?"

"It may not be your principles-before-money theory with this pigeon. Her shtick is investigative reporting. Same for her husband, although he's in PR now. We could end up disemboweled and splattered all over the news media."

"Fuck!" Kerwin spun around in his chair and stared at the nearest sooty brick wall. "What do you suggest?"

"Pull out while our asses are still intact."

"Bullshit! I've never given up on a case this early before, and I'm not about to do it this time. No pushy broad's

45

going to rattle my cage." He slowly turned back to face Pickerel. "Is there any way to neutralize her?"

Pickerel paced back and forth a couple of times. "Risky," he muttered. "Very risky." He saw the look in Kerwin's eyes and shrugged. "I'll work on it." He stopped as he was about to leave the office, turned around, and added, "But I don't promise anything."

Chapter 8

"I want that money, Paige," Sheryl shouted. "I'm not waiting for you and Max to have some kind of far-out personal adventure at my family's expense."

"But, Sheryl, you could have a hundred and twenty-five thousand dollars!"

"I'd rather have the sixty-two thousand five hundred dollars. Now!"

Paige dug her nails into her palm. The pain helped temper the recriminations she wanted to hurl at both her sister and her husband. She pulled the cordless phone away from her ear and stared at it while she regained her composure.

"This is a shared inheritance," Paige reminded her sister. "I'm not trying to cheat you out of anything."

"I never said you were, but that's not the point," Sheryl said in a calmer voice.

"Then what is it?"

"We . . . we're on the hook for twenty thousand dollars that we need to come up with, like, yesterday," Sheryl said, almost in a whisper.

"What happened?"

"Well, uh, George got involved in another one of his sure-thing, short-term investments and borrowed the money from what turned out to be some pretty shady people."

"And the investment turned sour again," Paige said. The last time this had happened, Sheryl had pressured her to lend them five thousand dollars because their credit lines were maxed out. Less than a thousand dollars had been repaid.

"It's a good investment," Sheryl pleaded. "It's just going to take longer than George anticipated for us to see a return and recoup our capital." There was a long pause. "Unfortunately, the lenders want their money back *now!*"

"You're putting me on the spot here, Sheryl. I mean, there's no way I can come up with twenty thousand bucks for you, even if you signed a note to repay it directly out of Uncle Jock's money."

"No, no, Paige, I'm not asking for a loan. Really. And I'm very much aware that we still owe you from the last time." After a short pause, she added, "If we could just get something on paper that said we will have the sixty-two thousand dollars from Heirs Apparent in ninety days, then maybe George could prevent any, uh, collection problems."

Paige rubbed hard at her eyes, trying to wipe away not only her anger, but also the unbearable heaviness that came over her whenever she had any kind of dealings with her sister.

"I don't know how to communicate with you anymore, Sheryl," Paige finally said. "We used to at least be able to talk about real things. Important things. What happened to us?"

The silence on the line filled Paige with a profound sadness. It was as if she'd not only lost her mother, father, and uncle, but now, finally, her sister.

"I'm not sure I know what you're taking about, Paige. We have a relationship. We still talk."

Paige spoke very softy: "Let's forget for the moment that

you and George still haven't totally repaid the last money I lent you. Okay? I can handle that. But I will not, cannot, advance you twenty thousand dollars."

"Then you're willing to sign the agreement with Heirs Apparent?"

Paige could hear the sound of victory in her sister's voice. "Sheryl, listen, and listen carefully—I'm not going to settle for one-half of what's coming to us. You and George are going to have to find some other way to solve your current cash problem."

"You bitch!"

The receiver at the other end slammed down so hard that a high-pitched ringing assaulted Paige's ear.

Paige was running late for work after the long, frustrating phone conversation with her sister. She glanced at her watch as she ran out the door: eleven thirty-five! The phone rang inside the condo just as the door clicked shut.

"Damn it!" She fumbled with the key. "All right, already!" she grumbled after the third ring. She didn't quite beat the answering machine.

"Neither Max nor Paige are here now to—"

She punched the stop button, waited for the irritating squawk to cease.

"This is the real Paige Alper," she snapped.

"Caught you," Max said. "Tried your cell phone but . . ."

"Can you believe it? I forgot to turn it on. It's been that kind of morning."

"Wanted to tell you that I put in for vacation time. I'm set to leave whenever you can wrap up whatever you're working on."

"No problem getting off?"

49

"Nah, it was easy. I asked. They said no. I quit."

"You're kidding?"

"Nope. We're now a one-income family . . . yours."

"Uh huh! And how do you feel about that?"

"I think I've been waiting for the right opportunity to get out of there for a long time. Of course, it would have been better if I had another job in my back pocket, but—"

"—but you did it and I'm glad." She slid down the wall to sit on the polished hardwood floor. "Seems you've just been putting in time there anyway. I don't think PR is really your shtick."

"Has it been that obvious?"

"Like a walking Excedrin headache."

He laughed. "Then you're not upset?"

"Upset? Hey, you're married to a woman who's about to come into money, remember?"

Max was lost in the Internet "Yellow Pages" for San Diego when Paige came home from the *Bay Sentinel*. The dining room table was covered with airline schedules, downloaded magazine articles, computer printouts, and other scraps of paper.

"You've been busy," she said, kissing him on the back of the neck.

"Do you have any idea how many banks and savings and loans there are in the San Diego area?" He turned and pulled her down onto his lap.

"How many?"

"Plenty!" He nibbled at her earlobe.

"Did you start anything for dinner? I'm starving!"

"I put *something* in the oven. I don't remember what it is."

"Ha! You really must be into this." She reached over

and ruffled through the papers on the table.

"Can't help it. I love a good chase. I get all sweaty just thinking about it."

She mussed his red, wavy hair and kissed him again. "I'm starving! I'm going to risk a peek in the oven to see if what's there is still edible."

Max and Paige shoved the piles of brochures, schedules, and printouts aside to make room for plates of steaming lasagna, a basket of garlic bread, and a bottle of Italian sparkling water.

"The man *can* cook!"

"One of my many talents."

"So what happened?" Paige asked. "Did you give two weeks' notice?"

"I tried, but Hawthorne was his normal shitty self: 'If you're going, go.' So I cleaned out my desk and went."

"Serves him right. And the timing couldn't be better."

"Hope so. What about you?"

"Tom said I could take off as soon as I finish the identity theft series. That should be no later than Wednesday."

"That soon?"

"Sure. And he said to take as much time as I need, just so it's not more than two weeks." She took a huge bite of garlic bread and pulled some of Max's research closer. "Looks like you think we should start in San Diego."

"Yeah ... at the nursing home where Jock was staying when he had his accident."

"Sounds right to me."

Max rummaged through the pile of papers on the far side of the table and came up with an airline schedule printout. He studied it while stuffing a forkful of lasagna into his mouth. "We can leave here for San Diego at almost any time of day."

"Okay. And if we don't learn anything at Ocean Shores?"

"We go to plan B."

"Which is?"

"I made a list of the banks in the area. Maybe he kept his money there."

"But Uncle Jock lived in a lot of different places. He spent his entire adult life at sea."

"Didn't he ever talk about one particular place?"

"Max, I don't think I actually saw him more than two or three times in my whole life. Most of what I know came from my mother, and all she ever did was scowl and clam up whenever I mentioned his name. There was some kind of serious pain there, but she would never discuss it."

"Didn't you say you heard from him regularly?"

"I did. I have a box full of cards and letters he sent us from all over the world. He never missed our birthdays, or Christmas, or anything like that."

"What about Chanukah?"

"That, too . . . just after I married you. Don't you re-member?"

"And I thought I was being *so* funny. Anyway, wasn't there at least one place in the States where he spent more time? Like San Diego, hopefully?"

"We're not going to be that lucky," Paige said. She wiped the last smudge of sauce from her plate with a tiny bit of crust. "A lot of stuff came from Hong Kong and Ceylon, though."

"You mean Sri Lanka?"

"Same difference. It's a long way from here, no matter what it's now called."

"So, we'll start in San Diego and hope we get lucky." He sifted through the papers again and came up with a page of handwritten notes. "Now pay close attention," he said with a flourish.

"I'm all ears, master."

"Here's what I found out from the California state controller's office: after seven years, an inactive account is declared abandoned, if attempts to contact the account holder prove unsuccessful." He ran a finger along his notes, found the place he was looking for. "After notifying the appropriate state agency, ads are placed in the major newspapers where the account holder was last known to have lived. If that doesn't do it, the funds are turned over to the state."

"Did you say *seven* years?"

"Yes."

"But Uncle Jock died just five years ago. I don't understand."

"There are a number of scenarios: Jock didn't touch the accounts for two years prior to his death; someone's played fast and loose with the rules; or maybe the accounts are in another state where the rules are different."

"What did Kerwin mean about the statute of limitations possibly expiring?"

"It didn't mean a damn thing. Just a bluff. His sneaky way of trying to pressure you into signing. The controller's office website said that even after the state gets the money, the account holder, or heir, could still reclaim it. But it does get complicated, and more expensive."

"That deceptive son-of-a-bitch!" She pushed her chair back and started gathering up the dishes. "I'm going to enjoy beating that bottom feeder at his own game."

Chapter 9

Journal—1996
Jock Ian Boylan

May 27—Port of Long Beach

Down with the fever again.

Two years since the last attack. Thought I had it whipped.

Too smug. Too stupid.

Eyes blurred, everything dim. Muscles keep cramping.

Hurt so much can barely lift the pen.

Need help. Don't know why I'm writing. Why I'm still here.

Not true.

Same egotistical fool I've always been, gambling with death, pushing the odds to the limit.

Dumb!

Got to think of Sallee. Got to be there for her.

It could get me this time, just the way it got Nolla. Don't trust those damn hospitals. Won't go there.

Must write down the address of the convalescent home in San Diego, pin it to my fucking shirt with the fare.

Ocean Shores will take me in. Lester will take care of me. Always has.

Air is stale. Can hardly breathe.

Damn bulkheads closing in. Got to leave the ship.

Gave Nolla the bug. Lost her in that frigging Colombo hospital.

Hospitals. Doctors. What do they know? Not a goddamn thing.

They let her die. Let her die right before my eyes.

Dead but not gone. Still with me, aren't you, Nolla? So hot. On fire. Shaking.

Last spasm was a pisser. Need to think.

Stay with me, Nolla. Help me.

Damn runs are twisting my guts into bowline knots. Keep puking up the fires of hell.

No need to tell *you*, Nolla. They stood by your bed. Wrung their hands while you tore at your chest. Tore at your throat. Gasped to breathe.

God help me. The fear, the panic in your eyes.

Cramps have me doubled over. Head's like a blazing furnace, searing my brain. Can't think. Throat swelling. Can't swallow.

Waited too long.

Afraid.

June 5—San Diego

That bout almost deep-sixed me. Can't remember ever being sicker.

Barely got to Ocean Shores in time.

Should find a place closer to the Port of Long Beach when I'm in the States.

Old habits hard to break. Been coming here too many years.

How terrible if I'd missed Sallee's graduation. She's worked so hard, done so well.

Must remember to tell her how proud I am.

Hard to believe my little girl will have a Master's Degree

55

in international relations. So idealistic. Wants to make the world a better place.

Not a cynic like her old man. Ha!

Seems like only yesterday she was sitting on my lap, pulling at my beard. Time keeps running away. Still think of her as my tiny little girl. Just fooling myself.

The kid's grown into a gorgeous woman.

Can't believe I helped create something so perfect.

Damn tears cloud my eyes when I look at her. Image of her mother. Seeing her helps keep Nolla alive in my heart.

Without Sallee there would be nothing.

Feeling stronger. Still not exactly in the best shape to travel.

Got to get to that graduation. Would crawl if I had to. Good thing it's in San Francisco and not back in Hong Kong.

June 10—San Francisco

Sallee and I leave tomorrow morning for Hong Kong.

So proud of her I could burst. Fresh out of school and she lands a big, big job. Liaison between an international trading company and the Chinese government.

Wait until she finds out there's a brand new BMW waiting for her at home.

Never told her I expected to retire when she graduated from UCLA. Figured sixty-six was more than old enough to give up the helm. Little scamp pulled the graduate school bit on me. Damn schools are so bloody expensive. Had to keep at it another couple of years.

Can't complain. Top of her class.

Nice of Paige to call from Europe to offer congratulations.

Don't know what happened to Sheryl.

Would be wonderful to see all three girls together sometime. If only Moira, God rest her soul, had not been so
bitter. Wonder if she ever felt guilty about not taking in
Sallee after Nolla's death? No matter. Moira was who she
was, and it was as much my fault as hers.

At least I can afford to retire now. About time!

Final scheduled voyage coming up soon. One more loop
around the Pacific—Kaohsiung, Busan, Yokohama, San
Francisco, and home again to Hong Kong.

Then what?

Have to think about that. Not used to having choices.

Rich wants me to come back to San Diego and help run
Sunair Ranch.

Great place to recuperate, but don't know if I want to
spend the rest of my life living in a nudist park.

Enjoy the area. Great memories of growing up there—
sailing on San Diego Bay, picnics on Coronado, wild trips
to Tijuana.

But damn it, Sallee is going to be in Hong Kong.

Don't have to make that decision for a while yet.

Be strange knowing I won't be going back to sea.

Can't just sit around and tell sea stories. What a bore I'd
be. Bet I could tell some real whoppers, though.

Been thinking about my woodcarvings. Some of them
are pretty good. Maybe I could become a famous artist.
Cap'n Moses. Ha!

Going to have to find something to keep busy. Don't
want to end up like other beached sailors, fat and full of
rum.

Chapter 10

"Strange that Martin Lester gave you such a bad time when you called to make an appointment," Max said.

"More like he was distant . . . cold." She thought for a moment, watching fog-rimmed San Francisco shrink into the distance as the airplane climbed. "No, he was reluctant."

"Yeah, well, nursing home administrators get rather sensitive about patients having fatal accidents on or near the premises."

"You have to admit he was solicitous when we went down there to arrange for Uncle Jock's cremation."

"Nauseatingly so," Max said.

"Right. Neither of us liked him then, did we?" She clutched at his arm with both hands. "What was that?"

He smiled, stroked her cheek with the back of his hand. "An air bump, love, that's all."

"I wish they wouldn't do that." She closed her eyes and pressed back into her seat. "I'd be so much happier if we could just take off and land immediately and be in San Diego."

"But it's so quiet and peaceful up here. Besides, it's the takeoffs and landings that are the most dangerous."

"Don't give me logic." She opened her eyes and gave him a weak smile. "Sorry. What were you saying?"

"Five years ago, I think this Lester guy was afraid you

and your sister might try to take them for a bundle . . .
wrongful death, breach of contract, any number of things."

Paige risked a glance out the window, watched a huge
cloud drift by, and finally relaxed her grip on Max's arm.

"Actually, I still think you and Sheryl should have sued
them. In fact, as I recall, Sheryl and George were talking
about it."

"But they gave it up. George lost interest when he found
out that kind of suit could take years, would be difficult to
win, and that the awards usually don't cover the costs. At
least not his inflated costs."

When the seatbelt light blinked out, Max loosened his
belt and stretched. Paige kept her belt cinched tightly
across her lap. He reached over and lightly poked her in
the ribs. "You got a high out of telling Sheryl that you
weren't going to sign the Heirs Apparent contract, didn't
you?"

Paige wrinkled her nose. "It *was* fun making her squirm
during that first conversation about the inheritance. But
this last time was truly awful. She made me feel like I was
throwing them to the wolves if I didn't go along with what
Heirs offered us."

She lifted the armrest that separated them and snuggled
into Max's shoulder. "All my sister can see is that we're on
some stupid wild goose chase at her expense."

"I'm sorry, kid."

"And this time it sounds like they're in really bad financial trouble. I got the impression George has been dealing
with some loan sharks."

"Sort of shark-to-shark."

"No kidding. But it's still awkward. Even though we
don't get along, I do feel for her."

"One of these days, you're going to have to iron out the

wrinkles in your relationship with your sister. Not for her sake, but for yours."

"I don't iron."

"You know what I mean."

"The truth is, it's never going to happen."

"How can you be so sure?"

"Our goals, our outlook on life, are just about as far apart as you can get. She's always wanted to be the wife–PTA mom–volunteer kind of person. You know, stay at home and enjoy the fruits of having a rich husband."

"You could say her quest has only been partially successful," Max said. "George doesn't quite fit into her ideal picture."

"Yeah, which makes the dangling carrot of Uncle Jock's money real crazy-making. But even if we do score the whole jackpot, there's not a hope that Sheryl and I will ever get together."

"I still don't see how you can be so certain."

"Because," Paige said with a giggle, "she keeps hanging up on me."

They arrived early for their ten a.m. appointment with Martin Lester, only to be told he was running a few minutes late and would be with them as soon as possible.

"Too bad I couldn't talk him into seeing us yesterday afternoon when we got here," Paige said, flipping through the pages of an old *Nursing Home Administrator*.

"No big deal," Max said. "It gave us time to relax and get out of the San Francisco fog, *and* end the day with a candlelit dinner overlooking Mission Bay." He leered at her. "My favorite part came later at the motel, after the moonlight stroll on the beach."

"Shh. The secretary's listening." She rolled her eyes and

nudged his arm. "Anyway, it did give us time to call Sacramento and learn that no Jock Boylan bank accounts have been turned over to the state . . . to date."

"I suppose we could check the local newspaper files for abandoned account ads, but that seems rather futile, since it hasn't been seven years since Jock's death."

"Which makes me wonder again what originally brought Uncle Jock to San Diego and Ocean Shores," Paige said. "And why didn't we think to ask that five years ago?" She tossed the dog-eared magazine aside.

"There wasn't any reason to ask then, Paige. Anyway, grieving people don't always ask the right questions."

"I know. It was all so sad . . . I couldn't believe he was suddenly gone and I was never going to get to see him again."

"And strangely enough, it appears even dead Captain Jock Boylan continues to be full of surprises."

Paige glanced at the secretary, then back at Max. "Here I thought that chapter of my life was over, then we discover dear old Uncle Jock died with two hundred and fifty thousand dollars in an unknown bank."

"So where do we look now?" Max said.

"Haven't the slightest. Maybe Sri Lanka, New York . . ."

". . . Hong Kong, Tokyo, Bangkok?"

Paige sighed, "Well, we knew it wasn't going to just fall into our laps."

"I hate it when we're right like that."

When the receptionist finally ushered them into the administrator's office, it was ten twenty.

"I'm sorry I kept you waiting," Lester said as they entered. He shook both of their hands. "It seems emergencies in this business never follow any sort of schedule." He sat down, twisted his neck inside his starched collar, and flipped through a pile of file folders.

Paige and Max eased into soft, cream-colored leather chairs and waited for him to give them his full attention.

"I'm not sure I understand why you've come all the way down from San Francisco for this meeting," Lester said, looking up. "We easily could have done this by telephone. However, as long as you're here, I don't mind reviewing the details of Captain Boylan's residence at Ocean Shores. But I doubt there's anything new to tell you."

"Perhaps," Paige said. "However, another matter has come up with respect to my uncle's death. Since it's been more than five years, we thought it would be better to meet with you personally."

Lester finally found the file he'd been looking for, opened it, and tapped the contents with a forefinger. "Ocean Shores was held blameless for your uncle's death. Had you taken the time to consult with either local or state authorities before coming here, you would know that nothing has happened since then to alter that official opinion.

"Simply stated, Mr. and Mrs. Alper," Lester continued, raising his head to peer at them over gold half-rim glasses, "Captain Boylan died as the result of a hit-and-run automobile accident. That could neither have been foreseen nor prevented, especially under his self-imposed terms and conditions with this institution."

Paige shifted her attention from Lester and gave Max a wry look, then turned back to the administrator. "Why are you so defensive, Mr. Lester? I never said I was here to question the circumstances of my uncle's death."

Max added, "You act as though you expect us to be suspicious."

"And for good reason," Lester said, leaning across the desk. "Most of our clients are placed here at great expense to the family, who usually feel guilty about putting their loved ones in a convalescent facility in the first place. They experience even more guilt when death comes, as it eventually does. Sometimes there's a need to alleviate that guilt. And this is a very litigious world."

"I understand. But my uncle wasn't your typical client, isn't that correct?"

"What's your point, Mrs. Alper?"

"She means," Max said, "you keep defending yourself without actually being accused of anything."

"*Are* you guilty of something?" Paige said, enjoying the unrehearsed cooperation between her and Max.

"Ridiculous!" Lester's smooth, round cheeks flushed a deep crimson.

"Then why are you so uneasy with having us here?"

"Again you've assumed, rather than asked, why we've come," Max added.

"All right, why *are* you here?" Lester conceded. He tugged at the cuffs of his shirt until a half-inch of white flashed from each coat sleeve.

Paige opened her purse and pulled out her steno pad. She deliberately prolonged the moment, slowly leafing through the pages of shorthand notes. Was it only the fear of legal action that was motivating Lester?

"We recently discovered," she said when she located the appropriate page, "that my uncle may have had assets other than those turned over to us at the time of his death. We thought you might have information that would be helpful."

Lester shrugged noncommittally.

"Don't you require your clients to submit some kind

of financial statement prior to being admitted?" Max asked.

"Yes."

"Then I'd like to have a copy of my uncle's statement," Paige said.

"Absolutely not!"

"Why?" Max demanded.

"It's against Ocean Shores' policy."

"For what possible reason?" Paige said. She stuffed the notebook back into her purse.

"Financial information is *always* confidential."

"To protect the privacy of your client, right?" Max said.

Lester glared at him. "Obviously!"

"Obviously?" Paige echoed. "But the patient is dead and I'm one of two legal heirs. Whose privacy are we talking about?"

Lester pulled off his glasses and massaged his forehead with one hand. He closed Jock Boylan's file, centered it on his desk, and leaned back in his chair. "What exactly is it you want to know?"

Paige and Max relaxed and crossed their legs almost in unison.

"This is a very expensive facility," Paige said. "Yet, when Uncle Jock died we found only a small checking account at a nearby bank. He must have listed other assets to qualify for admission."

"Captain Boylan had established his financial credibility with us over a long period of time."

"But he'd only been here a little over a month before he died," Max said.

"I'm talking about prior to his last admission."

"So he'd been here before?" Paige said.

"Many times over the years. He came here whenever he

had a relapse of Lassa fever."

"Lassa fever?"

"It's an African viral disease your uncle contracted during a voyage to Lagos, Nigeria. It requires specialized supportive treatment. He came here for that care."

"What *kind* of supportive treatment?" Max said.

"The best available. You need to understand that every time Captain Boylan was admitted, it was necessary to create an isolated area for him," Lester said. "He also required skilled nursing care. The point being that his admission was never run-of-the-mill, not by a long shot."

"Would you mind explaining?" Paige said.

Lester leaned further back in his chair, obviously more comfortable with the way the interview was going. "While Lassa is not highly contagious, it's certainly much more serious than contracting a severe case of influenza." He leaned forward to make his next point. "The facility had to be properly equipped, and the medical staff had to be more skillful than is the norm for our facility."

"Wouldn't Jock have been better off in a hospital?" Max asked.

"Captain Boylan had great distrust of hospitals and insisted on more personalized care."

"And my guess is that Uncle Jock paid you quite handsomely for that kind of attention," Paige said.

Lester gave her a piercing look. "This is not an inexpensive facility for anyone, Mrs. Alper."

"No charity cases, then," Max said.

Lester shook his head negatively. "I'm afraid not."

"So tell us more about my uncle's special circumstances," Paige said.

"Well, as I mentioned, it was necessary to isolate Captain Boylan from the other patients during the acute phase of each relapse. That meant a private room with experienced nursing care around-the-clock—using people who were accustomed to working with contagious diseases."

"If there was a possibility of his infecting other patients, I'm surprised you admitted him," Paige said.

Lester picked up his cup and took a sip of coffee, then looked at each of them. "I'm sorry, I should have offered you coffee . . . or tea?"

Paige and Max both declined.

"Let me repeat: this is a skilled nursing facility. We are able to provide barrier nursing skills when necessary, around the clock."

"You mean the staff is required to wear special protective clothing, like masks, gloves, gowns, eye protection," Max said.

"Plus, the strictest of equipment sterilization procedures." He took another sip of coffee and carefully placed the cup on the credenza behind his desk. "Believe me, Mr. and Mrs. Alper, we earned every dollar Captain Boylan paid us."

"So how did he get here from Hong Kong, or wherever he was when he had a relapse of Lassa, without exposing other people?"

"Fortunately, the virus is not spread through casual contact. Most of the time he had himself bought here by air ambulance services that had trained personnel on call. Other times, he seemed to sense when his health was running down, making him likely to fall ill again. Then he came directly here before he was incapacitated. And I must say he was rarely wrong."

"But what about when he was at sea?" Paige said.

"Sometimes he was treated at Asian facilities. But if at all possible, he arranged to come to Ocean Shores."

Paige's voice hushed, became tentative. "Was there much suffering?"

"We kept him as comfortable as possible," Lester said, his voice softening somewhat for the first time. "But frankly, the symptoms could be quite debilitating."

"What were the symptoms?"

"Are you sure you need to hear this?" Max said to her.

Paige squeezed his hand. "Please continue, Mr. Lester."

"Well, there were chills, fever, vomiting, diarrhea, and headaches. Sometimes these were accompanied by pharyngeal and severe abdominal pain . . ."

"I think that's enough," Max said. "We get the picture."

"I just don't understand," Paige said, tears welling in her eyes, "why have I never heard anything about this?"

"Captain Boylan kept the problem to himself," Lester said. "We were under the strictest orders not to discuss his condition with *anyone*. It often left him very fragile, and he was a very proud man."

"How did he happen to choose your facility as a place to recuperate?" Paige said.

"I can only suggest that it was by reputation." He opened a file folder in front of him, scanned the first page, pointed a finger, and said, "Yes, he came here the first time on a recommendation from the Los Angeles chapter of the International Organization of Masters, Mates and Pilots."

"So, from here he would go back to sea," Paige said.

"No, once the symptoms were under control, he would complete his recuperation at a place near El Cajon called Sunair Ranch."

"A ranch?" Max asked.

"It's a . . . uh . . . nudist park, about fifteen miles southeast of here."

Paige burst out laughing. "My uncle at a nudist park?"

"Jock seems to have been full of all kinds of surprises," Max said.

"Whatever possessed him to go there?" Paige asked.

Lester did not join in the laughter. "Sunair is owned by a retired sea captain, who happens to be a long-time personal friend of Captain Boylan's."

"This is all very fascinating," Max interjected, "but it doesn't explain how Jock paid for this expensive care from a local checking account where the balance, according to the bank, never totaled more than a thousand dollars."

Lester sighed and straightened the heavy gold watch on his wrist. "Originally, Captain Boylan covered anticipated expenses with a substantial cash deposit. However, that last time the bills were sent to a third party for payment."

"Who?" Max and Paige asked in unison.

Lester hesitated, then said: "A bank."

"What bank?" Paige insisted. "And where?"

Lester reopened Jock Boylan's file, leafed through the pages, and found what he wanted. He read as he followed a line with his index finger: "The Seamen's Bank in New York."

Max and Paige exchanged near imperceptible nods.

"Have you ever been contacted by a Russell D. Kerwin?" she asked.

"I'm not familiar with that name," Lester responded, almost before she'd finished saying it.

"You're certain?" Max asked softly. "Kerwin. K-E-R-W-I-N. Russell D."

"I said, no." He pushed himself back from his desk and stood. "Is there anything else?"

"We need the name of the person who handled my uncle's account at The Seamen's Bank," Paige said.

"See my secretary on your way out," Lester said, nodding toward the closed door of his office. Without looking at them, he called his secretary and instructed her to provide them with the trust officer's name.

Chapter 11

As soon as the office door closed behind the Alpers, Martin Lester unlocked the center desk drawer and retrieved a slim leather telephone book. When he found the Manhattan number he was looking for, he chose his cell rather than the office phone to punch in the necessary eleven digits. He waited impatiently for the call to ring through.

"Russell Kerwin or Alex Pickerel," he snapped when the secretary finally answered.

"Alex Pickerel speaking. How may I help you?"

"Paige Alper just left my office," Lester shouted into the phone. "She's looking for her uncle's money."

"Oh? Was the sister with her?"

"No, just the husband." Lester searched the top of his desk and found what he wanted. "Max. Max Alper."

"Yeah, well we know who the husband is," Pickerel said. "What did they want?"

"They wanted to know whether Captain Boylan had any assets other than those turned over to the two sisters at the time of his death."

"And you said?"

"I told them what I knew," Lester said. "I had no other choice."

"Uh-huh! C'mon, Lester, exactly what did you tell them?"

"I told them about the San Diego bank account,

which *was* and *is* empty."

"And?"

"And Seamen's Bank in New York."

There was a pause before Pickerel commented, "Rather you wouldn't have led them down that path, Mr. Lester. But what's done's done." Another pause. "Maybe you told them something else during the course of your conversation, like, a small mention of Heirs Apparent?"

Lester took a deep breath while he thought back over his conversation with the Alpers. "No," he said finally, "not a word."

"Good!"

"Good?" Lester shouted. "There's nothing good about any of this. You and Kerwin promised there would never be any kind of an investigation, promised that Ocean Shores and I would never be implicated in your operations."

"Hey, we're not talking investigation here, Mr. Lester. What we've got is one greedy relative, hoping to outsmart all of us."

"And if they decide to go to the authorities? What do I do then? You *assured me* there was no risk involved. I would *never* have given you the names of people like Boylan otherwise. Your puny finder's fee isn't worth that kind of hassle."

"Like I said, Mr. Lester, what's done's done," Pickerel said. "What we do need to do is take steps to keep the situation from escalating." He went on to explain the various precautions Heirs Apparent took to protect the confidentiality of sources.

Lester listened, eyes shifting from one part of the room to another, a finger tapping rapidly on his desktop.

"That's not good enough," Lester snapped. "I want you people to do something that will lead the Alpers as far away

71

from me as possible. Misdirect them! Work with them! Negotiate! Something!"

He lifted the Boylan file and weighed it in the palm of his hand, then slammed it down. Papers slipped from the clip and drifted down onto the floor.

"We are definitely taking care of things," Pickerel said. "You have our word on that."

"Your word?"

"Reassure me, Mr. Lester, tell me again you did *not* bring Heirs Apparent into your conversation with Mr. and Mrs. Alper?"

"I'm not stupid, goddamn it! Why would I mention you or your crooked organization? It's assholes like you who fuck up everything, not me. And I'm telling you right now, if there's even a hint of a scandal, or if I see the remotest possibility of losing my license over this, Heirs Apparent is going down the tubes with me. Count on it!"

"There is no need for threats, Mr. Lester." A pause. "Again, you only told them about the San Diego bank and Seamen's Bank in New York?"

"What's the matter with you? Those are the only Boylan banks I know anything about. Now fuck off and don't ever call me again . . . about Boylan or any other client of Ocean Shores!"

He banged the phone down and shoved his chair back. He stomped over to the huge picture window that overlooked the ocean.

He had to regain control before he made the next call.

Down below, he saw the Alpers standing at the knoll beyond the edge of the parking lot, obviously enjoying the day's clear view of the Pacific. They looked like any other young couple enjoying a spectacular panoramic scene. In fact, not much different from the newlyweds they'd been when they came to Ocean Shores just after Boylan's death.

While he'd barely remembered Paige Alper when she'd called from San Francisco a couple of days ago, he'd never forgotten the sea captain. Boylan had been a good-paying client. Ocean Shores had made huge amounts of money because of his health problems, but he had caused Lester grief like no other patient ever had.

His arrangement with Heirs Apparent was one thing. A few dollars here and there. But those others. They'd laid a small fortune on him. In cash. And unlike Kerwin, those people were very, very scary.

Lester turned from the window after the Alpers had gotten into their car and driven away. Slowly and methodically, he picked up the scattered papers from the Boylan file and re-clipped them into the folder. He sat down and reluctantly made the call to Hong Kong, even though it was two a.m. there.

The man who answered did not identify himself, merely asked what the call was about.

"An heir tracer has found some money Captain Jock Boylan stashed somewhere and has contacted the captain's nieces."

"Go on."

"One of the nieces, Paige Boylan Alper, is trying to find the money on her own, along with her husband."

"Max?"

"What?"

"Is the husband's name Max?"

"Yes."

"And what have you done about this?"

"Called you," Lester said. "That's what you told me to do, what you paid me to do."

"I see." A pause. "Where were they going next?"

"They didn't say."

There was a long pause.

"It would be most advantageous to all concerned if you could obtain that information."

"How am I going to do that?" Lester said, not liking the way the conversation was going.

"We have paid you quite generously over the years, Mr. Lester, have we not?"

"Yes, of course. But Boylan has been dead five years now. That should be the end of it."

"It ends when we say it ends, do you understand?"

Lester pulled out his handkerchief and wiped the sweat from his brow.

"Mr. Lester, I asked you a question."

"Yes, yes, I understand."

"Good. Then you will proceed to learn the Alpers' next destination and report back. Immediately!"

"But . . ." Lester was talking into dead air. The person at the other end had hung up. He wiped at the sweat that continued to blossom on his brow, and buzzed his secretary.

"Ms. Childs, did the Alpers happen to mention where they were going from here?"

"I heard them talking about Sunair Ranch," she said.

"Thank you." He hung up and referred once again to his small telephone directory. He made one final telephone call before deciding to take the rest of the day off.

Chapter 12

"So what's your take on Martin Lester?" Paige asked as they walked toward the Ocean Shores parking lot. "Guilty?"

"Guilty of something."

"All that nonsense about possible litigation didn't ring true. We're five years away from what happened. Something else has to be bugging him."

They walked out to the tree-shaded parking lot that overlooked the Pacific Ocean. Before getting into their rented Dodge Neon, Paige took Max's hand and they ambled out onto a small knoll.

"I wish we could spend our two-week vacation here." She pointed to the sparkling waters. "Wouldn't it be fun not having to do anything but play beach bum in La Jolla? Think of it . . . sand, sun, and sex." She inhaled and exhaled loudly. "But it wouldn't work for me. I'm too revved up over this whole business to relax. If we don't solve this puzzle, I'll go nuts."

Max wrapped an arm around her waist and held her tightly. "So what do you think, on to New York or back to San Francisco?"

"Let's try Sunair Ranch, then on to New York."

"It's worth a try. Jock's old seafarin' buddy might be able to shed light on some of this." He started laughing.

"What's so funny?"

"The thought of your salty old sea captain uncle running around in the buff."

"And just who do you think goes to nudist parks?"

"Have no idea. I've never been to one."

"Well, you're about to find out," she said.

"And they'll let us in?"

"Why not, if we're willing to blend in."

"What do you mean, 'blend'?" he asked, unlocking the car door.

"Remember when Maggie did that nudist park feature? She told me they made her and the photographer strip down to reveal the awful truth."

"Funny, I don't remember that part being in the story."

"You could always wait in the car."

"Oh, no, my lovely," he said, tapping her lightly on the tip of her nose. "Where that beautiful bod goes, I go . . . especially when it's nude."

On their way to Sunair, they stopped at a mall not too far from the nursing home and bought a bottle of water. Paige used her cell phone to call the nudist park while Max made flight reservations for New York.

"Best I could do were two coach seats on the redeye," Max said. "What did you find out?"

"Uncle Jock's friend wasn't in, but he should be back by the time we get there."

"Did you get directions?"

"Hey, think you're dealing with some cub reporter?"

They drove east on I-8 for several miles before leaving the freeway and cutting south, then picked up an eastbound, two-lane, paved road that wound its way through arid, rolling desert. Despite the blazing midday sun, they kept the windows open, preferring the whip of the hot breeze to being cooped up with the air-conditioning.

The road ribboned through a sparsely populated canyon, where many of the houses appeared to be long abandoned.

"Hard to believe that less than an hour ago we were standing by the ocean in the midst of a thriving metropolitan area of almost three million people," Paige said.

"Wish you could lay those cool ocean breezes on me right now." He looked around. "Are you sure this is the right road?"

Paige reread her notes, studied the map, and nodded as she chewed on the end of her pen. "Looks right."

"And somewhere out here there's supposed to be a huge pool surrounded by a lush lawn, towering trees, and naked sunbathers?"

"That's what the lady said. There's also tennis and volleyball."

"In this heat? Forget it."

Rounding a sharp curve, they came on a roadside grove of trees surrounding a small general store and diner. A pair of fifties-style gasoline pumps stood on a small concrete island a car-width away from the road.

"No golden arches, but civilization nonetheless," Max said. "Don't know about you, but I'm ready for a swim, suit or no suit."

"Hate to disappoint you, love, but I don't think this is Sunair. It's supposed to be protected by an eight-foot wood fence."

"Let's hit the store anyway. We could use some more bottled water."

"Good idea. I'm bone dry."

Max slowed as they approached the weather-beaten complex. "Wonder what kind of gas they sell?"

"Why, are we low?"

"No, but it's pretty desolate out here. Wouldn't hurt to have a full tank."

While the paint-chipped pumps had no brand label or other identifying marks, a woman was using one of them to fill the tank of a thirty-year-old GMC flatbed truck, proving at least one pump was working.

"Busy little place," Paige said, nodding toward several nondescript vehicles parked haphazardly outside the clapboard structure. "And look at that!"

She pointed to a four-wheel-drive, candy-apple red, Chevy pickup, riding on waist-high, all-terrain tires.

"Need a stepladder to get into that thing," Max said. He parked behind the Jimmy so he could use the pump next. "That's a real monster truck."

"Scares me and I'm fearless."

As they got out of the car and headed for the store, Paige pulled her blouse out of her skirt and flapped the tail in the air. "Look at me, I'm drenched."

She walked up to the bright red truck and tapped the bulging tread of one tire. "Can you believe this thing?"

"First one I've ever seen up close," Max said. He studied the chromed front bumper that stood as tall as the windows of their Neon.

They bought two bottles of water and drained them while they filled the small Dodge's gas tank, then got a six-pack of water to take along. When they came out of the store, two men were leaning against the driver's door of the customized monster pickup. Both were desert-scrawny, dressed in jeans, T-shirts, and gimme caps.

"Those guys are creepy," Paige said after they were back inside their car. "I don't like the way they were looking at us."

Max shrugged. "Just got an eye for a beautiful woman, that's all."

"I think it's trouble they have an eye for."

"So, we're out of here."

A quarter-mile down the serpentine road, she noticed Max concentrating more on the rearview mirror than on the road ahead. She turned and saw the high-riding Chevy coming up fast behind them.

"Don't play games with him," she said nervously.

"Who, me?"

"Yeah, you! This isn't our Porsche. And this is no autocross."

"Now you tell me."

The pickup moved up to less than a car-length behind. The center portion of the chrome front bumper and yellow-painted undercarriage filled the mirror of the dwarfed Neon.

"Let the jerk pass, Max!"

"As soon as the road straightens, it's all his."

Paige held onto the dash, staring ahead through the windshield. "Now!" she shouted as they came out of a curve. Ahead was a pencil-straight section of road.

Max eased over as far as possible, the tires gripping the edge of a drainage ditch. But the monster truck held its position a few feet off his rear bumper.

"Games!" he said. "They're playing fucking king-of-the-road with us." He floored the accelerator, but the small engine had little left to give. "How much further to Sunair?" he shouted.

"I don't know," she cried out. She turned to stare out the back window while searching around on the floorboards at the same time. "I can't find the goddamn map!"

"Shit!" Max yelled. "If this thing even hiccups he'll smear tire tracks all over the roof."

"Up ahead! A side road! Can you pull over and stop

without that bastard plowing into us?"

"I'll give it a shot." But as he tapped the brake pedal, the pickup rammed their back bumper, shoving them into a skid. He jammed the automatic transmission shifter into low, punched the accelerator, and twisted the steering wheel full circle. They catapulted onto the gravel road. The tires spun in the dirt, caught, and fired a fusillade of stones behind them. The car finally came to a shuddering halt amidst a thick cloud of dust.

Max and Paige coughed and wiped the grit away from their eyes, then twisted around to look out the back window.

As the air cleared, they could see the pickup stopped across the end of the side road, blocking their exit.

Chapter 13

"Lost?" came a voice from the glistening red truck.

Max started to open the door.

"Where're you going?" Paige demanded.

"To see what those pea-brains want."

"Are you kidding? Don't you dare go out there!" She held onto his arm.

"Hey! I'm talking to you folks," the man yelled. He swung down from the passenger side of the high-body Chevy truck.

Max reached across and locked Paige's door, then secured his own door. They both rolled up their windows just as the man came alongside the car.

"Guess you can't hear me with those windows rolled up," he shouted. He bent down to peer inside and motioned for Max to lower his window.

Max cracked the window a couple of inches. "What do you want?"

"Just wonderin' if you folks are lost. I mean, you just turned into the old Ryerson place." He scratched at his head. "Ain't nobody lived here . . . what? . . . maybe five, six years?"

"We're not lost," Paige said. She finally spotted the map on the floorboards, scooped it up, and fanned herself with it.

"Them city maps ain't worth a damn on these back

roads. Where you goin', anyways?"

"Don't tell him," Paige whispered, prodding Max.

"Nice of you to go out of your way," Max said, "but we're really okay."

"Trying to be friendly, that's all," the man said. He looked up at the sun and shook his head. "Gettin' frightfully hot out here to be cooped up in that little car of yours."

"Look, we're not too far from our destination," Paige said. She dabbed at her neck with a tissue. "If your friend would be kind enough to either back up or pull ahead so we can get out of here, we'll be on our way."

The man gave them a crooked grin, a salute, and sauntered back to the waiting customized pickup.

"I hope that's the end of that." Paige watched out the back window as Max put the car in reverse. When they reached the main road, the monster truck still hadn't moved. "If this is country humor, I can do without it," she said.

Max opened his window the rest of the way, leaned out, and yelled: "What's the problem now?"

"My friend here still thinks it wouldn't be neighborly of us to leave you wandering around this canyon in the heat of the day." The pickup driver nodded his agreement. "Could get stuck in a ditch or somethin' with that kiddy-car of yours, you know?"

"We already told you we're not far from where we're going."

The man pushed his hat back and wiped his forehead. "Well, now, the dude ranch is closed this year . . . nearest family's a fur piece down the road. Just where could you folks be goin'?" He tugged the bill of the cap down over his eyes and slapped the door of the truck. "Only one place anywhere near here, you know?" He turned to the driver, whooped, and pounded the side of the truck several times.

"Must be goin' over there to where all them nitwits prance around bare-assed," he shouted.

"Don't say a thing," Max cautioned. Perspiration trickled off his chin.

"Yep, that's it, isn't it?" The man yipped and pointed toward Paige and Max. When neither responded, he added, "Well, tell ya what . . . we're gonna see that you get to that skinny-dippin' place safe and sound." The red truck inched backward on its forty-inch tires. "We'll just follow you down the road and let you know where to turn off."

"Don't seem to have much choice, do we?" Max said.

"Yeah, either go along with them or sit here and roast to death."

They backed out into the road, turned, and continued in the direction they'd originally been going. The truck pulled up to tailgate.

"What do you think this is all about?" Paige asked.

"It's not about anything. They're probably bored and looking for a few laughs at our expense."

"Lucky us."

The truck's lights began flashing and the driver laid heavily on the horn. They looked back to find him pointing emphatically to the left. The passenger's arm popped out of the window and pointed up and over the cab of the truck.

"What do you think?" Max said, slowing. "I don't see the fence."

"They might know a back way in. They may be assholes, but the mileage seems about right."

They turned onto a narrow, one-lane gravel road. Paige waved a relieved farewell to their escorts and received a short toot in response. "I'm delighted to say goodbye to that pair."

"Now, if we can find the entrance, I could sure use a swim," Max said.

Paige smiled for the first time since their stop at the roadside grocery. "That's a lovely vision, you outdoors in the altogether."

"Don't count my freckles before they're aired." He stomped heavily on the brakes, slewing to a stop just short of an irrigation ditch. The road went no farther.

"They fucked us over, didn't they?" Paige slammed her fist against the dashboard.

"Vulgar, but true," Max said. He worked up a new sweat as he wrenched the steering wheel back and forth trying to turn around on the narrow road.

"How far in did we come?"

"Not more than half a mile," he said.

"I knew those guys were creeps the moment I saw them back at the store. Well, I hope they got their jollies."

"I'd sure like to catch up with them in something other than this econobox."

"You'd need a tank," she said. "Let's just chalk this one up in the loss column and get on to Sunair."

As they started back down the lane, the candy-apple red truck loomed up in front of them.

"Shit!" Max shouted, stopping the car again.

"This is too damn much."

They leaped out of the car, Max's hands balled into tight fists; Paige clenched a long flashlight at her side. The two men climbed down out of the truck and started toward them.

"Sort of led them down the primrose path, didn't you, Brad?" said the driver.

"Seemed the thing to do at the time," Brad said, his good-old-boy accent no longer evident.

"Don't you think this stupid game has gone on long enough?" Max snapped.

"It's not a game, man, and it's not over," the driver said.

"What is it then, money?" Paige demanded. "Credit cards?"

"Naw, lady, what we want is for you to get undressed," Brad said with a mean giggle.

"What?" Max and Paige said together.

"Look, we don't have time to repeat everything we say," the driver said. "Get undressed! Pretend this is the nudist park."

"No way!" Max said.

"Do it!" Brad snarled. He pulled a revolver from the back waistband of his Levis. "Do it now!"

"You don't seem to be getting the message," Max said, stepping in front of Paige. "She's *not* getting undressed for you."

"Look, Poppa Bear, pull in those claws," said the driver. "If you think we're out for a little recreational sex, forget it." He stepped forward. "Now, both of you: Get undressed!"

"No!" Max repeated.

"Aw, shit, man!" Brad said with a twist of his head. "Doesn't this here gun impress you?"

"Nothing about either one of you impresses me," Paige said.

The driver grabbed the gun away from his partner, quickly checked the load, and aimed it at Max's midsection. "Take . . . off . . . your . . . fucking . . . clothes!" He lowered the muzzle and fired off a round into the dirt between Max's feet.

Paige screamed.

Max spun around to find her clutching one calf, blood

trickling through her fingers.

"Get away from her," Brad ordered. "The broad'll live. It's only a rock chip."

"The next one'll take out her kneecap," the driver said.

"To hell with it," Paige said, unbuttoning her blouse. "It's not that important."

Max looked from her to the driver, and then started to undress also.

"That's more like it," the driver said. He turned to Brad. "Get their clothes out of that stupid Neon and take them to the Jimmy."

"What the hell are these guys looking for?" Max said to Paige, stepping out of his pants.

By the time Brad returned from the truck, the Alpers were standing naked in the blazing afternoon sun.

"Was there anything else in the car? Cell phone, PDA, that kind of shit?" the driver asked.

Brad rummaged around in the Neon again and finally held up a clamshell cell phone, a laptop computer, and Paige's cosmetic case. "Just these and one of those note-book thingies like secretaries use . . . with the curly wire on one end."

"Forget the *notebook thingie* and cosmetic case. If she needs to put some of that crap on her face out here, who cares?"

Brad dutifully took the phone and laptop to their truck.

"Now go through everything one more time," the driver said. "I want to make damn sure we haven't missed any-thing."

"Damn it, Bill, it's too fucking hot out here." He wiped his face on the bottom of his T-shirt while leering at Paige. "I guarantee, there's nothing there."

"Did you hear me, dude? Just do it!" The driver waited

silently for his partner to complete the task. When Brad came up empty-handed, he nodded and turned back to the Alpers.

"You're not going to strand us out here like this, are you?" Paige said.

"Sure as hell are," Bill said with a curt nod. "Now kick your clothes over here."

"You want them, come get them," Max said. He looked at Paige, who nodded in agreement.

The gunman slowly shook his head. "You two are too much." He ordered Brad to collect their clothing.

As Brad stooped in front of Paige, she nervously stepped back. "Now, now, little lady, I ain't gonna hurt a pretty thing like you." He reached up and trailed a finger across her stomach and down the length of one thigh.

Paige kicked him viciously in the genitals and then twisted away from him.

Brad squealed, cupped himself, and fell over in a heap. He'd no sooner hit the dirt than Max fell across him, pinning him to the ground.

"Run!" Max yelled. "Get out of here!" He struggled with the moaning man's body until he had it positioned between him and the driver.

"Just what the hell do you think you've done, Tarzan?" Bill sneered. He pointed off in the distance with the pistol.

Max looked in the indicated direction. Paige was standing only a few feet away. There was no place for her to run to in the open terrain. He slowly got to his feet, stepped back from Brad, and brushed away a coating of pebbles embedded in his skin.

Paige, blinking back tears, retraced her steps. As she approached Max, Brad reached out and encircled an ankle with one hand.

"You bitch!" the downed man grunted. His face was streaked with tears and dust. He grabbed her bloodied calf and used it, then her hip, waist, arm, and shoulder to pull himself upright until his face was less than an inch from hers. "No one kicks me in the balls and gets away with it."

Paige held his eyes, steadily, defiantly. She saw the hand coming, tried not to flinch, but the blow jarred her. She shook off the effects. "You hit like a wuss."

He held her by the neck with one hand, doubling the other into a fist. Before he could strike her again, Max jumped onto his back, tumbling all three of them to the ground.

"Knock it off!" Bill yelled, trying to take aim, first at Max, then at Paige. Giving up, he rushed into the melee, pinned Paige to the ground with one foot, and sapped Max with the pistol muzzle.

"Bastard!" Paige yelled. She squirmed out from under the driver's boot, crawled to Max, and cradled his head in her arms. "You've killed him!"

"I don't think so," the driver said. "That's not in the job description."

"What the hell's that supposed to mean?"

He ignored her as he helped the battered Brad to his feet. "Get the keys out of the ignition," he said, shaking his head. "How you managed to fuck up something this simple I'll never know."

Brad limped over to the Neon. "What about her purse and his wallet?" he asked.

"We don't need them."

"Lots of bucks here," Brad said, fingering Max's wallet.

"That's not why we're here." He waited for Brad to toss the purse and wallet back into the Neon. "Pick up their clothes and let's get the fuck out of here."

Paige rocked Max in her arms and watched the two men climb into the jacked-up truck. Instead of backing out the trail, though, the truck came forward, stopped only a few inches from Max's outstretched legs.

"One more thing," the driver yelled down from his perch. "This is your first and last warning, lady: forget this rinky-dink hunt of yours." He grinned and tugged at the bill of his gimme hat. "Go back to being pampered little yuppies. I hear they grow a lot of them up there in Frisco."

Chapter 14

Paige squinted into the blinding afternoon sun, then looked back at Max. His face, along with the rest of his naked body, was turning bright pink. She studied him closely for any signs of consciousness as she fingered the egg-sized lump on the top of his head. There was no change. No change in his shallow breathing, no change in his awareness. She smiled grimly: it was hotter than hell and her Max was out cold.

Their perspiration mingled and trickled down across her thighs. She lifted one wrist and took his pulse—rapid, much too rapid for a conditioned runner.

She had to get the two of them out of the sun, but the landscape of rocks and scrub offered no shelter. The only shade was inside the car, certain to be like an oven.

"Dammit, Max, what should I do?" she asked softly, gently rocking him in her arms. "My head's spinning. I can't think straight." Tears trailed down her cheeks as she looked back at the Neon again. She swiped at her face with the back of her hand. "Not much choice—either sunstroke or heat prostration."

She eased out from under him and lowered his head onto the hard ground. She walked gingerly across the baked earth to the car, opened all four doors, and cringed as the trapped heat parched her exposed skin. She started to lean inside, then quickly withdrew her hand—the upholstery was blistering hot.

"I'll never get him into this tin box without making some room," she muttered.

She winced at the hot surface of the steering wheel, released the passenger seat latch, and pushed forward until the seat came off its tracks. She wrestled the cumbersome seat out of the car and tossed it onto the ground. She'd done this before, but it was so much easier when she and Max did it together while cleaning their autocross car. The other side was even more difficult because she had to fight with the steering wheel jutting out into the driver's space.

She stopped for a moment, sweaty hands braced against knees, and waited for the adrenaline rush to subside. When the tremors stopped, she took a bottle of water from the six-pack they'd bought and went back to Max.

"Oh, baby, look at you!" His skin was dry, deepening in color from pink to angry red. She quickly twisted off the bottle cap, poured a small amount of water into the palm of her hand, and washed it across his forehead. Tipping the bottle to her lips, she swallowed half of the warm water before pouring the rest onto Max's hair.

Squatting, she took a deep breath, slipped her hands under his shoulders, and curled her fingers into his armpits. She straightened and inched backward toward the Neon. Max's heels dug twin furrows into the sandy soil. After a few steps, Max slipped from her grasp, bounced off her flexed thighs, and tumbled onto the ground with a grunt.

"Max!" She stumbled backward and fell into the prickly branches of a dead bush. "Dammit!"

She ignored the pain and bleeding scratches and struggled back to her feet. She examined Max again, but found he was no worse off than before. After drying her palms on the ground, she reached under his arms, locked her hands across his chest, and lifted him up. He groaned and mumbled incoherently.

"We're going to do it, Max . . . I swear, we're going to make it."

When she felt her calves bump up against the doorsill of the car, she continued on, straining to pull him up and inside. She collapsed on the carpeting, Max's a hundred and seventy-six pounds crushing down on top of her. She wedged her elbows against the floorboards and shoved at him until she could squirm out from under his dead weight.

Sweat cascaded down her body and a veil of black dots danced before her eyes. Blinking to clear her vision, she waited for her thundering heart to slow down. When she saw Max's sunlit feet still hanging outside the small vehicle, she started to cry.

"Okay, okay," she told herself. "Enough already!" She crawled over Max's inert body, bent his uncooperative legs, and wrestled his feet inside.

Paige twisted around in the small car, propped his head and shoulders against the rear seat. The compounded heat of the car interior and their bodies squeezed together was almost unbearable.

Even though they'd cursed the Neon for its lack of power, she was grateful they didn't have their two-seater Porsche.

As she reached across him to get another bottle of water, he moaned. A hand twitched; his eyes fluttered open, then closed.

"Wake up," she whispered and kissed his cheeks with parched lips. She sprinkled more water on his face, then took a handful and spread it across her chest.

"I'll be glad to do that for you," Max said, smiling weakly up at her.

"You're awake!" She cupped his face in her hands.

"My God," he said groggily as he looked around. "I take a little nap and you start to disassemble the car."

"You're incorrigible." She held the water bottle to his lips.

Max drank eagerly, draining the bottle. "My throat feels like someone used a hair dryer on it."

Paige opened another bottle and held it to his lips.

"What happened to the joy boys?" He groaned and shifted carefully into a more comfortable position.

"Gone, I hope. They took our cell phone, car keys, clothes, and laptop, then drove away."

"What did they want with the seats to the car?"

She laughed. "I did that. I needed the room so I could drag you in here out of the sun."

"And without your weightlifting belt." He ran a finger across her bare tummy before taking another drink. "Surprised they didn't take the water, too," he said.

"If you think that's strange, they didn't even take our wallets."

"Then it was just a game for them, after all," he said, sitting up.

"No, I don't think so. Someone sent them, but I can't figure out who or why."

"I vaguely remember thinking the same thing." He ran a hand across the top of his head, flinched. "God, my head hurts."

"Are you all right, other than that?"

"I think so. My head's pounding like a drum, but the rest of me seems to be in working order." He flexed his fingers and wiggled his toes. "Now if I could get you to turn on the air-conditioning—"

"Max, I'm worried. Those jerks told me we should bug

off and go home. Now!"

"Well, we'll have to see about that." He levered himself up onto the rear seat. "How close do you think we are to Sunair?"

"We can't be more than a quarter-mile away."

"Do you think we can hoof it?"

Paige shook her head. "We can't risk it. It's hotter than hell out there, and even if it wasn't, you shouldn't be going on any hikes with that goose egg on your noggin. Besides, what if I'm wrong and we're miles from there?"

"Okay, we go to Plan B."

She laughed and sat down next to him. "What, pray tell, is Plan B?"

Max moved off the seat and crawled towards the dashboard.

"What are you up to?" she asked.

"I'm going to hot-wire it." He reached up under the dashboard and pulled down a handful of colored wires.

"Aren't these new cars supposed to be burglar-proof?"

"Bullshit! If I don't have this friggin' Dodge running and reassembled before dark, we can walk out of here under the stars without having to worry about getting sunburned, or embarrassed."

Chapter 15

Journal—1996
Jock Ian Boylan

July 4—Hong Kong
Independence Day!
An auspicious day to start my last sea voyage.
Little more than a month and I'll be back here in Hong Kong, retired. Independence, indeed.
Not much time left to decide what I'm going to do, where I'm going to live.
Sure not interested in a shoreside maritime job. But don't want to sit around doing nothing, either.
There must be something here in Hong Kong that I could do to stay out of mischief.
Mattos wants me to go to San Diego to help him run his nudist park. Tempting, but can't leave the Far East and Sallee.
Sallee, my little grown-up woman. Has her own life to lead. Doesn't need me hanging around, getting in her way.
Got to find something to keep me busy or I'll end up driving her crazy, and everyone else I come in contact with.
Still amazed at her prestigious job offer. They came after her waving big bucks even before she was graduated. Knew she was doing well in school, but didn't know she'd become a genius. Her company has already sent her off to Shanghai

on a multinational trade deal. And her not even settled yet in her new apartment.

Hope she's back by the time I complete this voyage. Want to celebrate her new job with her.

To think my daughter's never seen a Fourth of July parade. Only been in the States during the school year.

Hell of a student. Always studying. Said there'd be plenty of time to see things after she was finished with school. Hope she does that and doesn't get all bogged down in a demanding job at her age.

She says she has no desire to return to Sri Lanka, where she was born. No interest in working in the States, either. Strange.

Might change her mind when the Chinese absorb Hong Kong next year. She'll be glad I went through all that red tape to make certain she has U.S. citizenship.

What to do?

Should ask her advice. Hard to share my thoughts with her. Never able to do that with Nolla, either, damn fool that I am.

July 7—At Sea

Taiwan Strait pirates tried to board us during the night. Had to break out the small arms to drive them off. Second mate wounded. Slug shattered his shoulder. Radioed for a helicopter to take him to Taipei. He'll be okay.

Will pick up a replacement crewman in Busan.

No other injuries to the crew and the ship didn't suffer any damage. Lucky.

This bunch wasn't very bright, though. I fired a few rounds into the air and they high-tailed it.

Don't know what they thought they were going to do with a shipload of forty-foot empty containers. Dummies didn't seem to know they would need special equipment to offload the boxes in the first place.

Even if we'd had loaded containers aboard and they'd been after one particular box, chances of it being where they could get into it would be almost impossible.

Nothing discourages them. They used to operate mostly in the South China Sea. Now find them almost anywhere. Get bolder every year. Another good reason to get my ass out of this business.

July 14—At Sea

Tried to call Sallee while we were docked in Yokohama. Her Shanghai hotel said she had checked out. No answer at her apartment. Will try again when we dock in Oakland.

July 24—Oakland

Still can't reach Sallee. Confusion at her office as to her whereabouts. Trying to convince myself it has to do with her being a new employee.

Shouldn't worry so much. She is an adult and has better things to do with her time than sit by the phone and wait for her daddy to call.

Did manage to reach Paige. She's back from a year in Europe. Got hired as an intern on a Frisco daily newspaper. Hoped we might get together, but there just isn't enough time in port anymore.

Docked at the container terminal in the evening, sailed through the Golden Gate by midmorning the next day.

Damn accelerated schedules have taken most of the fun out of going to sea.

Will try to reach Sallee via ship-to-shore. If I'm not successful, it's going to be a long two weeks back to Hong Kong.

Chapter 16

Captain Rich Mattos shook his head. His long, curly white hair flew out in all directions. "I'm really worried about this," he said, gently fingering the lump on Max's head. "You seem to be okay, but I'll feel better after we run you into town for the X-ray Doc ordered."

"Like this?" Max said. He looked down at his nude body, then at the equally nude, brown-skinned bear of a man hovering over him.

Rich laughed. "I'm sure we can find something around here to make the two of you acceptable in El Cajon."

"I'll bet not many of your guests arrive in the buff," Paige said, laughing nervously.

"Well, most of them start stripping the moment they clear the gate, but I can't remember the last time anyone arrived starkers, and cat-scratched from head to toe." He pressed the tape around the bandage on Paige's leg, and then led them into the living room of his sprawling, hillside house. A huge picture window provided a panoramic view of the nudist park.

"Are either of you hungry?" Mattos asked. "I'm a great cook, if I do say so myself." When neither answered, he realized they were looking uncertainly at the beach towels spread across the upholstered furniture. "They're a lot kinder to your bare rump than that scratchy fabric. Also help keep things sanitary."

Max sat down gingerly. "All I want is more water," he said.

"You're going to explode," Paige said and tapped him playfully on the stomach.

"I must say, the two of you look much better than when you dragged yourselves in here," Mattos said.

They were beginning to act more like first-time nudists now that they'd had a chance to clean up and get their wounds tended to. Paige moved stiffly, self-consciously. Max worked at appearing to be at ease. But both glanced nervously and repeatedly at the nudists walking back and forth outside the picture windows.

He was amused as he studied the Alpers: there were definite advantages to clothing—this pair would have looked a lot less silly with *something* covering all the tic-tac-toe dressings the resident doctor had plastered on their cuts and scratches. They'd been damn lucky to escape the searing desert at all, after being attacked and stranded by a couple of thugs.

"So you're one of Jocko's nieces," Mattos said. "Probably would have recognized you or your sister, given enough time . . . and under more normal circumstances. You still look pretty much like the skinny little girls in the photos he was always showing me. Kept a regular album, he did—you and your sister, and of Sallee, too, of course. But I never could tell you and your twin apart."

"They're definitely different," Max said. He laughed and stroked Paige's cheek.

"So tell me," Mattos said, "about this thing with the two goons. Do you have any idea why they ran you off into the boondocks like that?"

"Not a clue," Paige said. "They insisted that we should go back to San Francisco, no ifs, ands, or buts. Definitely wasn't a spur-of-the-moment kind of thing . . . someone hired them to attack us. I'd bet on it."

"And they were adamant that we should stop looking for Jock's money," Max added.

"What money is that?" Mattos asked.

"There's apparently a quarter-million dollars floating around someplace," Paige said. "We learned that from an heir tracer."

"That's odd. I knew he had some money stashed some-place. Didn't think it was that much, though. I would have thought he'd have left it to you and your sister in his will."

"If there's a will, we haven't found it," Max said.

"We think the New York heir tracer hired those guys to rough us up," Paige said. "Like, who else could it be?"

"It's almost certain the people at Heirs Apparent are up to something fishy."

"Possibly," Mattos said. He studied Paige for a moment, captivated by the intensity of her piercing green eyes. He'd seen that stubborn look before. Determination was obviously a family trait. Despite her ordeal in the hot, arid backcountry, she was still full of piss and vinegar.

"Do you have any thoughts about our little run-in?" Max asked.

Mattos hesitated. This unexpected appearance of his old friend's niece and her husband made him realize he should have gotten in touch with the sisters long before this. He'd just kept putting it off and putting it off, thinking he was protecting them. Well, he'd done a poor job of that, and it was way past time to get the story out into the open.

"Been a lot of people coming around here in recent years asking questions about Captain Jock Boylan," he said finally. "Especially since his death. Some were smooth talkers; others were really mean blokes, bad as any of the waterfront brawlers Jock and I tangled with in all those seedy bars around the Pacific."

"That's strange," Paige said and moved to the edge of the sofa.

"What were they after?" Max added.

"Well, it wasn't his money, that's for certain. Doubt if anyone knew he had any money hidden away. I sure didn't." He paused, looking from Paige to Max, then back to Paige. He'd promised to keep his old friend's secret, but Jock was dead and his family had a right to know. "I think they were looking for your uncle's journals."

"What kind of journals?" Max asked.

Mattos held up a hand, then pointed a finger at Max. "You're not the only parched one. First we drink . . . then we talk." He went into the kitchen, and in a few minutes came back with three large glasses of lemonade.

"Keeping a log's required when you're a ship's captain," Mattos finally said. "But Jocko took it a step further than most. He started keeping a personal journal from the time he entered the California Maritime Academy."

"But why would Heirs Apparent be interested in something like a personal history?" Paige interrupted.

Mattos shook his head. "I really don't think those fellows amount to much."

"But as far as we can tell, they're the only ones who could be interested," Max said.

Mattos shook his head again, more to himself than to the Alpers. "What do you know about your uncle?" he asked Paige. "I mean, the years between Sallee's death and your Uncle Jock's death?"

"Not very much at all," Paige said, spreading her hands out at her sides. "My mother always refused to talk about him."

101

"Well, maybe Jock wasn't much of a brother, but he was a damn good father. There wasn't anything he wouldn't have done for Sallee. When she was murdered, he went off his rocker, swore he would avenge her death one way or the other."

"Oh, my God!" Paige said. "Sallee was murdered? Uncle Jock wrote that she'd been killed in an accident."

"I know, I know. He didn't want to upset you and your sister again, so soon after your parents' death." He paused for a moment, surprised that even after all this time, memories of Jock could still make him so sad. "The real story's in the journals. You'll have to read them for yourself." Tears welled and ran down his cheeks. "It's not something I can talk about."

"You have the journals here?" Max asked.

"Some of them . . . the ones from the time Nolla died until just after Sallee was killed."

"Do you think we could read them?" Paige asked softly.

"Probably long overdue."

"And Jock's other journals you mentioned?" Max asked. "Where are they?"

"Haven't the slightest idea. Maybe Hong Kong, maybe Sri Lanka, maybe New York. He wouldn't tell me. Said what I didn't know couldn't hurt me." He laughed harshly. "Of course, your uncle wasn't right about *everything!*"

"Were you threatened?" Max asked.

"I suppose you could call it that, only I don't push too easy. When a couple of rather nasty blokes kept insisting I turn the journals over to them, I had to beat on them and throw them out of the park." He paused and drank some lemonade. "Either those bastards, or someone else, decided to get even—they trashed the house one night when I was out. Probably would have burned it to the ground, if

102

someone hadn't heard the racket. Found a half-empty gasoline can out behind the house the next day."

He got up and stomped around the room. "If I ever get my hands on those . . ."

"I know how you feel," Max interrupted. "I'd like to carve off a large chunk of the guys who attacked us. I can still see that creep leering at Paige . . . never felt so vulnerable, so damn defenseless in my life."

Mattos sat down again and looked at Max. "Didn't mean to get so fired up," he said. "Just an old fool who hates not getting in the last blow. Guess I'm not too much different from you or Jocko, for that matter."

"How long were the two of you friends?" Paige asked.

"We went back a long way. Met at the Academy. Couldn't stay out of trouble the whole four years we were there. Seems like we were almost always on the verge of getting expelled for one dumb stunt or another."

Paige shook her head. "I guess I never thought of Uncle Jock as a student. I always fantasized a swashbuckling sea captain, sailing from one exotic port to another."

"Oh, he would have lived up to your fantasies, all right. We had a lot of wild times out there in the Pacific. There are some crazy stories I could tell you, that's for sure. Some of them are so unbelievable I'm not even certain they actually happened. Time has a way of doing that, I guess. Anyway, once Jocko met Nolla, everything changed. Going to sea became just a job to him. He was truly devoted to her and that daughter of theirs." More tears trickled across his leathery cheeks. "I really miss the old bastard." He got up and went into the kitchen and brought back the lemonade pitcher.

As he refilled their glasses, Max and Paige were admiring a matched pair of wood-carved dolphins on an end table.

"Your uncle's work," Mattos said.

"He made these?" Paige asked. When Mattos nodded, she added, "There's so much I didn't know about him." She picked up one of the carvings. "I never knew he was an artist."

"Quite a good one. You should see some of the elaborate Oriental carvings he created. They're exquisite. Carved most of them at sea."

"What made *you* decide to go to sea?" Max said.

Mattos sat back in his chair, looked out the window. "Damn good question." He thought for a moment. "Got hooked on Jack London when I was a kid. Got the bug to see the world. But, when you get right down to it, it was the sea itself that lured me . . . its vastness, its power. After my first training voyage, everything else became ordinary, empty."

"And Uncle Jock, is that how he felt, too?"

"Hah! Who ever knew what that old coot thought?" He ran his fingers through his unruly hair. "Well, he did love the stars. Spent hours studying them. Best damn celestial navigator I ever knew. He used to talk all the time about how much closer the stars were at sea . . . even got me to believing it. Now, when I can't sleep at night, I go out to the bay and crawl into my boat, lay back, and look at the stars."

"But you retired, why didn't Uncle Jock?"

"He was going to. I even asked him to become my partner in Sunair. But then the triad murdered Sallee. After that, he was obsessed with revenge. Poor old guy. Her death sucked the joy of life right out of him. Might as well have cut his throat at the same time."

"You said a triad killed Sallee," Max said. "You mean a Chinese triad?"

"That's what I mean."

"When? Which one?"

"Slow down, Paige," Mattos said. "It's a long, complicated story. I think reading the journals I do have here will answer at least some of your questions . . . and probably give you a better sense of your Uncle Jock."

Chapter 17

Jock Ian Boylan

August 8—Hong Kong
  Sallee has vanished.
  Lai-ping says there's been no message from her at my place. Sallee's apartment looks like she just stepped out, might return at any moment.
  Sallee's office said she came back from Shanghai, spent one day at her desk, and hasn't been seen or heard from since.
  Police have been no help. Put out the word along the waterfront. Calling in every favor.
  Damn scared.

August 11—Hong Kong
  Flying to Bangkok.

August 13—Bangkok
  Two days sitting in a hotel room and nothing has changed. Can't even get drunk. Pointless. Everything is pointless.
  Sallee is gone.
  No, not gone. Gone would be tolerable, endurable. Just an absence, a temporary thing. Gone would be transient,

106

reversible, exist somewhere else.

That beautiful, sweet being has been destroyed.

My little girl.

My baby is dead.

August 14—Bangkok

Must force myself to write this down, no matter the pain. Must write every detail of what happened to my Sallee. Will record every action from this moment forward. If anything happens to me, my notes may help bring to justice whoever is responsible for this terrible deed.

Police say a well-financed prostitution ring kidnaps young women off the streets of Hong Kong. Circulate the women from brothel to brothel throughout the Far East. Never keep them in one location for more than thirty days. Impossible to track down the culprits.

Evidence indicates that's what happened to my Sallee.

Morning after she returned from Shanghai, she had an appointment to meet a friend in the park for an early run. She never showed up. Her friend was never able to reach her after that.

Can only speculate. Reliable informants say the usual procedure is to hold the women in an old warehouse or on a derelict ship. Wait until they have enough women for a *shipment*, maybe a half-dozen or so. A junk or old yacht is usually used for transportation.

Apparently the bastards had a good outing this time—twenty-seven women!

Some demented genius came up with the idea of equipping a twenty-foot cargo container with sleeping mats, water, food, and air vents.

They shipped the box out on a tramp steamer to Bangkok.

Idiots didn't realize containers are stowed so closely together in a ship's hold that air vents are blocked off.

God, how my baby must have suffered. How all of them must have suffered. Crowded, trapped, suffocating in a dark box, a dark hole.

I retch every time I think about their fate. Sallee's fate.

The stench coming from the container attracted Bangkok port officials. When they broke into the box, all the women were dead.

Of course, no one called at the Bangkok port to claim the death container. The consignee's name and address were fictitious. The women carried no identification.

Port officials determined the container's origin from the manifest—Hong Kong.

Because of the missing person's report I'd filed on Sallee, the Hong Kong police told me about the hideous crime in Thailand. Couldn't imagine this had anything to do with Sallee. Flew there anyway. Had to see for myself. Had to know.

The morgue was too small to hold all the bodies. They had to use a cold-storage warehouse.

Walked down the long row of corpses, lifted the sheet from each of their young faces. Hoped against hope it would prove to be a wasted trip.

But Sallee was there.

So small. So lost.

So dead.

August 15—Hong Kong

I've been gutted.

How could anyone do something that vicious?

The emptiness is unbearable.

August 21—Hong Kong
Can't bring my Sallee back to life.

Know she's gone forever, but I will find whoever did this. Find them and make them pay with their worthless lives. I swear I will make them suffer . . . suffer over and over again. As long as there is a breath left in my body, I will make them feel my pain.

Sallee's pain.

Chapter 18

Paige rolled over onto her back, her eyes watery and red. She closed the final journal and set it aside.

"What a terrible, terrible waste." She reached out to Max, lying next to her on the Sunair lawn. "Poor Uncle Jock. First Nolla, then Sallee."

"No wonder he became so obsessed with revenge," Max said. "He'd lost everyone that ever mattered to him."

Paige raised up on one elbow and gazed at the swimming pool, where a group of teenagers was making comic dives into the water.

"Sallee could have grown up with Sheryl and me . . . she would have been like a sister to us." A sob caught in her throat. "We never even met. Whatever possessed my mother to be so cruel, to refuse to take Sallee in?"

Max reached out and rubbed her back. "I know how much you loved your mother and father. But parents make the same stupid mistakes as everyone else. Your mother allowed her animosity toward Jock to interfere with her good judgment."

Paige rolled away. "And maybe she was just an out-and-out bigot."

"That's not fair, Paige. You only have a few words written in a journal to counter a lifetime of experiences. Don't forget, Jock had just gone through hell when he made those entries."

"I know, but Sallee was just a year older than we are. It's hard not to identify with her. And she's gone because some despicable cretins abducted her. Money! Can you believe it? It's all about money. Selling women for sleazy sex. If only she'd been allowed to come live with us . . ."

"You have to let it go, Paige. It's done. Over with."

She nodded and fell back against him. "I thought I knew . . . understood my mother . . . but I didn't really know her at all. I'm so angry with her. Sallee and Uncle Jock should have been a real part of our lives."

A door slammed, caught their attention. Rich Mattos came out of the house and headed in their direction.

"I wonder if *he* knows what Jock was up to that year after Sallee was killed?" Max nodded toward their host.

"Maybe, maybe not."

It took time for Mattos to reach them. He wasn't able to slip past any group or individual without stopping for a few words and a big smile or a hearty laugh.

"You seem very happy here," Paige said as Mattos dropped down on the grass beside them.

"I love it." He took in the scope of the park with a sweep of his hand. "Look at all these people—everything from babes in arms to grandparents enjoying the sunshine and fresh air without having to hide anything." He waved at one of the kids calling to him from the diving board. "I went through too many wars, saw too many young people die. Turned me into a pacifist." He interrupted himself with a booming laugh. "I guess the plain fact is that it's difficult to be angry or want to fight when your dingus is dangling in the breeze."

Paige laughed. "Uncle Jock should have taken you up on your offer to become your partner."

Mattos nodded with a sigh. "What did you think of his journals?"

111

"They made me feel empty," Paige said.

Max nodded. "And they were disturbing. But I didn't see anything about the triads you mentioned. You said they were the ones responsible for Sallee's death."

"Nothing but criminal gangs," Mattos said, driving a fist into the grass. "Mean, vicious bastards. Snuff you out without thinking twice."

"And you think one of the triads was responsible for what happened to Sallee," Max said.

"I would bet my life on it," Mattos said.

"I've heard rumors that they're even active in San Francisco," Paige said.

"I've heard that, too," Mattos said. "Not much different than the Mafia . . . the Mafia with a Southeast Asian flavor. Most are based in Hong Kong, but they can show up anywhere."

"Did Uncle Jock know which triad was responsible for Sallee's death?" Paige asked.

"I don't know. I didn't hear from him that last year, and when he came back to Ocean Shores, he was pretty damn ill. We didn't have many conversations during that time."

"You were close, I can see that," Max said. "It must have been terrible to lose such a long-time friend."

Mattos smiled grimly. "Like losing my right hand." He reached out and took one of Paige's hands in both of his. "Listen, you two, go to New York and find Jock's money. Enjoy it! I'm sure that's what he would have wanted."

Paige sat up and stretched. "Well, if that's what we're going to do, then we'd better check flights and make a reservation."

"You can use the computer in my office," Mattos said.

"And maybe we can scare up some of those clothes you

mentioned earlier," Max said. "I'm not at my best traveling nude."

Mattos laughed, stood up, and stretched. "My best advice is for you to forget about triads and all the other stuff in Jocko's journals. That was such a long time ago. It's over and done with, and there's nothing you can do about any of it anyway."

The next day, on the way to the airport, Max and Paige shipped Jock's journals north to their friends Rita and Mike in San Rafael. Then they went looking for a shopping mall, so they could replace their clothes and luggage.

When they finally dropped off the now-less-than-primo Neon, the car rental agency raised hell. They apologized, left the mess for their credit card company to sort out, and jumped on the terminal shuttle to catch their late-afternoon flight to New York.

Chapter 19

"Bankers! Phooey!" Max slammed down the telephone receiver and flung himself back onto the hotel bed.

"So?" Paige poked her head out of the steamy bathroom, a terrycloth towel wrapped around her.

"Frustrating," he said. "They're more asinine here in New York than they are back home."

"Did you reach that guy Lester's secretary told us about, the one at The Seamen's Bank?"

"The very same Northrup Leeds, for all the good it did me." He affected a falsetto voice: " 'Can't discuss client accounts without proper identification and authorization, and certainly not over the telephone.' He wouldn't even admit Jock had an account at the bank, much less say what the balance might be."

"Maybe he'll change his mind, if we go down there and wave the death certificate and power of attorney in his pink face."

"How do you know he has a pink face?" Max laughed. He pulled her down onto the bed, so he could re-bandage her wounded leg.

"Don't all bankers have pink faces?" She giggled and tickled his knee with her toes.

"Will you hold still?" He trapped her foot with one hand and wrapped the last piece of tape around her calf.

"No other way . . . we'll have to go to the bank and talk

114

to this guy Leeds in person."

"He said we would have to have a New York state tax waiver and an affidavit to cover a lost passbook, *if* there is an account."

Paige started laughing.

"What's so funny?"

"I keep imagining what Sheryl would say, if she knew I'd held onto that power of attorney for Jock's estate all this time. I meant to give it back to her after the funeral, but I forgot all about it."

"Surprised old lawyer George didn't jump all over you."

"Oh, I think once he found out Uncle Jock didn't have any money, he lost all interest. And it's too late now." She stood and pirouetted on the bandaged leg. "Ha! Almost as good as new."

Max nodded his appreciation. "You know, if we're doing this thing, we better do it right."

"What do you mean?"

"I think we should first arm ourselves with some research on New York banking and abandoned property laws."

"They're probably not too much different than California, but you're right, we need to check first. Wish those jerks hadn't taken our laptop." She picked up the 'Hotel Services' folder. "Maybe the hotel has computers for guest use."

"Thought of that . . . their system is down." He slipped on his shoes. "Tell you what: you check out Albany and I'll go out for some croissants and coffee."

"No! You promised you'd treat me to deli when we got to New York."

"It's not even ten a.m.," Max said.

"And what about those breakfast burritos you insisted on

when we were in Mazatlan?"

Max laughed. "I'm on my way."

"Come back soon. I'm starved."

Paige was sitting cross-legged in the middle of the bed when Max returned with a large bag filled with chopped chicken liver sandwiches, half-sours, German potato salad, and Dr. Brown's cream soda. There were scribbled notes on hotel stationery scattered all around her.

"Basically," she said, sweeping the scraps of paper aside to make room for the food, "accounts can be declared abandoned in New York after only five years of no activity, instead of seven years in California."

"That explains the timing of Kerwin's letter."

She dug a finger into the potato salad and licked it clean. "My guess is that originally Uncle Jock stashed away the two hundred fifty thousand dollars for his retirement. Then, when Sallee was killed, everything changed. He gave up his retirement plans and the money just sat in The Seamen's Bank, drawing interest, while he went looking for Sallee's killers."

"That sounds logical," Max said.

"Then Uncle Jock died. So after a total of five years of inactivity, the account was declared abandoned. Simple."

"But wouldn't he have listed a beneficiary, or next-of-kin? Like you and Sheryl, since you were the only family he had left?"

"You know as well as I do that I've never heard from Seamen's or any other bank. And you can be damn sure Sheryl would have been in touch if she'd heard anything."

"Yet, Heirs Apparent had no trouble finding you." He handed her a sandwich. "Weird."

"Very." Paige examined her overflowing sandwich,

trying to decide where to take the first bite, so chopped chicken liver wouldn't ooze out all over her and the bed. She found a perfect spot and liberated a mouthful.

"I mean," she continued, licking mayonnaise from her lips, "the New York Office of Unclaimed Funds said the banks are required to annually publish a list of these accounts in a local English-language newspaper. Guys like Russell D. Kerwin must pee their pants in anticipation of these lists coming out every year. All those accounts become ripe for the plucking."

"When are they published?"

"They start in late August and go into early September."

"That fits: Kerwin's letter to you and Sheryl was dated August twenty-sixth, right?"

"Right."

"Which means he was able to find you almost immediately." He snatched a chunk of pickle from her plate and held her at bay while he took a bite. "Anyway, how about we go right now and talk to your rosy-cheeked banker?"

"Not until you give me back my pickle, you thief."

Northrup Leeds was neither uncooperative nor pink-faced.

"Jock Ian Boylan has a checking account balance of slightly less than one thousand dollars," the black banker said, turning from his computer terminal. "It's too bad," he continued, "that the safe deposit box rental fees have been chipping away at it. He rented one of the largest boxes we offer."

"Only a thousand dollars?" Paige asked.

"That's it," Leeds said. "Anyway, it's too small to require a tax waiver. And since you have the other necessary papers with you, I'll cut you a check and close the account.

The safe deposit box, though, is a much more complicated matter."

"Just a checking account and a safe deposit box?" Paige said, shaking her head.

"Were you expecting something more?" Leeds asked.

"Something in the neighborhood of two hundred and fifty thousand dollars," she blurted.

"Maybe it's in the box," Leeds said.

"I don't think so . . . based on the information we have," Max said. "But we didn't even know Jock Boylan had a safe deposit box, until you mentioned it."

"Then I don't understand," Leeds said.

Paige and Max looked at each other quizzically. "Kerwin must have a line on an account in some other bank," she said.

"Excuse me, but if you're referring to Russell Kerwin of Heirs Apparent, you're definitely in the wrong bank." Leeds placed his palms flat atop his desk.

"You know Kerwin?" Max asked.

"Know *of* him. There is a distinct difference."

"Oh?"

Leeds glanced around, lowered his voice. "Look, you seem to be nice people, so I'm going to tell you something." He paused and once again surveyed the desks closest to him, then leaned toward the Alpers. "But if you ever tell anyone where you got this information, I'll absolutely deny it. Is that clear?"

Max and Paige nodded.

The banker leaned even farther over his desktop. "There are *some* people in *some* banks who cooperate with Mr. Kerwin, and other heir tracers. They let the tracers know in advance when a sizeable account is going to be declared abandoned. At one time the minimum figure that attracted those vultures was ten thousand dollars. I don't know what it is now."

"So you're saying Kerwin wouldn't have been interested in Uncle Jock's account at your bank," Paige said.

"For a couple of reasons: first, there's never been more than ten thousand dollars in it from the time it was opened; second, we don't cooperate with *any* of the heir tracers." He shook his head and leaned back.

"That's nice to know, but—"

"Also, our abandoned account newspaper ads don't run until tomorrow, which is the deadline. So there's no way Heirs Apparent could have known about Captain Boylan's account here."

"And you say the account was active until about five years ago, or around the time of Jock's death," Max said.

"That's the way it looks." The banker turned back to his computer terminal. After a moment, he said, "It seems the account was used strictly to make payments to a San Diego nursing home and to automatically pay the safe deposit box rental. The last activity was the day after your uncle's death, a draft made payable to Ocean Shores."

"Good old Lester. Probably scared he wouldn't get paid," Paige said. She pointed to the computer. "Wasn't anyone listed as beneficiary?"

"Paige Boylan Alper and Sheryl Boylan Fenster," Leeds said. "Unfortunately, he didn't provide any addresses, which isn't all that uncommon." He looked at the computer screen again and smiled. "That's nice: I see both you and your sister decided to hold onto the family name."

Paige laughed. "Actually, it's my mother's family name. She was afraid we'd forget our Irish heritage. I was Paige Boylan Tait before I married Max."

"Well, I hope you find the two hundred and fifty thousand dollars." He laughed to himself. "I'd sure like to see *someone* outsmart Russell Kerwin."

"Any suggestions?" Max asked.

"Are you sure the money's here in New York?" Leeds asked.

"We hoped it was," Paige said. "Now, who knows?"

"If it were me," Leeds said, tilting his head back, "I'd go to the library and start looking at the newspaper files for the dates around the time of Kerwin's letter to you."

"Do the banks publish the unclaimed accounts on their web pages?" Paige asked.

"Not that I'm aware of," Leeds said. "We do pretty much what the law requires and let it go at that."

"Okay, then it's off to the library," Max said and turned to Paige. "Like we did in San Diego."

"And what do we do about the safe deposit box?" Paige asked.

"It can be opened only before or after regular banking hours," Leeds said. "It has be drilled open in your presence and that of a bank officer, and someone from the IRS."

"That figures," she said. "Is there any possibility at all we can do it later today?"

"Hold on! I'll need to make a couple of calls," Leeds said. He covered the telephone mouthpiece during the second call, and asked: "Five thirty this evening all right?"

Max rolled out of the library booth where he was going through back issue newspapers and peeked in at Paige in the adjoining cubicle. She was sound asleep under a flickering fluorescent light, her head resting on the side of the enclosure. Rather than wake her, he slipped her newspaper binder off her table and took it back to his booth. He'd already gone through the major dailies. He knew Paige had completed the Bronx weeklies and was working on the Brooklyn community papers.

"Hey, someone stole my newspapers," came a groggy voice from the other side of the partition a few minutes later.

"I've got them over here."

"Find anything?" She rolled her chair around behind him and rested her chin on his shoulder. "This place is really dismal. How many floors underground are we?"

"Dante's fourth circle," he laughed, stretching his arms. "Anyway, I'm up to September eighth, and haven't found anything. And this is our last New York City metro newspaper."

"God, I hope he didn't do it over in New Jersey, or someplace upstate. I'll go blind if I have to read through many more of those ads."

They both watched as Max flipped through the pages. He rushed past the news pages, slowing whenever there was an ad for any kind of bank or savings and loan.

"Go back!" Paige ordered. She pounded on Max's arm.

"See something?"

"I don't know. It looked right, but it was only a quarter-pager."

"I suppose it's possible, but everything else we've seen has been a full page or double-truck."

"I know. I know. Just humor me."

Max slowly turned the pages, one by one.

"There!" she shouted. Her voice echoed in the small room. "Lower right-hand corner—Atlantic-Pacific Trust."

It was the only "B" listing: Jock Ian Boylan, #66-313527.

"We did it!" she screamed, jumping up. "We did it!" She grabbed Max's hand and pulled him out of his chair and started dancing him around in a circle.

"Look at it, Maxie," she said breathlessly, pointing at the newspaper page.

"Yeah, and look at the date: two weeks *after* Kerwin's letter to you."

"That son-of-a-bitch!"

Chapter 20

Journal—1997
Jock Ian Boylan

March 22—Hong Kong

A breakthrough today!

Think I finally have a solid lead on the bastards responsible for Sallee's death.

Damn!

Never thought it would take almost eight months. Guess I'm lucky to have found *anything*.

What a dummy to think all my years in Hong Kong made me an insider.

But spread enough money around, eventually something useful is bound to pop up. Hell, that's the way it's always been.

Looks like it was the Shan Triad. Told it's the most notorious of the Hong Kong-based crime groups.

Always thought the triads were almost exclusively involved in hauling contraband into mainland China—televisions, VCRs, cigarettes, automobiles. That sort of thing.

Too naive at times.

Why wouldn't they be involved in white slavery?

Or any other illegal activity for that matter?

Document, document!

Must be diligent in keeping track of everything I learn,

make copies of every related news clipping and piece of paper I find.

March 23—Hong Kong

Stopped by the Royal Hong Kong Marine Police today. Talked to Inspector Hsieh. Told him what I'd found out about the Shan Triad.

Only reaction was to remind me once again that he doesn't appreciate my snooping around. Told me to mind my own business.

He can suggest all he wants. If he doesn't want me to ask any questions, fine. I won't feed him any information, either.

Besides, if the Hong Kong or Bangkok police have any clues or suspicions, they're certainly not sharing them with me.

Get the feeling Hsieh may be about to take the case off the active list. Who cares about a bunch of dead prostitutes?

Damn them!

The triads get bolder and bolder every day. There's even talk about taking legislative action against them. All very interesting. Believe it when I see it.

March 25—Hong Kong

Have learned the Shan Triad's top man is a Tan Mong Kuan. Also called Fan-tan because of his addiction to that particular gambling game. I'm sure he's not as simple as that ancient bean-counting game.

And if Mr. Tan is the one I want, what then? Odds on my getting close enough to strangle the son-of-a-bitch aren't worth calculating.

Yes, I hear you Nolla: control that Irish temper, try a little patience.

If it *is* this Fan-tan guy, will have to make him come to me, draw him out. Need to wound him, need to hit where it hurts him the most.

Want him to know it's happening, who's doing it, and why. Most of all, don't want him to be able to do a goddamn thing about it.

Need trustworthy information about both Tan and the Shan Triad. Where and how do they operate? Where's their base of operations? What kind of business do they use as a front? Where are they weak?

Time! It's going to take time and planning. And money. I can handle that. Got to do it right.

Must.

Go charging in like a meat-starved pit bull and I'll end up one dead Irishman.

Can't let that happen. Need to clamp my teeth onto something solid.

Sallee deserves my best effort.

Can still barely write her name without tears.

When does the pain stop? Maybe when I get my hands on those animals who savaged her.

March 26—Hong Kong

Put in a request for reactivation.

Retirement will have to wait until I have the funds to operate on my own.

Company didn't seem to mind. Said they hadn't wanted to lose me in the first place. Nice to be wanted.

Would be perfect if I could prove it *is* Tan and get this over and done with immediately.

No! That's not really what I want. What I really want is for the bastard to suffer.

Suffer the way he made my Sallee suffer.

Chapter 21

Paige pushed down on the skirt of her dotted-Swiss summer dress to keep it from swirling in the late-afternoon breeze. "If only we could have squeezed in an appointment at Atlantic-Pacific Trust for this afternoon, what a perfect day this would have been."

"Well, this evening or tomorrow we should know whether or not we actually found the two hundred and fifty thousand dollars."

"Can I wait that long?" She jumped ahead of him and walked backwards while she talked. "What are we going to do with our share, Max?"

"Financially speaking, twenty percent should go into blue chips, thirty-five percent into a money market fund . . ."

"I should have known better than to ask, you nut. I'm talking about fun. F-U-N, fun!"

"Oh, *that* stuff. I guess we could budget that in someplace."

"Of course," she added, falling in step with him, "I suppose we should get our hands on it first."

"Don't forget: we still have to finish up at The Seamen's Bank later this afternoon."

"Ah, yes, dear Mr. Northrup Leeds. Wasn't *he* cooperative once we showed him the documents? And finding that safe deposit box . . . what an unexpected bonus."

Max nodded. He chewed on a doughy pretzel he'd bought from a street vendor. "You could have knocked me over when he said they would bring in a locksmith at closing time today."

"What do you think we'll find?"

"Who knows? But with a box that size, probably more journals."

"I hope so," she said. "They're so fascinating. Wouldn't you love to lead that kind of life, sailing around the world, calling at exotic ports? Think of all the different kinds of people he must have met, the places he must have seen."

"Yeah, but look at the downside." His face settled into a frown. "He ended up alone, torn apart by loss, the loss of all the people who mattered to him, all the people he loved." He squeezed her hand. "The more I think about the journals, the more uneasy I become. Maybe we should just stash them in the attic and forget about them."

"I can't do that." Her eyes welled with tears. "Jock was a missing part of my life for too many years. His diaries have changed that. I *need* to know what he was trying to do . . . need to know if we can finish it for him."

"Finish it?" Max nodded slowly. "I understand how you feel . . . I feel the same. But still, the smart move would be to get out now."

"There's this connection, Max, even an obligation. I have to honor that. I can't turn my back on my uncle the way my mother did. If there're more journals, I have to read them . . . study them." She held onto his arm and looked up at him. "Why are you so hesitant? It isn't like you not to be at least curious."

"Oh, I'm curious, all right, but after what happened in the desert—"

"Are you trying to protect me again, Max Alper?"

127

"It's strictly selfish. I just don't know what I'd do without you." He suddenly wrapped his arms around her on the busy corner of Broadway and 47th and kissed her.

They wandered down Broadway, gawking like tourists. Street sounds reached out, surrounded them with the dissonance of blaring horns and garbled voices until they were caught up in a massive stream of restless, scurrying people—walking, running, even crawling along the littered sidewalks. The variety was endless—smiling, frowning, yelling pedestrians; hustlers; pan-handlers; characters with steely, watchful eyes offering food, magazines, tickets, pencils, drugs, sex.

"This really is something, isn't it?"

"New York, New York!" Paige said. "An amazing city. Almost too much to take in."

"It's difficult to comprehend what it took for them to get through what happened on 9/11."

"It takes more than courage to get through that kind of disaster without it destroying you."

"You know, we talk about Jock's far-out life," he said. "But what could be more exciting or more frightening than being in the heart of Manhattan after 9/11? If these aren't brave, exciting people, who are?"

She punched him lightly in the arm. "That's not what I meant and you know it. This isn't exciting, Max, it's crazy."

"Okay! Okay! But it's a wonderful crazy. There's no other place quite like it. In fact, I think New Yorkers generally are given a bum rap by the media." He wiped crystals of loose pretzel salt from his mouth with the back of his hand and licked them away. "You've got to admit, everyone we've met so far has been terrific."

A messenger on rollerblades caromed off Paige. She laughed. "I suppose you're right. Hell, that guy in the subway even got up and gave us his seat so we could sit together."

Max nodded toward the stream of taxis passing them. "Speaking of riding, how do you feel about walking back to the hotel in those heels?"

"Let's be decadent and take a cab. I would love to kick back for a while, at least until it's time to go to the bank for the grand opening."

"A woman after my own heart." He poked two fingers into his mouth and whistled. A taxi screeched to a halt in front of them. "And if 'kicking back' means what I hope it means, I know I'm going to love it." He ran a hand along her thigh as she climbed into the taxi.

"Max!"

The cabby smiled as he dropped the flag on the meter.

Max chased Paige down the seventh floor corridor of their hotel. "You can't get away. I've got the room card key."

She removed her heels as she ran, tossing them over her shoulder at him. "I've got one, too," she yelled, waving a key card over the top of her head. "I may just lock you out."

"No fair." He snatched up her shoes on the run, caught up to her just as she slid the card into the slot.

"Thanks *ever* so much, Mr. Alper," she said, twisting out of his grasp. "It's been an . . . an . . . *illuminating* afternoon. But I *really* must go in now."

"Don't hand me that blarney, Paige *Boylan* Alper." He swept her up into his arms. "You can't pull that sexy stuff in the cab and think you're going to get a free pass."

"What stuff?" she taunted. "I was only teasing."

"That's what you think." He pushed the key card in the lock and kicked open the door.

A small Asian man was sitting in the room's only upholstered armchair, a pile of crumpled notepaper in his lap.

"Mr. and Mrs. Alper, I believe," the man said. Next to him stood a sumo-sized companion, his bulk straining the fabric of a cheap, shiny suit. The giant smiled at them through perfect teeth, as though he'd just found a jade necklace in a Cracker Jack box.

Max and Paige looked at each other, then back at the intruders.

"What an enchanting entrance," said the seated man. His delicate, parchment-like skin looked as if it had been carefully draped over his tiny skull; small, black pearl-like eyes stared coldly at them.

"Put her down, please," he ordered quietly. He emphasized the command with a gesture from what appeared to be a .357 magnum. "And close the door. Quietly."

Max lowered Paige onto the plush carpet, keeping her hand gripped tightly in his. He eased one foot back toward the open doorway.

"Do not do that!"

As the door began to swing shut behind them, the man waved the muzzle of the pistol toward the bed. The bigger man stepped toward them, deceptively fast for his size. He grabbed them by the backs of their necks and flung them onto the bedspread-covered mattress.

"Hey, watch it, buster!" Paige cried out, almost rolling off the far side.

Max tossed a protective arm around her to keep her from tumbling onto the floor.

"You present quite a lovely picture," the seated man said. "Very romantic." His voice was soft and coaxing as he carefully articulated every syllable. Then, a harsh, rapid-fire guttural command in another language brought his companion back to his side.

"Get to it," Max said. "What do you want from us?"

The man slid off the chair, the crumpled notes in one hand. He walked in measured steps to the window, where the bright afternoon light streaming through the glass made his skin appear translucent. He stared down onto Central Park. "Soon the leaves will turn to red and gold, and if good fortune smiles on us, we will all live to see another spectacular autumn."

"Skip the scenic monologue," Paige said.

The man turned from the window, sighed, and returned to stand behind the chair. "You Americans have so little appreciation of nature's offerings. No wonder your artists are treated like second-class citizens."

"What the hell do you want?" Max said, springing to his feet.

The muscleman stretched out and chopped Max across the chest. He fell back with a grunt. Paige screamed. The giant clamped his huge hand across her face to silence her. She twisted her head frantically, beat on his chest, and pried at his fingers.

Max launched himself from the bed, lunged a shoulder into the man's stomach. His reward was to have his own face smothered by the other massive hand.

"Ah, why is it young people today have so little respect for their elders?" questioned the smaller man. "*I* am asking the questions. Do I make myself clear?"

Paige and Max thrashed helplessly. A staccato order punctuated the room. The two of them were flung effortlessly onto the bed again. They both sucked in huge gulps of air.

"You are Captain Jock Boylan's niece."

Paige, still gasping for air, glared at him. "What if . . . I . . . am?"

131

The small man's eyes flashed anger; he nodded almost imperceptibly to the other man. His enforcer reached out and yanked Paige up by the hair, then shook her violently.

"Let her go!" Max yelled. He smashed a fist into the attacker's jaw. The man let Paige's hair slip through his fingers, grunted, and kneed Max in the stomach.

"You Neanderthal!" Paige shouted, crawling to Max. She pulled him to her and rocked him back and forth.

"You are trying my patience," said the man in charge. His eyes signaled the bruiser, who returned to his side like a trained dog. "I will not tolerate disobedience, especially from a woman."

Max sat up. Paige smoothed his hair, kissed his cheek. "How many times have I told you not to hit the other kids in the sandbox," she said, "especially when they're bigger than you?"

"Guess I forgot."

"Are you okay?" His face was a pasty white. "Did he . . ."

"Enough!"

The Alpers turned. The tiny Asian's face was an expressionless mask, but his eyes sparked with cruelty.

"Did you have a successful visit to The Seamen's Bank today?" He emphasized his questions by holding her notes up for them to see. "You saw a Mr. Northrup Leeds, according to the scribbling on this paper." He slid the pistol and the hand holding it into the side pocket of his seersucker jacket. "Tell me about that visit."

Paige and Max looked quickly at each other, then back at the intruder.

"We were there on a family matter," Max said. "Nothing that could possibly be of interest to you or anyone you represent."

"No, it is of considerable interest to me. Your so-called family business is certainly connected with Captain Boylan, an old nemesis."

"What could my uncle have had to do with the likes of you? He was just an old sweetheart . . ."

"Very funny, Mrs. Alper. And very stupid. You know exactly what I'm talking about."

"No, I don't. You need to be more explicit."

He flicked an impatient hand at them.

"We have kept track of you and your sister ever since your uncle died." He offered them a humorless smile. "And how was your visit with Captain Mattos?"

"We've been followed?"

"You Americans think you are so clever, and yet you cannot see what is under your very noses. There hasn't been a day since Captain Boylan died that we were not aware of where you were or what you were doing."

"Why would you want to follow Paige and Sheryl?" Max said. "And who the hell are you?"

The Asian man ignored the question and stared at Max with eyes that were dark and flat. "Where are the journals you received from Captain Mattos?"

"What journals?" Paige said.

"Kim!"

The rotund man moved quickly away from his boss and jerked Paige off the bed. He clamped a forearm tightly across her throat, kept his eyes on Max.

"It has always been assumed that Captain Boylan left his journals with his nudist friend," said the Asian.

"And your attempts to beat the information out of him never produced a thing, did they?" Max said.

"You will tell me whether or not you were given the journals, or I will have Kim break your wife's neck." He nodded at Kim, who cupped Paige's chin with one hand and began to turn her head to one side.

"Yes, he gave us the journals!" Max shouted. "Now let her go."

"Ah, yes, of course he did." He looked slowly around room. "And they are where?"

"Where you can't get your hands on them," Paige whispered.

"Your defiance is stupid. One of you will tell me what happened to those journals or I will have Kim finish the task at hand."

"They were shipped to San Francisco," Max said quickly. He carefully pulled out his wallet and handed the man the UPS receipt.

"I hope for your sake that you are telling me the truth," he said.

"Why would we lie to you?" Paige whispered.

"Why do Americans do anything?" He glanced from the scattered contents of the Alpers' suitcases to the ransacked closet. "You really expect me to believe that two journalists would simply mail off such fascinating documents without first reading them?" He tilted his head toward the bed, and Kim responded by tossing Paige back down beside Max.

"Believe what you like," she said.

"You are an ignorant woman, Mrs. Alper. It is a shame you do not have the benefit of having been raised in a Chinese household."

"I barely knew my uncle," Paige said, rubbing her neck. "We're only here trying to find an inheritance."

"At The Seamen's Bank, yes? I believe that has been well-established."

The Asian stepped near them, grabbed Paige's purse, and dumped the contents on the dresser. He picked up her steno pad and mumbled, "Gregg" as he leafed through the pages of shorthand.

"Ah, here, Mrs. Alper," he said, "a notation to meet Mr. Leeds at The Seamen's Bank at five thirty p.m. this evening, along with the number B1735. A safe deposit box number, perhaps?" He waited, then added, "Am I correct in my deductions?"

"Not even close," Paige said.

"Please! You are insulting my intelligence." He pulled the gun from his pocket again and said something to Kim, who swiftly retrieved a pillow from the bed.

Paige and Max watched as the pillow was wrapped tightly around the revolver. The man stepped forward and pushed the pillow against Paige's forehead.

"Are you or are you not going back to the bank this evening?" He steadied his gaze on Max. "Perhaps you are more reasonable than your childish wife, Mr. Alper."

"We have an appointment at the bank," Max said.

The man threw the pillow on the bed and walked back to the window again. He tapped the muzzle of the gun gently against the glass several times. "I am sixty years old. I have had to rid myself of three wives like yours, Mr. Alper. All hotheaded women, wayward children. I don't know why I'm so unfortunate as to keep getting involved with that type of woman." His voice trailed off as he stared down at the street below.

Only the nervous breathing of Max and Paige, and the muffled sound of car horns outside broke the silence. They watched expectantly as the man abruptly spun around and held them with a cold, calculating glare.

"You and I, Mrs. Alper, will go to the bank and retrieve whatever it is Mr. Northrup Leeds has there for you." He turned to smile at his companion. "This will probably disappoint Kim, whom I am certain would have enjoyed having the opportunity to teach you some manners." The large man nodded slowly while appraising Paige's body.

The smaller man crossed the room, reached down, and took Paige's nose between thumb and forefinger. He pinched viciously until she was forced to move off the bed. Her eyes watered. She stared helplessly at a tattoo of a small, colorful butterfly displayed between the two fingers. The man carefully watched Max, whose hands were balled into fists.

"Don't be rash, Mr. Alper. You will have plenty of time to express your complaints to Kim while I accompany your wife to the bank." He turned to his companion and added, "If I am not back in two hours, kill him and return to Hong Kong immediately."

Chapter 22

Journal—1997
Jock Ian Boylan

April 3—Hong Kong

Persistence. And a few more bribes.

Now have a connection between the Shan Triad and the tramp steamer *Mariposa*—the ship that carried Sallee and the other women to their deaths.

The *Mariposa* and two sister ships, the *Farfalla* and the *Schmetterling*, are all operated by a small intra-Asia steamship company, Papilio Coastal Line. One of several subsidiaries of Papillon Enterprises, Ltd.

Peeled away layer upon layer of multinational corporate camouflage to expose the lead investor—M. K. Tan, who owns or controls ninety percent of the common stock.

Corporate games. Façades of legitimacy to hide illegal activities. No different here than in the States. Anything to make a buck, anything to keep from getting caught. Under which of the three shells is the corporate criminal hiding?

Games, games, games.

I have no doubt that Western-style M. K. Tan and Asian-style Tan Mong Kuan are the same guy. Evil under any name.

Coincidence doesn't stop there.

Shan, mariposa, farfalla, Schmetterling, papilio, and

papillon all mean "butterfly."

Now isn't *that* cute?

Don't know why I didn't make the *Mariposa*-Shan-butterfly connection before. Shouldn't have stopped working crossword puzzles.

Tempted to try this out on Inspector Hsieh and see what reaction I get. Probably just get pissed at me again for not minding my own business.

Convinced that if anything is going to get done, I'm going to have to do it myself.

April 4—Hong Kong

Asked to be assigned exclusively to the intra-Asia trade routes. Will allow me to move around the Pacific Rim and gather more information on Tan's Papilio ships and his other operations without it costing me an arm and a leg for airfare.

April 5—At Sea

Trail is still cold as a penguin's backside.

Agreed to take a containership to the U.S. and back—Hong Kong, Keelung, Busan, Los Angeles, New York, and Savannah, then return via the same ports.

Hate putting everything on hold for two months. Pay's too good to pass up.

This investigation is beginning to cost some serious money.

Being careful, but eventually someone is going to tell the Shan Triad I've been around asking questions.

Would be better if my funds were stashed someplace where the triad can't get at them. Will move all my bank accounts to New York. As far away from Hong Kong as possible.

June 10—Hong Kong

Back home.

Checked in with Inspector Hsieh. Nothing new. Surprise, surprise.

Feel less vulnerable. All liquid assets have been transferred to New York.

Made arrangements with one of the banks to pay Ocean Shores in case the Lassa comes back and my medical insurance won't cover everything. Rented a safe deposit box.

Dreary details. But necessary.

Worried about Mattos' offer to have me mail him my journals and any incriminating evidence I find. Don't like putting him at risk. But seems unlikely anyone would look for that kind of stuff at a nudist park.

Need to get busy with the investigation again.

Still two months before I'm scheduled to go to sea again.

Bless the union.

June 12—Hong Kong

Have a lead on a brother of one of the girls who died with Sallee. They say he belongs to another triad, a rival to the Shan.

June 22—Hong Kong

Hsieh is angry. Don't care. For all I know, the Shan may have gotten to him.

If those goddamn punks had listened to reason, I wouldn't have had to scuttle two of their junks and roll a taxi through the front of their cabaret. Needed to find Jennie Tsao's brother. How else to convince them?

Thought Hsieh was going to have me locked up, indefinitely.

That would have really put a crimp in my plans.

Did find Raphael Tsao. Took some convincing, but he eventually saw the wisdom in telling me what I needed to know. The death container is definitely linked to a Shan Triad prostitution operation.

Tsao's a little shortsighted, or very smart. He's going after the guy who screwed up the positioning of the container on the *Mariposa*.

I'm going after Tan.

Chapter 23

"Need I remind you, Mrs. Alper, that if you do anything foolish you will never see your husband again?" The Asian shoved her roughly into the elevator when she hesitated at its threshold.

Moving to the back of the empty car, Paige turned and leaned heavily on the handrail. She looked out into the empty hotel corridor, waiting for the doors to close. Was it only moments ago that she and Max were there, laughing and playing? A flood of memories washed over her—times of doing things together, times of loving, the very first time they met.

Paige had been drawn to Max the instant they'd been introduced at the *Bay Tribune*. It had been her first day as an intern, fresh out of journalism school. There'd been stars in her eyes—everyone and everything at the busy daily newspaper captivated her. But Max Alper had stood out from all the rest.

She discreetly asked around the office about him. Gossip had it that he'd been an itinerant little-bit-of-this, little-bit-of-that kind of guy before settling down to journalism and calling San Francisco his home.

He wasn't wildly handsome, but his ruggedness had an uncanny kind of magnetism and, along with his shock of red hair and ready smile, he drew attention wherever he went.

She marveled at how most people immediately warmed to him. It didn't take her long to discover his secret: he had the ability to be genuinely interested in anyone he talked to, whether at work or socially. He listened and made people feel they mattered, that he cared about them.

As the months passed, she settled into her job and became even more curious about Max Alper. Sometimes, sitting at her desk searching for a lead to a story, she'd drift away, lose concentration. Inevitably, she would find herself staring, satisfying an unexplainable craving for the sight of him. When he caught her at it, she would play eye tag, retreating into the safety of her work.

Eventually, she was given her first big feature assignment.

She knew the city editor was relishing the pained expression on her face when he assigned her the difficult story of putting together a cross-section of Californian attitudes about legalized euthanasia. The impetus for the story was another state initiative for legalization that had qualified for the ballot. The original proposition was narrowly defeated the year before; early projections were that the voters might pass the measure this time.

She did a tremendous amount of research for the assignment—talked to nurses, doctors, families of the dying, and, hardest of all, the dying themselves. She began to have nightmares, like the ones she'd had when she lost her parents.

One night she awoke drenched in sweat. Chilled and shaking, she fumbled for the phone and called her sister in Albuquerque.

"They're coming back again, Sheryl," she said, her voice quavering. "The nightmares are coming back."

"Oh, Paige, it's been more than a year. You've got to let

Mom and Dad go. It's all over. We can't bring them back."

"God, how I wish we could. Don't you?"

"You know I'd give anything . . ."

"I keep seeing them skiing, Sheryl, then the horrible growing rumble of the avalanche . . . the snow racing after them . . . crashing down . . ."

"Paige."

". . . smothering them."

"Paige!"

"Their stiff frozen fingers clawing at the mountain of snow . . ."

"Stop it!"

"Don't you understand, they were buried . . . alive."

"You shouldn't be alone, Paige. Call your friend, Marilyn. Spend the night with her. Do it! Please?"

She'd known her twin was right. "I'll call."

But she didn't. Instead, she'd dressed, fled from the apartment with no idea where she was going.

She ended up at the newspaper at two a.m. The security guard let her into the silent offices. She sat numbly before her computer, the monitor's dull glow and her desk lamp the only illumination in the cavernous office. Hands poised over the keyboard, she waited for inspiration, willed herself to think, to compose. When the words wouldn't come, she lowered her head onto the desk. Soon she was sobbing.

"Trying to court the muse can really be a bitch sometimes," said a voice behind her.

She raised her head and spun around. She hadn't heard anyone come in, but there was Max, only a few feet away.

"It's not that." She offered him a shrug of frustration. "I just . . . can't . . ." Tears gushed and before she realized it, she was sobbing into his shoulder. He stroked her hair, held her in his arms.

"What is it? Is there anything I can do?"

"It's so unfair. One moment they were here, just as I always thought they'd be, then . . . then . . . they were gone."

"Who?"

"My parents."

"I'm sorry."

He'd rocked her gently in his arms for a long time, murmured soothing words and sounds of comfort. Without knowing how or when the moment arrived, they kissed. He'd been so warm, so alive. There to love, there to hang on to.

What if that maniac Kim hurts Max? My God, what if he kills him?

Tears washed her cheeks; her stomach spun itself into a tight, painful knot. She swallowed hard to keep from gagging.

I may never see him again.

Her legs gave way. She grabbed the handrail, overcome by a wave of alienation so intense she was startled by the sound of the elevator doors when they finally clunked shut. She clutched at her throat. Her anxiety increased as each floor number flashed on the brass panel. She was suffocating.

Then, as quickly as the fear flared, it was replaced by blazing anger. She couldn't allow this evil little man to just walk into their lives and indifferently destroy them.

"Don't even consider causing any trouble, Mrs. Alper," the man said. His black eyes bored into hers. "Believe me, I shall not hesitate to kill you at the slightest provocation. If that is not sufficient to deter you, then I should remind you that any foolishness on your part will precipitate your husband's demise. Is that clear?"

Paige snapped her head around, tearing her eyes from his. She stared into the closed elevator doors, drilling holes through them. "Yes, it's very clear."

On the ground floor, they weaved through the hustle-bustle of the lobby, the man gripping her arm painfully. When she missed a step and bumped heavily into him, she felt the hard bulge of the pistol in his side pocket. She looked frantically around the busy room, trying to catch the eye of any of the lobby groupies. But it was as if the two of them were in a magic corridor, allowing them to see, but not be seen.

It took ten excruciating minutes before the doorman was able to flag down a taxi. The Asian gave the cabby the address and nearest cross-street for The Seamen's Bank. The cab pulled away from the curb, then stopped, caught up in a late afternoon traffic jam. Paige repeatedly glanced at her watch.

"Patience is its own reward, Mrs. Alper."

"Don't give me that philosophical bullshit," Paige snapped. "If this traffic doesn't break, we're never going to make the bank by five thirty."

"You have a filthy mouth, especially for a woman."

"You told that clown to kill my husband if we weren't back in two hours, and I'm supposed to sit here and act nonchalant?" She tapped her foot nervously, out of synch with the cab's blaring radio. Up ahead, she could see the flashing lights of a police car.

"Please lower your voice," her escort hissed. "And smile! Mr. Alper's life depends on your cooperation." He looked up at the rearview mirror and offered a small smile of his own for the cabby's benefit.

The driver, who had been attracted by Paige's raised voice, shrugged and looked away. He turned up the volume on the radio and shifted restlessly in his seat, batting half-heartedly at a pair of large, discolored Styrofoam dice hanging from his mirror.

"Goddamn jerks really clobbered each other," the cabby groused, indicating a two-car accident up ahead. "Damn drivers oughta take a cab, or bus, for chrissakes. Stay off the goddamn streets!" He shook his head. "Lousy way to make a buck, hacking."

"What's your connection to Martin Lester and his San Diego convalescent home?" Paige blurted, hoping to catch her captor off-guard.

He studied her for several seconds, smiling benignly. "Mr. Lester," he said finally, "has been extremely useful to us."

"In what way?"

"He has kept us informed about certain matters."

"Concerning my uncle?"

He glanced past the cabby's shoulder to check on the situation ahead of them, then said, "Did Mr. Lester mention our, uh, arrangement with him?"

"Would that make a difference?"

"Not to you, my dear Mrs. Alper. But it could make a considerable difference to Mr. Lester, a man who has grown very accustomed to the great wealth we have bestowed upon him."

"And Heirs Apparent? Do you have a similar arrangement with them?"

"Son-of-a-bitch!" the cabby yelled. "It's about time!" He edged past a police cruiser with red and blue flashing lights, then barely missed a traffic-directing policeman. A tow truck had already hooked onto one of the damaged automobiles.

"Mrs. Alper, you are a very trying person, more so than

most females of your race, whom I find extremely repugnant." He looked around and nodded approvingly as the cabby hurried the taxi through the cross-streets. "Now I must insist: either be silent, or I will kill you here and now."

"Before you get the journals?" Paige taunted. "What will your superiors think about that?"

He pulled the gun from his pocket and jabbed it painfully into her breast. "You sorely tempt me, but—"

"—but you have your orders, don't you?" She shoved the gun away.

The Asian glared at her for several beats before slipping the weapon back into his jacket pocket. "We will continue this discussion later . . . *after* we have collected the journals from the bank."

They arrived forty minutes after the hour.

"We'd just about given you up to the New York rush hour," Northrup Leeds said. He turned and led the procession of locksmith, security guard, IRS man, Paige, and her "attorney" toward the huge safe deposit vault of The Seamen's Bank.

"Thanks for waiting," Paige said. "I really appreciate it."

Leeds unlocked the deposit box with the bank key as the locksmith plugged in his drill and began boring into the renter's key slot. The banker stepped back and joined the others down the aisle away from the whining, grinding sound.

"It can be difficult getting everybody together in these situations," Leeds said, smiling at Paige. "But these guys don't mind a little overtime now and then."

Paige returned his smile, her mind in a whirlwind.

Can I get to his gun before anyone gets hurt? What if I miss? He'll take out the guard and everyone else. Then go for Max.

She glanced at each of the men around her, then into a pair of waiting eyes. The Asian stared back at her and pressed his elbow against the gun in his side pocket and smiled.

It was unsettling to think he was aware of her every thought. She had no choice but to continue on with the charade. But she would stay alert, not allow herself to become distracted with what was happening with the safe deposit box.

Paige was certain an opportunity would present itself to take some kind of positive action, and she intended to be ready for it when it happened.

Chapter 24

Max and Kim stood a few feet apart, their eyes locked as the door to the hotel room clicked shut behind Paige and her escort.

"Just the two of us now," Kim said softly, the thin slash of a smile bisecting his moon-shaped face.

Max's thoughts were still on Paige. The click of the door latch echoed like a thunderbolt in his mind; his heart sank to the pit of his stomach. He was consumed by the memory of the last time he thought he'd lost her forever.

"They're crooks," Paige had yelled at him.

He'd stood looking at her open-mouthed, not expecting this kind of reaction to his news. He'd thought she would be proud—it was the first public relations account he'd landed on his own. He hadn't been sure about going into PR, but one of them had to leave the newspaper after they got married. He'd accepted the outcome of the coin toss, and this was the first solid indication he was going to make any money as a flack.

"What are you talking about?" He'd been stung by her outburst. "ConLease has been around for years. There's never been any hint of illegal operations."

"I'm talking about Zorn Industries," Paige said.

"The big holding company, right?"

"Exactly."

"So?"

"So, Zorn owns both CWF Forest Products and ConLease, and—"

"—and CWF is part of the exposé you're working on . . . their plan to clear-cut old-growth redwoods."

"Right! Money-grubbing con men. They rape the land and try to snow the public into believing they're conservationists."

"But ConLease doesn't have anything to do with the redwoods. They lease ocean containers. Period!"

"Come on, Max! How's it going to look if you're out there beating the drum for one Zorn subsidiary while I'm doing a series showing how slimy its sister company is?"

"That's not fair. ConLease means a big raise, enough to pay off a large stack of our bills."

"Are you telling me that's more important than saving the earth?"

"That's unfair. Besides, I'm not part of your exposé. Maybe *you* should be the flack, so I can get the hell back to journalism, where I should have stayed."

"What's that supposed to mean?"

After that, it had degenerated into a spiteful, name-calling fight that had nothing to do with the original discussion. He'd allowed hateful things to escape his mouth, things he'd wanted to retrieve and cancel, but couldn't. It had gone too far. It was all too much for their eight-month-old marriage.

Paige had gone silent, packed a bag, and left their apartment, not with an angry slam of the door, but with an almost imperceptible click of the lock, a sound of sickening finality.

At that moment, he'd known he was losing the only person in the world he truly loved. He went after her, made things right, and swore to himself he would do everything humanly possible not to ever lose her again.

Max refocused on Kim, who had metamorphosed from underling to master. Oddly graceful, the huge man moved cat-like toward the upholstered chair his boss had recently shown such a fondness for.

"I don't like you, Mr. Alper." He lowered himself into the chair with deliberation—a king taking his rightful throne. As he slid down, he synchronously unbuttoned his jacket, milliseconds before the cheap material threatened to split from the pressure of his expanding bulk.

"It is not personal," he added, slowly cracking his knuckles in sequence. "I've never met an Occidental I liked, although your women can be sexually amusing."

Max was noncommittal, his eyes irresistibly drawn to a dark, hairy mole in the center of Kim's forehead, an inch below the stubble of a buzz-cut that thinly covered the man's white scalp. The two of them continued to pace the perimeter of an imaginary arena.

"You have a very provocative wife," Kim continued, his eyes surveying the expanse of mattress where Max sat.

Max allowed himself no more than a blink.

What the hell am I going to do with this guy?

Kim wasn't just a fat man; he'd already demonstrated that beneath his thick layer of blubber was a dangerous powerhouse. Max rubbed at his chest, pain throbbing with every heartbeat.

"I look forward to seeing more of Mrs. Alper," Kim said with a smirk. A sheen of perspiration coated his forehead.

"As soon as she and your boss come back, we're out of here," Max said. It was an assurance he didn't feel.

Kim shook with a roar of laughter. "You are a stupid man."

"Don't count on it," Max said. He couldn't help wincing at the repetitive crunch of Kim's knuckles. "Besides, my wife and I pose no threat to you."

The man waggled a plump forefinger at him, as if chastising a fractious child. "That is most certainly true," he giggled. "We only want the journals. If they are found at the bank, then your usefulness ends."

"What if there are no journals in the safe deposit box? What then?"

Kim shifted uncomfortably in the chair, caught between its restricting arms. "Then your fates will be decided by others. I do not possess that information."

Max shrugged. "We only came here for my wife's inheritance."

"You should have stayed in San Francisco and accepted the offer of the heir tracers. Now, you and Mrs. Alper—and her sister—will die for your foolishness, just as that interfering captain had to die."

"What are you talking about? Are you saying Jock's death wasn't the result of a hit-and-run accident?"

"It was a final payment for his cowardly larceny."

"But why Paige and Sheryl? They barely knew the man."

"Some debts are passed on as an unexpected part of an inheritance."

"That makes no sense."

Kim's face was impassive as he continued to crack the knuckles of his meaty fingers. "Your wife, she's good in bed?" His lips stretched back into a lascivious grin.

Max studied Kim's eyes, as lifeless as those of the man who had taken Paige away. Dead eyes. Assassin's eyes. This man would make Paige suffer, violate her with his grubby hands, and crush her with his gross body.

Max knew that Kim was merely toying with him to pass

the time, like slowly pulling the wings off a housefly. But he knew the thug would eventually grow tired of the game. Max envisioned Kim breaking his neck with no more thought than he gave to cracking his knuckles. He wouldn't be that merciful with Paige. Max was certain of that.

"Hey, I hate to interrupt this fascinating repartee," Max said, ignoring the taunts, "but I've got to take a leak."

Kim glanced around the room and grunted his approval. "Don't try anything stupid, Mr. Alper," he said, shifting, trying to find more room for his body in the inadequate chair.

"Yeah, yeah, I know you're a big, tough guy," Max said, starting toward the bathroom. "But I'll bet what's really tough is trying to find clothes to cover all that lard."

He saw Kim's face redden as he pulled the bathroom door shut. He quickly scanned the tiny, windowless space, looking for something, anything he could use as a weapon.

He turned on a water faucet, adjusting the flow to a trickle with the hope that it would sound like him peeing.

His head spun, he could barely breathe.

Damn it, Paige! What am I going to do?

He rifled through his toilet kit, but the most dangerous thing he could find was a pair of nail clippers. His electric razor, still plugged into the wall socket, mocked him—convenient, but lacking the potential of an old-fashioned razor blade.

Shit!

He peeked behind the shower curtain. Nothing! The single drawer in the washbasin cabinet didn't even yield dust.

If I don't outsmart this imbecile now, it's all over for us.

He turned off the water and stole a moment to rummage through Paige's cosmetic kit. He nodded slightly as he

153

pulled out a huge bottle of shampoo. He smiled grimly as he remembered the aggravation it always caused during packing. Threads of a plan started to come together.

"Don't make me come in and pull you out of there, Mr. Alper," Kim called out.

Max was certain the man was still wedged in the chair.

Probably take a pry bar to lever him out of it.

He hefted the plastic shampoo bottle in his hand.

Think, damn it! Think!

"Give me a moment!" he called out.

I've got to nail the bastard while he's still stuck in that fucking chair.

"I'll be right out."

He looked around and focused on the ice bucket. It had potential. He flushed the toilet, spun the cap off the shampoo bottle, and dumped the nearly full contents into the container.

Paige Boylan Alper, I'll never complain again about your toting this monster.

Max took a deep breath, worked up moisture for his bone-dry mouth, and tried to affect a casual exit. He held the ice bucket tightly against his thigh on the off-side away from Kim, who was still seated in the chair when the door swung open. Murderous eyes held him motionless for a beat.

Max stepped forward. His legs seemed to move slowly, like a lazy swimmer out of synch with the sledgehammer pounding of his heart.

He saw Kim's eyes flash with understanding a split-second too late. The shampoo was already halfway out of the bucket, flying towards the chair-bound assassin's face. Kim's hands came up fast, but not fast enough. He instinctively wiped at his burning eyes, rubbing the soap deeper into the sockets.

"You fucking asshole!" Kim screamed as he tried to launch himself from the chair.

Max smashed the man repeatedly in the face, first with the flimsy ice bucket, then with his fists. Both were ineffectual. The huge man stood, crouched, the chair still stuck to his backside.

Frustrated, Max grabbed the bedside lamp and pulled its cord free from the outlet. As Kim stumbled blindly toward him, roaring his anger, Max coiled the cord around one groping hand, then the other.

"I'll crush your skull!" Kim growled. "I'll rip out your worthless heart!" He tensed his arms and snapped the electrical wire as if it were string.

Max skipped out of Kim's way, scooped up the telephone, and jumped onto the bed. "Sorry we can't finish this conversation," he wheezed, "but I've really got to go." He raised the telephone high over his head and brought it down with all his strength.

Kim staggered into the edge of the bed, lost his balance, and toppled over backwards, landing like an upturned tortoise, arms and legs flailing weakly in the air.

Chapter 25

A wall of noise abruptly halted Max's frantic rush from the Fifth Avenue hotel. The street was a sea of bumper-to-bumper traffic—horns blared, drivers shouted. He scowled and shook his head defensively against the deafening point-counterpoint of the pandemonium.

To his left he could see the blinking lights of a tow truck slowly removing a crumpled Ford under the careful direction of a policeman, who was waving furiously at the same time at the confusion of traffic in the intersection.

"No use trying to get a cab now, sir," the doorman said. "You might be better off walking over to Park Avenue. This will probably be a big mess for another half-hour or so."

"Thanks!" Max said. He checked his watch, nodded grimly, and took off at a trot south to take the next cross-street. He had to get to the bank before Paige left with the Asian.

The air was hot and sticky; the late afternoon sun pressed down heavily on him. He shrugged off his suit jacket and tied the sleeves around his waist without losing a step.

He picked up the pace when he reached 69th, weaving in and out of pedestrian traffic, jumping into and out of the street when the sidewalk was blocked. His legs ached and his feet burned inside his leather-soled shoes. He tugged at his sweat-soaked clothes, trying to free himself from the restriction.

Max drained his mind, surrendering to the rhythm of his feet pounding the pavement, moving him forward. He allowed no fears or what-ifs to break his concentration. When he finally reached the intersection of 69th and Park, a sense of dread displaced his detachment as cab after cab sped by, ignoring his wildly waving arms.

He took to the street again and continued south at a trot, watching for an empty taxi. Suddenly, a cab pulled to a stop a car-length ahead of him. Max breathed a sigh of relief and held the door open for the exiting passenger. But before he could enter, an expensively dressed man, reeking of cologne, darted past him and ducked down to enter the cab.

"What the hell do you think you're doing?" Max shouted in the man's ear. He yanked the man back by the coat collar and spun him around toward the sidewalk. "Enough is enough!" He shoved the man up over the curb, jumped into the back of the cab, and slammed the door shut.

"I'll call the police!" the man screeched from the sidewalk, his face a fiery red.

"God, I wish someone would," Max said under his breath.

"Where to, man?" the driver asked, waving impatiently at the discordant chorus of horns behind him.

Max looked at his watch: 5:55. "There's an extra fifty in it if you can get me to The Seamen's Bank in less than five minutes."

The cabby grinned. "Fifty, huh?" The cab's tires chirped as the driver launched the vehicle into the flow of traffic. A new blast of horns assaulted them as they sped through the first tint of a red light.

Max leaned back, closed his eyes, and took a deep breath. When images of Kim and his boss popped into his mind, he opened his eyes with a shake of the head and tried to concentrate on clearing the dense traffic ahead of them.

Paige stuffed a pair of journals into a white and blue plastic bag imprinted with the bank's stylized schooner logo. She, the Asian, and Northrup Leeds left the safe deposit box vault and returned to the banker's office.

"Thank you very much for your cooperation," Paige told Leeds after signing all the necessary release documents. "And I do appreciate the carry-all."

"My pleasure, Mrs. Alper. It's always nice when things work out so perfectly for everyone concerned." He laughed. "I do think the IRS man was a tad disappointed that Captain Boylan's safe deposit box didn't yield a nice bundle of taxable cash."

"I feel a bit the same way," Paige said, "but retrieving these journals means a great deal to me."

Paige winced as her captor dug his fingers harshly into the flesh of her upper arm, urging her to hurry. She wanted to jerk her arm free, but didn't dare risk making a scene.

"Well, I think we've taken up enough of your time, Mr. Leeds," Paige said. She stepped toward the banker, leaving the Asian no option but to release her arm. "Again, thank you for all your help." She reached across the desk to shake his hand.

"This has all gone quite efficiently," said the Asian. "Thank you." He turned to Paige. "Allow me to carry that heavy bag for you." He grabbed at the plastic bag containing the journals.

"Don't trouble yourself," Paige said with a sickeningly sweet smile. She refused to let go of the drawstring tote.

"No trouble, at all, Mrs. Alper." He countered with a wide, pasted-on smile that never quite reached his eyes.

The two of them turned and headed out across the lobby of the bank toward the front door, where a guard stood waiting to let them out.

Paige tried to slow the pace, but the Asian wouldn't allow it.

Max, Max! What are we going to do?

Max jumped out of the still-moving cab, his eyes searching the bank entrance. He'd taken no more than a couple of steps when he saw Paige and her escort stepping past a bank guard holding the door open for them. He ducked into the nearest doorway and watched as the mismatched couple edged through the surge of the after-work pedestrian traffic.

At the curb, the Asian signaled for a taxi with one arm while holding onto Paige with his other hand. She held her chin high, but Max could see that she was frightened. Her eyes darted in every direction, like a trapped animal. The gunman's face reflected supreme confidence, the kind of expression people only wear when they assume fate and the gods are solidly on their side.

Max had to do something, and do it fast. Paige would soon be pushed into a cab and whisked away. He shook his head to get rid of the anger that kept interfering with his ability to come up with a viable rescue plan.

It made no difference whether his rage roiled because the little man clutched possessively at Paige's arm, or because of the man's condescending self-assurance, or from the way he and Kim had abused them, treated them like worthless scraps of meat. Right now, all that mattered was preventing the bastard from stealing Paige away. He stuck his thumb and middle finger into his mouth and blew as hard as he could.

★ ★ ★ ★ ★

Paige heard the distinctive, shrill whistle through the competition of the raucous street noise all around her. She whipped her head around to see where it had come from. Only her Max whistled with that peculiar atonal screech that could drive other 49er football fans crazy.

Then she saw him, charging through the crowd like a Super Bowl linebacker. She laughed and jerked free of her captor, who was momentarily distracted as he reached out to open the door of a taxi. The Asian recovered quickly, tried to grab her arm, but she was already too far away. He moved quickly toward her, one hand reaching into his jacket pocket for the pistol.

Paige surprised him by stepping forward, close enough to grind her heel hard against his instep. The man squealed; the pistol clattered into the gutter.

"Save some for me," Max shouted. He grabbed the kidnapper by the lapels and rapidly pounded his fist into the gunman's face again and again.

The delicately featured man folded like the water-starved petals of a dying flower. Legs crossed first, then his arms neatly overlapped as he slid to the sidewalk, out cold.

The flow of the crowd never slackened. Max looked down at the pistol, debated for a moment whether to pick it up, then kicked it hard in the direction of a traffic control officer standing in the middle of the intersection.

"In or out?" the cabby demanded.

Paige scooped up the journals, which had slipped out of the tote bag onto the pavement. Max grabbed the bag and gave the Asian a final kick in the ribs. The two of them tumbled into the taxi.

"Wait!" yelled the traffic officer as the pistol slid to a stop in front of him. It was too late.

The cabby accelerated and merged into traffic. "Tax collector after you?" he asked with a barked laugh.

"If only it were that simple," Paige said, looking into Max's eyes.

"Where to, folks?"

"Just drive," Max, said as they fell into each other's arms.

Chapter 26

August 12—Hong Kong
Bad day.

One year ago today I learned about Sallee's death.

Still see her everywhere.

Still see bits and pieces of our life together.

Maybe I shouldn't have moved back to Hong Kong. But we'd been here so long I couldn't give up the apartment, couldn't risk losing all the memories of Sallee growing up, all the happy moments.

Pulled a box of her toys down from the closet and wept. Could still see my little girl playing with all her dolls, fire engines, colored marbles.

Feel so old, so tired. Every part of me aches.

Would like to close my eyes and never open them again.

But as long as Tan Mong Kuan is alive, I will keep going.

August 14—At Sea
Good to be back aboard ship.

Hanging around the apartment feeling sorry for myself wasn't accomplishing much of anything. Made me feel worse.

Spent my last night ashore hobnobbing with Hong Kong and Japanese businessmen at Club Ferrari.

Passed myself off as a wealthy steamship company executive, so I could sit in and listen to them making *sub rosa* business deals.

Hated watching them make asses of themselves by taking part in the club's sophisticated pay-for-play sex. Patience and forbearance paid off, though.

One mainland bureaucrat actually took a liking to me. Wanted to know if I could deliver TVs, DVD players, and other name-brand consumer electronics to any of several uncharted ports, if he made sure there were no problems at the receiving end. Said payment could be in any currency.

Politely refused. He just laughed and had another drink.

Did make me think that getting involved in contraband might be a way to get to Tan.

Shouldn't have stuck around after that. One of the club's hostesses looked too much like Sallee. All I could do to keep from slugging the drunken slob who was groping her.

Had to remind myself of the only time when I did interfere. Girl lost her job and wanted to kill me. Can still hear her screaming. Accused me of stealing the food from her family's table.

She was right. Wasn't my place to disrupt the flow of commerce, no matter how distasteful.

Prostitute or Material Girl, it made no difference.

Can't stick my nose in where it doesn't belong.

The concept still bothers me. Never been able to understand what possesses men to behave like rutting animals in public places. But have learned to keep my fists under the table. Bite my tongue. Women don't lose their source of income. I don't get my head cracked open.

Was able to carry off the rest of the night's subterfuge

with restraint and sobriety.

Paid off. Much better than I had expected.

Learned that Tan Mong Kuan has a reputation for supplying almost any commodity, in almost any quantity, on very short notice. No written contracts. No backing out on a deal. Tough business.

Among the lead items in the Shan Triad's catalog of contraband and hijacked goodies are rare and exotic spices.

Couple of discreet inquiries revealed his ships are equipped for ship-to-boat, at-sea transfers. These are easily accomplished out among the hundreds of islands that lie between Hong Kong and the Leizhou Peninsula.

Think I can use that little piece of information to my advantage.

August 29—Singapore

Took time to check out the local boat builders.

Tan's smuggling activities and his illicit trade in spices has given me an idea.

One yard said it could build and deliver the latest smuggler-type speedboat on relatively short notice—forty-foot catamaran with steel-capped bow and steel plates to protect the propulsion units.

Fully equipped with the latest in electronics and propelled by four 1,000-hp waterjet engines, it would have a top speed of about sixty knots with a full three-ton load.

Said they'd just finished one and put her into the water. Wouldn't give me a ride, or even allow me to get close to her. Said the people who ordered her were very security conscious.

Got the impression the boat builders were afraid they might lose something more than future business.

Took a chance and ordered one.

Hope she will do the job. Eighty thousand dollars is a lot of cash.

August 31—Hong Kong

Found the perfect hideout for my new smuggler's boat—empty yacht storage building on one of the out-of-the-way New Territories islands. Inside dock, crane, and ten thousand square feet of storage space.

Paid the owner cash for six months' rent up front. Kept him from asking too many questions.

Never realized how much money it takes to get into the business of being a crook.

Heard from the Singapore boatyard.

My offshore speedster will be ready next week. Good timing.

Plan to bring the boat back on the containership as deck cargo and drop her off in Macao to keep from raising any suspicions around Hong Kong.

Will fly to Macao the next available weekend and run her back to Hong Kong under cover of darkness. The forty-mile jaunt will give me a chance to give her a thorough wringing out. Find out exactly what my new toy can and cannot do.

Next step: trap that rare, venomous butterfly, Tan Mong Kuan.

September 20—Hong Kong

Shakedown cruise accomplished without a hitch.

She's a real beauty. Does keep a one-man crew occupied full-time, though.

Most potent piece of sea-going machinery I've ever laid hand to.

The Racal Doppler log indicated a top speed of sixty-two knots.

165

Can't afford to let your attention wander for a second with that much power on tap.

Neither the Hong Kong nor Chinese marine police have anything that can catch her.

Hope Tan doesn't either.

Decided to christen her the *Nolla*. Be like the two of us going out together to make the bastards pay for our Sallee's death.

September 29—Hong Kong

Only one boatload of hijacked cargo and already the shed smells like a spice factory.

Can't believe how well it went.

Came up on the stern of the *Farfalla* just after nightfall as she rounded Castle Peak on her way to Malaysia.

Pulled even and bumped her lightly just aft of the bow. Make them think they'd hit something. It worked. Cut speed. Hit them again near the stern and backed off. Came to a dead stop, just as I'd hoped.

While the ship's crew worried over the origins of the empty drums tossed into the water to starboard, lashed the *Nolla* to their port side, pulled the knit mask down over my face, and boarded.

Everyone except the captain was staring into the water, chasing the drums with a spotlight. Easy to sneak up to the wheelhouse without being seen.

Captain heard me enter. Uzi kept him from doing anything other than glare at me. Pretended he didn't understand English. Threatened in Cantonese to shoot off his kneecaps. Cooperation improved dramatically.

With the captain under my control, the five crewmen went along with the drill. Didn't even struggle when I tied them up and left them in the wheelhouse.

Advance preparation paid off.

Took less than half an hour to locate and offload the spices into my boat, using the freighter's on-board gear.

Would have liked to take entire cargo. New speedster doesn't have that kind of capacity. Quantity isn't the name of this game.

Disabled communications. Fixed it so one of them could eventually work loose his bonds.

By the time I'd tucked the *Nolla* out of sight behind a small island, they still weren't underway.

Everything smooth as silk.

Keeps going this well, will need another warehouse.

Can't let this initial success to go to my head.

Tan and his rotten triad may not be so easily suckered next time out.

Chapter 27

The food was just so-so and the service was terrible. But the cabby had been right—the little neighborhood pizzeria was cozy and private. Max and Paige sat close together in a tiny booth at the rear of the restaurant and exchanged horror stories.

The waiter who brought their order spilled the drinks as he dumped everything onto the table. But on the good side, the smell of garlic permeated the whole restaurant.

Paige took her first bite from a wedge of pizza with cheese, tomato, and a generous spread of anchovies. She looked at Max, and frowned. "You're not eating."

"Guess I'm not so hungry after all," he said, twirling straggling strings of cheese around a finger.

"This is not *my* Max, the walking, talking, eating machine, the man I've grown to love and adore." She poked at his stomach and laughed. "An alien must have taken up residence in there, maybe an anorexic one."

He smiled, slipped an arm around her. His blue eyes were filled with sadness.

"What's the matter, baby?" she said, planting a kiss on his forehead.

"It's been a long time since I've had to face the possibility of losing you," he whispered. He shifted uncomfortably on the lumpy seat. "Not since the time—"

"Don't think about that. Max, please forget it. It was

just a silly lovers' quarrel from eons ago. I've forgotten all about it."

He laughed in spite of himself. "Sure you have." He kissed her cheek and slipped a lock of hair out of her eyes.

"There's something else, isn't there?" she asked

"Yeah." He twirled more cheese around a finger then let it slide back to his plate. "I just don't know how . . . how to tell you."

She laid her head on his shoulder and nudged his ear with her nose. "Whatever it is . . . just say it. The last thing we need is secrets coming between us."

He sat up straighter and gazed into her eyes. "That hulk back in the hotel room said your uncle was murdered."

"Uncle Jock was murdered?" She grabbed his leg with both hands. "Someone deliberately killed him?"

"That's what that piece of lard, Kim, said." He gulped down some Chianti and refilled his glass. "Payback because Jock had stolen from them."

"No! He was toying with you, trying to make you angry."

He pulled her closer, whispered in her ear, "I'm so sorry, Paige. But I think we both know these people are capable of anything." He jiggled the bag with the diaries. "Kim said they never intended to let us go, whether they got the journals or not. We both knew that, didn't we?"

"So they must have killed Uncle Jock because he was a danger to them in some way," Paige said. "Either he knew something and he was going to tell the authorities, or he had something they desperately wanted."

"Whatever it was, we're next on their hit list. Sheryl and George, too. Maybe even Rich Mattos."

"I just don't get it, why?"

"Kim said you and Sheryl not only inherited Jock's

wealth, but his debts as well."

"Debts? What debts? No one came after us before. Why now? It's been five years since Jock died."

"But we now know they've been watching you and Sheryl all this time," Max said. "There had to be some kind of reason for keeping you under surveillance."

"I suppose they never considered us a real threat, at least until we got involved with Heirs Apparent and went looking for Uncle Jock's money." She thought for a moment. "Then we suddenly go nosing around . . . stirring things up . . . messing in Jock's affairs *and* collecting his journals."

"So now, we've really made someone very nervous."

"There must be *very* critical information in those journals, Max. Why else murder Jock, threaten us?"

"That blubbery beast didn't say. My guess: they're all members of the triad Mattos told us about."

"But what about Martin Lester, do you think he was in on it, too?"

"Almost anything seems possible. Right now, I don't trust anyone except thee and me . . . and I'm not so sure about thee."

"Not funny!" She punched him in the shoulder. "You better trust me, Max Alper, or you won't share in the goodies when I become a rich woman."

He gave her a long, hard kiss. "I am your devoted servant."

"That's better." She tore off a big bite of pizza. "I wonder whether those guys who attacked us in San Diego and the two who grabbed us today are connected in some way."

"And if the two in the hotel had orders to kill us, why didn't the pickup truck pair do us in when they had us isolated in the desert?"

"Maybe these new journals will give us some solid answers," Paige said. She threw her wedge of pizza back on the plate as a flood of tears suddenly spilled down her cheeks. "My God, Max, what kind of black cloud is my family living under?" She covered her face with her hands.

Max eased her hands away and kissed one damp cheek, then the other. "You can't think of it that way, Paige. There's an explanation; we just have to find it."

She toyed with the crust of her pizza, then began tearing the napkin into smaller and smaller pieces. Soon bits were scattered across the table. "I know you're right, Max. But Jock and Sallee and Nolla's deaths make me think about how my parents died in that avalanche. Then I get lost in dark thoughts." She looked into his eyes. "So much suffering, so much violence. And now someone wants to kill the rest of my family."

"To quote my beautiful live-in newshawk, 'What they want, and what they get, ain't necessarily the same thing.' "

"I never say *ain't*." Her lips curved into the hint of a smile.

"Sez you." He pulled Jock's journals out of the bag and they began reading them in chronological order. About halfway through the first book, he slid a hand under a piece of pizza and took a huge bite without taking his eyes off the journal.

Paige laughed. "Ah, now that's my Max."

"Poor Jock," Paige said. "Reading these journals breaks my heart . . . and makes me madder than hell." She trailed her fingertips across the bound volumes. "So alone, filled with hatred and obsessed with revenge."

"This changes everything," Max said. "I thought they killed him for what he knew about them. But that was only one part of it—they were mostly pissed because he cost them money and made fools of them."

"He was clever . . . and brave," Paige said.

"Damn shame he didn't get away with it."

Paige tore the napkin into smaller pieces. "I wouldn't be too sure about that. Why are they still chasing after his journals?"

"Yeah, and anyone with half a brain could have figured Jock would turn up at Ocean Shores sooner or later," Max said. "Lassa fever and his distrust of hospitals made him far too vulnerable."

"And remember how we thought Lester was guilty of something?"

"Maybe now we have the answer."

"If he was involved with the triad," Paige said, "I'm going to find some way to nail the bastard."

The waiter interrupted, asking if they wanted dessert. Max looked at Paige and she shook her head. "Just the check, please."

"If Lester was part of it, he must have thought he was home free until we showed up," Max said. "What about this scenario: Lester was on Tan Mong Kuan's payroll, *and* also collected finder's fees from good old Kerwin."

"Heirs is small potatoes compared with this Hong Kong crew."

"But why did the triad kill Jock before they got their hands on the journals? How did they expect to find the merchandise he'd stolen from them?"

"The hit-and-run must have been a mistake. The people in the death car may have panicked, thought Jock was running away. And I'll bet he had a journal or two with him."

"Then you don't think these are the last of them?" Max said, pointing to the books on the table.

"No, these only take us to September ninety-seven. What happened between then and when Uncle Jock was killed?"

"Okay, let's assume the triad does have the last journals. Whatever they found obviously didn't satisfy them."

"In other words, they have part of the puzzle, we have a part, and there's still a part missing."

"Which puts us in a very dangerous position."

Chapter 28

Martin Lester stared at the rococo-styled clock perched on the far corner of his mahogany desk. Gold-tinted glass enclosed the brass works and the face was heavily decorated with gold-leaf curlicues. Petite Roman numerals of an ancient font jumped out in dramatic contrast to the broad, smooth lines of the rest of his office furnishings.

For the most part, Lester liked contemporary things. A clean, uncluttered, almost simplistic look made him feel peaceful, allowed him the pretense that life could be uncomplicated.

As he stared at the clock, he acknowledged once again that historical objects often made him uneasy, made him ponder the role and responsibilities of the individual in a complex society. Those kinds of thoughts only accentuated his lack of contributions to a very needy world. But, after all was said and done, he was who he was.

His father had given him the antique clock, and he liked to keep it where he could see it throughout the day. It was symbolic, a constant reminder that money *was* important. Without it, he would have been nothing, had nothing.

But it had been many years since he needed prodding to remember that. All he had to do was settle into his chauffeur-driven Cadillac and be taken to his four-acre estate overlooking the Pacific Ocean, where the view was far more expansive than the one from his office at Ocean Shores.

Late in the evening, he liked to stand naked on his bedroom balcony, where not a soul could see him. He would spend several minutes gazing down on the grounds and his private stretch of beach, enjoying the fact that his was a truly privileged life.

Now, in his office, the clock chimed eight. It was a delicate, unobtrusive, series of notes that he found soothing, when he actually listened to them.

He stared at the dusky sky through the picture window across the room. Another beautiful California evening unfolding. For a brief moment, he thought about what he might like to have for dinner. Since his wife died two years ago, food hadn't held much interest for him. He would probably have a simple sandwich and let it go at that.

Mesmerized, he watched the little golden balls spin in the clock's glass encasement.

His father's presentation of the antique clock many years earlier—while Lester was living in an attic apartment—had been accompanied by a humiliating denunciation of his lifestyle and choice of careers.

"Writing is not a profession for a real man," his father had said. "Puerile and ridiculous! It will eventually destroy you." His father went on to mock the tattered and stained mattress that rested on the rough, raw wood floor next to the door-less icebox.

His final gesture had been to place the gleaming, expensive clock on Lester's rickety plank-and-sawhorse desk. "Return home when you come to your senses, when you see the wisdom of making a living at a real job."

In that desolate room, the clock became a beacon. Lester would stare at it for long periods of time until one day, cradling the clock in one arm, he returned home and took over Ocean Shores. He never again attempted to express his thoughts on paper, and he never again had to worry about money.

Lester turned his attention from the clock to the folder containing Jock Boylan's records. The papers still rested in the middle of the desk where he'd placed them during the Alpers' visit. For some reason, he hadn't put the folder into his out-basket so his secretary could return it to the inactive files.

He'd liked Jack Boylan even though the man was a definite pain in the ass. The captain became a success story for Ocean Shores, for Lester. Most of the patients that arrived at his facility rarely left on their own two feet. But Boylan would come in sick as a dog and depart in relatively good health, time after time. At least until that final admission five years earlier.

He ran his hand lightly across the folder, then flipped it open. As he scanned the pages, he became engrossed in the story they told. He was surprised when he realized someone was knocking at his office door.

"Come in!"

His secretary popped her head in. "I've finished the paperwork for that late arrival," she said. "Is there anything else?"

"No, no. Thanks for staying late, Ms. Childs. I appreciate it." He gave her a dismissive hand gesture. "Have a nice evening."

With everyone now gone except him, it was quiet in the administration wing of the facility. He looked around, but there was nothing else for him to do. He started to close the Boylan file, but was drawn back into it again.

Over the years, Captain Jack Boylan had been a cash cow for both Ocean Shores and him personally.

The funds from Hong Kong, of course, were never entered into a ledger. There was a taint to that money and the arrangement made him nervous, but, as much as he wanted to, he couldn't turn down that kind of cash offer.

It had all been easy until Boylan's last visit. There'd been a new twist: Hong Kong had demanded that their "specialist" have access to the captain. Their only explanation was an extra ten thousand dollars. He'd done as requested and asked no further questions.

When the hit-and-run driver killed Boylan, Lester was afraid Hong Kong might blame him. But Hong Kong only asked for continuing information, if anyone came asking about the old sea captain.

No one came and he continued to collect easy money.

Then the Alpers came. Now Hong Kong had him hanging on the end of a line tied not only to the Captain, but to the Alpers.

Paige and Max Alper had to be stopped. Lester had to make them turn around and go back to San Francisco before they ruined everything.

If those thugs had done their job, the two grand he'd paid them would have been well worth it and the Alpers would have turned tail and gone home. Hong Kong would never know.

He put the Boylan file into his out-basket and stood to leave. There was another knock at his door, probably his secretary, who may have forgotten something. Perhaps the janitorial staff, looking to hurry him along so they could clean the office.

"Come in!" he said impatiently. "I'm just leaving."

The door eased open and two well-dressed Asian men entered. They closed the door quietly behind them.

"Yes?" Lester said.

"Mr. Martin Lester?"

Lester nodded, then froze. While he had never before seen either man, his heart became a trip-hammer. He looked around quickly for someplace to run, but the men stood between him and the door.

"What do you want?" he asked.

"You were told not to interfere with the Alpers."

"I . . . I didn't do . . ."

"The men you hired are much more loyal to one-hundred-dollar bills than they are to you."

"I don't know what you're talking about."

"You are not a truthful man, Mr. Martin Lester. Your usefulness has come to an end."

Lester bit into his lower lip, tasted blood. *Goddamn Alpers. This is all their fault.* He needed to explain, he needed to . . .

The other man's arm whipped around from behind his back with such speed that his hand was a mere blur.

Lester had only an instant before a sharp object lodged in his neck. He opened his mouth to speak, but all that escaped was a faint gurgle.

His legs gave way and he reached out to the desk for support. His hand only found air, groped towards his father's gift. The last thing he heard was the crash of the clock as it shattered on the floor.

Chapter 29

Paige and Max constantly glanced back over their shoulders after they left the pizzeria. In record time, they covered four long blocks to a small, commercial hotel the restaurant owner had suggested. Convinced no one was following them, they climbed a short flight of stairs and entered a cramped lobby. Upholstered but threadbare armchairs stood next to a pair of scratched end tables topped with tattered magazines.

Crossing the cracked marble floor, they stood in front of a wrought iron cage that served as the hotel's registration desk. Paige, toeing the unraveling edges of an imitation Persian rug, crinkled her nose at the pervasive aroma of disinfectant, stale tobacco smoke, and rancid urine.

The night clerk, poised on a high stool, eyed them suspiciously as they registered under "Mr. and Mrs. Mick Wood, Los Angeles," and paid in cash.

"Will you require a receipt?" the clerk asked. He assumed a pretentious attitude of upscale respectability while watching their every move.

"Yes," Max said.

"Luggage?"

"Uh, the airline lost it. They promised to have it sent to us by tomorrow morning."

The clerk frowned his disbelief as he pushed the receipt across to Max. He openly eyed them up and down, taking in their sweaty, rumpled clothes. A barely perceptible shake of his head expressed his disapproval as he shoved a key through the opening of his cage.

Once out of his sight, they each gave him the digital salute and broke out laughing.

"What a prick!" Max said.

"I thought he was cute, in a sleazy kind of way."

In the room, Paige kicked off her shoes and plopped down on the faded chenille bedspread. She reached for the telephone.

"Where the hell have you been?" Sheryl screamed. Paige held the phone away from ear. "We've been trying to reach you for *days* . . . Don't you ever check your answering machine? . . . Even the newspaper didn't know where you were . . . and the PR agency said Max resigned . . . What's going on, Paige? . . . Do you hear me? . . . Do you . . ."

"Take a breath, Sheryl," Paige said. She held the phone a few inches from her ear. "If you'll just give me a chance . . ."

"I'm not playing games with you anymore, Paige Boylan Alper. Do you understand? We need that money. I want you to sign those Heirs Apparent papers, and I want you to sign them right now! Do you hear me?" Her voice had risen to a shriek.

Paige squeezed her eyes shut, grit her teeth. "Oh, yes! I hear you quite clearly, Sheryl," she said in a low, firm voice. "But for a change, you're going to have to hear *me*—and there isn't much time."

"For God's sake, Paige, much time for what?"

"You, George, and the kid—"

"Can't you say George Junior? Is that so hard to say? You're supposed to be a hotshot reporter and you still can't remember your own nephew's name."

"—you're all going to have to pack and leave town. Now! And you can't come back until you get an all-clear from either Max or me."

Silence.

"Did you hear me, Sheryl?"

"I heard you. I just want to know whether you've totally lost your friggin' mind or what? Like, what is all this nonsense about leaving town?"

"Have George pick up the extension, so I won't have to repeat everything."

"Do you think they'll leave?" Max asked.

"I think I convinced them of the danger, but I'm not convinced they'll take the precautions I suggested to keep from being followed."

"We can only hope they'll listen to someone else for a change."

"I know, but with the financial mess they're in, plus their total obsession with Uncle Jock's money, I'm afraid they'll be careless . . . do something stupid."

"We'd better keep that in mind ourselves."

Paige shivered as she stepped out of her dress. "It's not turning out the way we thought it would, Max. It's gotten away from us."

"That chunk of dough was an enticing carrot." He pulled her into his arms and held her. "And the chase sounded like great fun at first."

"But it's gone way beyond that, hasn't it?" She slipped away and walked into the bathroom. The showerhead sputtered, then gave way to a drizzle of water. "Before we started reading Uncle Jock's journals, all I could think about was Heirs screwing us out of fifty percent."

"And now?"

"Oh, I haven't given up on exposing Kerwin and Heirs Apparent. Not for one second. I don't like the way their kind does business. They take advantage of people who don't have the smarts or the time to find an inheritance on their own."

"So, when this is all over, we'll dig deeper, see if we can nail their hides," Max said. "We'll do a freelance piece . . . win a Pulitzer or something."

"Man, I like the sound of that, but maybe we first better plan on getting through this with our skin intact." She took off her bra and stepped out her panties.

"Tan Mong Kuan and his triad have thrown us a curve . . . a dangerous curve."

She paused. "I can't back down."

"Spoken like a true Boylan," Max said. "A true, nude Boylan."

She grimaced at the grungy shower stall, then stepped in and huddled under the defective nozzle to get as much water as possible.

"That triad murdered my uncle . . . and Sallee . . . and God knows how many others. Someone needs to stand up to them."

"It's not as though we have a choice. Tan Mong Kuan isn't going to allow us to walk away from this, my love. We *have* to finish what your uncle started, whether we like it or not."

Naked, he reached into the shower for Paige's hand, their eyes locked. She yanked him into the tiny stall where they huddled under spitting drops of water.

"First thing in the morning," he said, "we'll get some new clothes, collect the quarter million, and get the hell out of Dodge."

Chapter 30

At daybreak, Max eased out of bed and cringed as he pulled on his soiled, wrinkled slacks and sweat-stained shirt. He tossed the socks, unable to look at them, let alone wear them one more day.

He stood for a moment at the bedside and silently watched Paige's chest rise and fall. They'd slept fitfully, waking each other every so often to add another detail or two to their master plan. Now, she was finally in a deep sleep, clutching a bunched-up pillow beneath her head. He smiled, trailed a finger down her cheek, turned, and tiptoed out of the room.

From the safety of the sheltered hotel entrance, he scanned the street in both directions, tried to peer into the entryways across from him. The night shadows were gone. A few homeless people shuffled away with their crumpled bedrolls, melting from the sight and mind of the early morning foot traffic. He sniffed at the hot, humid air, then frowned as the rank aroma of stale perspiration wafted up from the grungy clothing sticking to his body. Stepping out in the direction of a coffee shop's flickering neon sign, he continued to survey his surroundings. No one seemed to have any interest in him.

Within a short time, he was back with hot coffee and a bag filled with toasted and buttered English muffins. As he slid the key into the hotel room lock, the door flung open, wresting the key from his fingers. Paige wrapped her arms around his neck, almost knocking their breakfast out of his hand.

"Where have you been?" she cried, burying her head in his shoulder. "I woke up and you were gone!"

"Hey, it's okay." He could feel goose bumps on her bare arms. He rubbed his cheek against her loose hair. "I just went to get us some breakfast."

She pulled him into the room and closed the door behind them. "God, I sound like such a wuss." She smiled weakly. "I'm sorry. It's just that . . . that I woke up and I was all alone. I wasn't sure whether I was awake or dreaming."

He curled a finger under her chin and tilted her face. "A *real* wuss wouldn't have made it past San Diego."

Paige looked into the department store dressing room's mirror. Since their clothes had been heisted in the desert, she'd been forced into garments she wouldn't even think of wearing. Now, she'd had to buy clothes she wouldn't even dream of wearing.

She made sure her telltale long, black hair was tucked out of sight beneath a poorly made synthetic blond wig. She studied her scrubbed-clean face and ran fingers through the unruly mop of brassy shoulder-length hair that was certain to twirl and tangle in the slightest breeze. Tugging and adjusting her blouse, she tried to keep the thin cotton material neatly in place, but it was hopeless—she knew it would bag and sag again within a few minutes.

It had taken them less than an hour to outfit themselves, but she was regretting the cheap neutral flats she'd hurriedly purchased. They were already marred by scuff marks and starting to pinch.

"I feel so . . . so dowdy," she told Max when she came out of the dressing room.

"That's part of the plan," Max said. "But it's definitely not working in your case." He shook his head. "I could toss you into a barrel of mud and those green eyes would still sparkle like emeralds."

"I'm sure you exaggerate, my prince, but don't stop." She quickly glanced around the store as they started to leave. "I've never bought clothes and walked out with them on my back."

The insistent dong-dong-dong of an alarm startled them. Everyone in their vicinity paused to gawk as a security guard moved quickly toward them.

"Did you just purchase that luggage, sir?" the guard asked Max politely.

"Yes, why?"

"I'm sorry, but I'll have to ask you to step this way."

As soon as they moved away from the exit, the alarm ceased. People openly stared at them as they stood waiting at a nearby counter.

"Open the suitcase, please. I'd like to see the receipts for your purchases."

Max flipped open the latches to reveal an array of packaged blouses, shirts, pants, skirts, and underwear. Price tags peeked from the folds of the clothing. Max retrieved a wad of receipts from the elastic storage pocket and handed them to the guard.

"I think you'll find everything accounted for, including the clothes we're wearing."

The guard checked the VISA charge slips against the purchases, item-by-item, moving with irritating thoroughness. Straight-faced, he turned to Paige: "Mrs. Alper, you might want to cut the tickets off of your skirt." He pointed at two red tags dangling from her waistband. "You also seem to have a sensor still affixed to the hem of your skirt in back."

Paige knew her face had flushed to a bright red. "This definitely is not one of my better days." A saleswoman led her behind the counter and struggled to unclamp the offending device, then pulled out a pair of scissors to snip off the price tags.

"That's what I get for pushing my budget and buying an upscale skirt," Paige said.

"Honey, that alarm goes off all day long. And don't let that security man bother you . . . we don't get the brightest of the bright of them to work here, you know." She smiled sympathetically. "There!" she declared to the guard, slapping her tools back down on the counter. "That should take care of big brother."

This time, Max and Paige exited the store without incident.

"I hope we catch on to this cloak and dagger stuff soon," Paige said outside. "So far, we look pretty lame."

"Don't sweat the small stuff," he said. "I mean, we're still alive, aren't we?"

"Oh, boy, are you encouraging!"

They stood across the street from the Atlantic-Pacific Trust, fidgeting in their new clothes as they studied the pedestrian flow in front of the bank. Anyone who paused longer than a few seconds became suspect.

"What do you think?" Max asked.

She shrugged. "We can't wait here forever. Besides, it all hangs on whether or not the Hong Kong people have a tie-in with Heirs. If they do, there's probably someone looking for us right now."

186

"If not, the triads are going to have to start from scratch, since I doubt if they'll be sending the wiry Asian or his buddy Kim after us or anyone again. Those people don't tolerate mistakes."

"But I'm not counting on anything," Paige said. "I say we stick to the plan . . . not stand here any longer than we have to." She moved a few feet away.

"You know, we don't have to settle this money thing right now. It'll still be here when we get back from Hong Kong."

"No. I promised Sheryl we'd take care of it while we were here. It was the only way she would agree to go into hiding." Paige shook her head for emphasis. "A promise is a promise, no matter how much of a twit she is."

"I suppose you're right," he said. "I wish I could go in there for you, love, but no matter what I do I'm never going to be taken for Paige Boylan Alper."

She kissed him quickly on the cheek. "Hey, it's going to be a breeze." She moved away with a thumbs-up over her shoulder and melted with the tempo of the fast-paced crowd.

Paige glanced at the Corinthian columns flanking the bank entrance, expecting an equally ornate interior. But the building had been remodeled, turned into a nondescript series of teller windows and executive cubicles, most of them empty.

She walked up to the customer service desk and waited her turn. The woman listened to her query and passed her on to a female loan officer, who shook her head and passed her on to a bank trust officer, who sighed and handed her off to the assistant branch manager.

The corpulent bank officer rose from his chair and took

Paige's hand, shaking it with an unnecessary intimacy. "Ralph Linus!" he announced. "How may I be of service?"

Towering over her, Linus offered her a seat and sank heavily back into his own chair, where he twirled, licked, and stroked a large cigar before stuffing it into his mouth.

"Still can't get used to the fact the law says a man can't smoke a fine panatela at his own desk anymore."

"The world does change," Paige said. "Sometimes for the better."

His patronizing smile remained pasted on his face, but the unlit cigar quivered slightly between his clamped teeth. "I understand you are seeking information concerning disposition of abandoned and inactive accounts."

"No, just one specific account, Number 66-313527, in the name of Jock Ian Boylan."

"And what is your relationship to Mr. Boylan?"

"Niece."

Linus turned to his computer, turned the screen so Paige couldn't see it, and then typed in some information. "And your interest in this account?"

"I want to claim it, close it out."

Linus shifted the cigar from one side of his mouth to the other. "It's not quite that simple, my dear."

"I do *not* appreciate being patronized, Mr. Linus. I'm quite aware there is a formal procedure."

"I see."

"So tell me," she asked, "is there an account here for my uncle or not?"

"First, my . . . uh . . . Mrs. Alper, right?"

"Correct."

"Yes, well, I will need to see some kind of identification, plus verification that you are related to Mr. Boylan, and have a claim on his estate. If he is deceased, I also will need a copy of the death certificate, a New York state tax waiver, an affidavit to cover a lost passbook, and a power of attorney." He paused. "*Then* we can discuss the particulars of Boylan's account."

Paige smiled pleasantly, unsnapped her purse, and withdrew the envelope containing the death certificate and power of attorney, which she placed in front of Linus. "I've done this little dance before, Mr. Linus, so I know this is all that's required for you to verify existence of the account and the dollar amount."

Linus pulled the documents toward him and scanned their contents.

"That one," Paige said, tapping a fingernail on one of the papers, "is a power of attorney from my sister, Sheryl Boylan Fenster, the only other heir. As for the tax waiver and lost passbook affidavit, I believe the bank supplies those prior to the account being turned over to my sister and me."

Linus glared at her.

"I'm glad we have that straight. Now, Mr. Linus, is there an account in this bank in the name of my uncle, as indicated by your abandoned accounts newspaper ad?"

Linus sighed. "Yes, Mrs. Alper, there is."

"And the size of that account?"

"Quite sizable."

"How sizable?"

"We must go through certain procedures step-by-step before I can tell you that."

"Oh? Well, tell me, Mr. Linus, are you the only bank officer who handles the disposition of abandoned accounts?"

"It's one of my responsibilities. Why?"

"Then you must be the person who has the working relationship with Heirs Apparent, Incorporated."

Linus blanched. The cigar fell from his mouth. He snatched it out of the air as it bounced off his ample belly. He took a moment to compose himself, and then leaned across the desk to get as close to Paige as possible.

"Mrs. Alper," he growled, "do not antagonize me. You are here requesting my assistance." He waved a hand across the array of documents on his desk. "I can make this very simple, or make it so excruciatingly difficult and time-consuming . . ." He raised both hands, palms up. "I think you get the picture."

"Oh, I get the picture all right, Mr. Linus, and it's an ugly one. What I get is a portrait of a corrupt bank officer who is pocketing kickbacks from heir tracers."

"You have absolutely no proof of that."

"Would you care to bet your career on it?" When he didn't respond, she added, "I didn't think so." Paige reached across the desk and pulled the power of attorney and death certificate back in front of her. "Now that *that's* settled, let's discuss your connection to the Shan Triad."

Linus' blank expression told her what she needed to know—Kerwin and Tan apparently were not interlinked.

"All right, Mr. Linus, let's get on with the matter at hand. It would be in your best interest if you started carrying out your fiduciary responsibilities without any further delay." She shifted in her chair and gave him a sickeningly sweet smile. "And this whole transaction had better go as smooth as silk, or the virile part of someone's anatomy is going to be surgically amputated and tossed to the wolves, mixed-metaphorically speaking."

The banker stuffed the cigar back into his mouth and re-arranged it several times with his tongue before taking his wary eyes off Paige to glance at the Jock Ian Boylan file. "The principal, Mrs. Alper, is two hundred and fifty thousand dollars. In addition, there is accrued and compounded interest."

"And the total figure?"

He punched a couple of computer keys. "Brings it to three hundred nineteen thousand, seventy dollars and thirty-eight cents."

"Thank you very much. Now what say you get busy putting together whatever documents that need to be signed so checks can be cut for my sister and me."

Linus nodded. "When would it be convenient for you come in? Tomorrow?"

"I'll wait," she said.

Paige bounded across Houston Street, darting between swearing cabbies and digital-saluting delivery drivers.

"It's there! It really is there!" she shouted.

He wrapped his arms around her and swung her off the pavement. "I was beginning to think you were never coming out of there."

"I wasn't about to leave that bank until everything was disclosed, signed, and witnessed."

She held up a copy of the receipt for closing out Jock's account, waved it in front of his face, then pressed a forefinger against the tip of his nose: "See? *Now* you're really married to a woman of means."

He started to spin her around, then stopped. Paige saw him looking past her into the crowd. People were starting to stare.

"We still have to get out of New York with our skins intact," he said, lowering her to the ground.

"I know." She tugged, straightening her wig, which had tipped to one side of her head. "But damn it, Max, we did it. You and I. We did it!"

Chapter 31

"Better take this call," Alex Pickerel told Russell Kerwin over the intercom.

"Who is it?"

"Ralph Linus over at Atlantic-Pacific Trust."

"It's a little late in the year, isn't it?" Kerwin said. "He must have stumbled on a good one."

"I'd say we're the ones who stumbled," Pickerel said.

"Don't care for the sound of that. You must be talking Boylan?"

"Afraid so."

"Hm-m." He started to punch into the outside line, then told Pickerel: "Listen in, but let me do the talking."

"What else?"

Kerwin had kept the Boylan file on his desk ever since hearing from that twit Martin Lester at Ocean Shores in San Diego. *God, how I hate dealing with Californians!*

"Good morning, Ralph, what can I do for you?" Kerwin said.

"Paige Boylan Alper just cleaned out Jock Boylan's savings account to the tune of some three hundred nineteen thousand dollars," Linus said.

"How did that happen?"

"Don't ask *me* how that happened. I thought you and Pickerel had the Boylan nieces all nicely wrapped." When Kerwin didn't immediately respond, he added, "Well?"

192

"In this instance, Paige Boylan Alper turned out to be a wild card—she's an investigative reporter for a San Francisco newspaper. It also means she was not happy with Heirs Apparent's SOP and decided to go looking for the inheritance on her own."

"Are you saying I'm not going to get my finder's fee, that I'm not going to have my daughter's fall semester college tuition?" Linus said.

"There's always CCNY."

"That's not funny."

"I wasn't trying to be funny, Ralph. We're out almost a hundred seventy-nine thousand ourselves." He heard a muffled gasp from Pickerel and realized he'd said more than he should have.

Linus was silent for a few seconds. "That doesn't exactly compute, Russell."

"What doesn't compute?"

"I shouldn't have to do the math for you, Russell, but I will," Linus said. "I'm supposed to get ten percent of what you get, or sixteen thousand out of your hundred sixty thousand. So what's this hundred and seventy-nine grand business?"

"Okay, okay, Ralph." Kerwin took in a deep breath. "Let's put it this way: as a rule, people don't track down the money themselves, so we don't tell them about accumulated interest, unless they make a point of it."

"Asshole! How much have you cheated *me* over the past several years?"

"Heirs Apparent does all the work; all you have to do is give us an advance heads-up on the names," Kerwin said. "But this is one of those times when it would have been nice if you could have exerted yourself just the tiniest bit."

"What are you talking about?"

"If you had put your mind to it, chances are you could have delayed Mrs. Alper, even if only for a day. Then we would have had more time to pressure the twin sister to go for the original offer."

"Look, Kerwin, that Alper woman came in here un- announced with a very good working knowledge of New York banking laws, plus she had every piece of identifica- tion and documentation she needed to claim Jock Ian Boylan's dormant savings account. She was beyond stalling. Let's face it, you failed to reel this one in." There was a deep sigh. "She rolled right over us."

"Did she say how she got on to you?" Kerwin asked.

"On to me? She didn't know *shit* about me until she sat down in front of my desk. But she sure as hell had the goods on Heirs Apparent, Inc."

"She mentioned us by name?"

"The company, yes. You specifically, no."

There were several beats before Kerwin said, "Tough one to lose."

"That's the prize understatement of the year." Another deep sigh. "An investigative reporter, for chrissake! *Shit!* I sure as hell hope she's going to be satisfied with the three hundred twenty grand and not give us a bunch of trouble by going to the authorities."

"Time will tell," Kerwin said and hung up. "Well?" he asked Pickerel, who he knew was still on the line.

"I'm thinking about taking up full-time residence in that little beachfront villa I built in the Caymans," Pickerel said.

"Are you nice to your neighbors?" Kerwin said.

Chapter 32

"We probably should have driven to Boston," Paige said as they walked toward the United Airlines ticket counter at JFK.

"I don't think they'll figure us for a Miami flight, no matter where we leave from," Max said.

"Miami?"

"Yeah." They got in line with the other unticketed passengers. "I thought maybe we could take a regional flight to Miami—"

"—grab a direct flight from there to San Francisco—"

"No, L.A. first, then San Jose—"

"—and try to shake anyone who may be following us. Then pick up our passports and go on to Hong Kong."

"You got it," Max said.

"Pretty smart, Alper."

"Hope so." There was only one person ahead of them now in the ticket line. Max moved closer and whispered in Paige's ear. "We have to assume they'll only cover flights headed for the West Coast, expecting us to run for home."

"I can't believe they have enough people to cover every ticket counter at JFK, LaGuardia, and Newark."

"True, but we have no idea what kind of word-of-mouth network they might have, or how much money they spread around to informants."

Paige scanned the crowd, studying faces and clothing.

195

"Since 9/11, everyone looks so damn shifty," she whispered, then clapped a hand over her mouth.

"What's wrong?" Max said.

"Do you realize today is the second anniversary of the attack on the World Trade Center?"

Max checked the date on his watch and shook his head. "I haven't been paying attention to the actual date since we got to San Diego." He looked around. "Amazing . . . life just keeps going on, doesn't it?"

"Normally, I'd only be on the lookout for some crazed-looking passenger. But our government has us so paranoid that everyone looks like a potential terrorist. I keep expecting someone to step out of the crowd and start shooting, or detonate a bomb."

"I'd say the best thing right now is for us to keep from looking suspicious ourselves," Max said. "With all this extra homeland security, we don't want to be singled out and risk attracting the attention of one of the triad's people."

A clerk raised an arm and indicated they were next.

"How may I help you, sir?" the young woman asked with a dazzling smile when the Alpers stepped up to the counter.

"I phoned in a reservation earlier for two seats on your three-fifteen flight to Miami—Paige and Max Alper." As he waited for her to consult the computer, Paige frowned at him. With just a slight twitch of his head, he warned Paige not to say anything. At the same time he tugged at the brim of the straw hat covering his red hair, which was too distinctive, too easy to spot, too easy to remember. Maybe he should have dyed it or gotten a wig when Paige did.

The clerk's long burgundy nails clicked at the keys, paused, then resumed their practiced rhythm. She looked up at Max, then tried the computer again. "Did you say Alper?"

"Yes. Paige and Max."

"And you phoned in your reservation."

"From the hotel," Paige said, joining in on the subterfuge. "Why, is there a problem?"

Max looked at his wife and wanted to burst out laughing. Even lying they worked well together.

"I don't find any record of your reservation," the clerk said. "Did they give you a confirmation number?"

Max pursed his lips. "Yes! Yes, they did." He pulled out his wallet, looked through it, and shook his head. "I know I have it here someplace." He went through all of his pockets.

"Did I give that confirmation number to you?" he asked Paige.

She shook her head, barely able to keep from laughing.

"I called about ten this morning," Max said. "They gave me one window and one aisle seat, just behind the wing," Max said. "Then I wrote down the confirmation number." He patted his pockets again. "For the life of me I can't remember where I put it."

"And they took your credit card information?" asked the clerk.

"Oh, yes. Yes. All of that. I remember having to read the expiration date twice . . . oh-two, oh-seven."

The clerk sighed. "I'm afraid this is one of those times when the system didn't work."

"You mean we can't get on the flight?" Paige asked.

"The best I can do is put you on standby."

"Damn! If we miss the wedding . . ." Max put on his best sorrowful expression.

The clerk gave them a sympathetic look. "Tell you what: I'm going to cheat a little and put you at the head of the list. There're almost always people who don't show."

"We really appreciate that," Max said, picking up their suitcase.

The Alpers were no more than a couple of steps away when the clerk called them back.

"I can't believe this," she said. "Two adjoining seats up front just became available."

"I think we can handle that," Max said. "Thank you. Thank you very much."

"You're welcome." She started to punch out the tickets, then said, "I will need photo identification for you each of you."

Once their faces had been confirmed by their driver's licenses, Max paid for the tickets by credit card.

"Enjoy the wedding," the clerk said. She held up her left hand and wiggled her ring finger. "I'm getting married myself in October."

"Congratulations," Paige said.

Away from the congestion of the ticket counter, Max said, "Let's go find some out-of-the-way place to wait for the flight."

Paige put an arm around him and began to laugh. "You are too much, Max Alper."

"We got the tickets, didn't we?"

"Just hope it didn't cost us too much karma."

When they were finally seated, Paige tugged at Max's sleeve. "What?"

"Do you suppose these guys can hack into airline passenger manifests and credit card transactions?"

"That same thought hit me when I saw I didn't have enough cash to pay for the tickets and would have to charge them," he said.

"Got an idea."

"Go."

"Let's ticket ourselves to two or three other cities, on different airlines," she said. "Maybe by the time they figure out our real flight plan, we'll have made it back to San Francisco, picked up our passports, and be on a flight to Hong Kong."

By the time United started boarding passengers for their Miami flight, Max and Paige were also booked on flights to Chicago, Dallas, and Atlanta, via three different airlines other than United.

"Now this is what I call summer," Max said several hours later as he watched the fog spill across the Northern California coastal hills. They hurried through the San Jose airport and boarded the first hotel courtesy van that pulled up to the curb, not caring which one it was as long as they got out of the area in a hurry.

Once they were settled in a seat near the door, Paige huddled against Max and surveyed the other passengers. "Do you think we got away clean?"

"Looks good so far."

She took a deep breath and looked out the window. "Can you believe the differences in temperatures? This morning I was so hot I wanted to tear off my clothes."

Max wrapped an arm around her. "Promises, promises."

"Now, I'm freezing." She let out a loud yawn. "I'm not complaining though. Just to plant my two feet on Mother Earth again is good enough."

"Only tore my arm off twice during the last flight."

"Very funny." She burrowed her head into his chest. "I don't care what you say, Max Alper. If the airlines really cared about passengers, they'd offer complimentary knockout drops instead of peanuts."

The van driver drummed his fingers on the steering

wheel, apparently waiting for another incoming flight. Every now and then he revved the engine to smooth out the tick-tick-tick of an out-of-adjustment valve. After checking his watch once more, he gave a final thump to the accelerator and reached for the door lever. Before he could secure it, the door was blocked from the outside.

"Thanks!" a man called up to the startled driver. "I'm on a tight schedule." He looked around as he climbed into the bus, then slid into the aisle seat directly across from Max and Paige.

As the van driver wove his way through airport traffic, Paige casually peeked around Max's chest to study the late arrival: tall, ordinary looking, somewhere in his thirties, briefcase but no luggage. She almost lost interest as the rhythmic motion of the van caused her eyelids to droop. Then she dreamily saw the late-arriving passenger shift around and look directly at Max, who also was beginning to nod off. Through half-closed lids, she saw the appraising eyes shift from Max to her. A chill rippled from the base of her spine to the curve of her neck.

"Max!" she whispered urgently, nudging him with her free hand.

"What is it?"

"Lower your voice!"

"Yeah?" he whispered.

"I don't like the looks of that guy across from you."

"Me, either. But we haven't liked the looks of anyone since we left San Diego." He kissed her on the forehead. "I think we're both jumpy and imagining things. A good night's sleep will slay the dragons."

"Wish we could go back to our place, at least for one night."

"Yeah, kick back in the hot tub, put some perspective on

everything that's occurred since you received that letter from Heirs Apparent."

"I know. Everything has happened so fast. One part of me is still trying to digest the thing with Heirs, while at the same time we're on the run from a bunch of Hong Kong cut-throats."

Max leaned his head back. "I think I'm beginning to understand how Jock must have felt toward the end."

"Rootless and vulnerable." She peeked at the man again, but he had turned away to look out the side window. "It was smart to send the journals back UPS ground to Rita and Mike. One less thing to worry about. Now, if we can just get our passports out of the safe deposit box without any problems."

"This is the first time I've ever seen any logic in your carrying that damn key with you all the time," Max said.

"Hey, some people accumulate loose change, I collect keys. Never saw a key I didn't like."

"One day you won't be able to lift that valise you call a purse." He laughed. "Sometimes I feel like I'm married to a call girl."

"Not funny, Alper."

As the shuttle turned into the hotel driveway, everyone stood and began moving toward the front of the van. Max started to step into the aisle to beat the rush, then paused to allow the man across from them to go first.

"After you," the man countered.

As Max and Paige exited the bus, the suspect passenger followed a few steps behind. At the registration desk inside, Paige whispered in Max's ear: "That guy still gives me the creeps."

"But he's always said such nice things about you."

She slugged him in the shoulder.

Max signed them in as Mr. and Mrs. M. Wood while the man from the van registered next to him.

The three of them entered the elevator at the same time. Paige never took her eyes off the other passenger.

Max punched Four. "What's your pleasure?" he asked, finger poised. The door slid shut.

"Doesn't matter, dude." The man quickly thrust a hand into his jacket pocket.

Paige swung her purse around full force, catching the man square in the face. His eyes went from dazed to vacant as she hit him twice more. He crumpled to the floor just as the elevator came to stop.

"Great reflexes," Max said, peeking out into the empty corridor of the fourth floor.

"Buying all those tickets didn't do us a damn bit of good, did it?"

"Nope."

"Anything in his pockets?"

Max reached down, ran a quick search, and came up with a small semi-automatic. "Ugly looking, isn't it?" he said, hefting it in his hand.

"You're not going to keep that thing, are you?" Paige backed out of the elevator.

"No, it's his. Taking it wouldn't be nice." He released the clip, jacked the round out of the chamber, and dropped both into his pocket. He then positioned the gun in the unconscious man's hand and stepped out of the elevator, then reached back in to push the Lobby button.

"He's going to have a lot of explaining to do," Paige said, grabbing for Max's hand. "But right now, I think we'd better get the hell out of here."

They ran toward the fire exit, threw open the door, and raced down the stairs.

Chapter 33

Journal—1997
Jock Ian Boylan

November 2—Hong Kong

A reaction at last!

After five raids in five weeks on Tan's ships, one of the newspapers finally ran a front-page story about "The Mysterious Spice Pirates."

Nice touch. Not many details. Doubt Tan cooperates much with the media.

Marine Police also had very little to say, according to the newspaper. Do they really care about Tan's misfortunes?

Speculation up and down the waterfront about the identity of the perpetrators of those forays has been prize scuttlebutt for the past week.

Everyone has a theory about who has the balls to challenge the mighty Shan Triad.

Damn it, I do.

Got to be careful, though. Getting more and more difficult to keep my mouth shut as the barroom stories get wilder and wilder. Want to tell them it's me, Jock Ian Boylan. Tell them I'm getting even with the scum who killed my little girl.

Can't do that. Not yet. Only irritated the bear. Need to lure him out of his den.

Heard rumors that Tan is offering a fifty-thousand-dollar reward for the name of the person breaching the moat to his castle.

Never thought I'd become notorious, or find myself with a price on my head. Should frighten me. Couldn't care less.

Does amuse me that Tan's freighter crews obviously haven't told him the truth about being hijacked by only one man. Don't blame them.

Tonight, heard one blowhard claim he was part of the crew during my second raid on the *Farfalla*. Said a dozen Spice Pirates boarded her. Even described the attacking vessel as a police-type cutter. Claimed they were forced to heave to after shots were fired across their bow. Man had a vivid imagination.

Wanted to drive my fist into his face when he said one of his shipmates had been shot down in cold blood for doing nothing more than speaking out of turn.

The man I shot wasn't a seaman. He was one of the armed thugs Tan put aboard after the first raid. This one tried to be a hero—jammed a knife in me while I was herding everyone into a cabin. Had to kill the son-of-a-bitch.

Have managed to avoid that until now. He just wouldn't leave it alone.

It was only a minor flesh wound and I hated going to a hospital with it. But I was bleeding like a stuck pig.

Told the ER people it happened in a barroom brawl. They were willing enough to accept that. Said they get several of those every night.

Would like to squelch the scuttlebutt, but how?

Worried the Marine Police may get more actively involved if there's a suspicion of murder.

Certainly can't go to Inspector Hsieh and fess up to what I've been doing.

Suppose a physical confrontation was bound to happen sooner or later. Has made things trickier, since Tan increased the complement of guards aboard each ship. Takes a lot more planning on my part.

Look at me. Caught up in the damned challenge of it. Me against them. Good guy versus the bad guys. Sounds like a dumb B-movie script.

Who the hell do I think I am, Steven Segal?

Questions: Has the doing of the thing become more important than the reason? Am I cultivating a taste for this? Am I beginning to enjoy it too much? Have I lost sight of my objective?

Best give it all some serious thought.

Shit!

November 2—At Sea

Have hit the *Mariposa* twice and the *Farfalla* three times.

Was going to go for Sallee's death ship again last night, but decided to let things cool for a couple of weeks.

Have yet to see the *Schmetterling,* reportedly the queen of Tan's fleet. Does he have some special use for her? Maybe she's just on a long voyage.

Doesn't seem likely. Papilio Coastal Line supposedly sticks close to the area between Taiwan and Southeast Asia.

Continues to trouble me that I had to kill one of Tan's hoodlums.

Would I feel the same if I knew he'd been directly involved in Sallee's death?

Know the answer to that. Just can't bring myself to put it down on paper.

November 15—Hong Kong

My vendetta against Tan has become all-consuming, both physically and mentally. Affecting my performance at sea.

Maybe my crew hasn't noticed, but I know. Not right to endanger their lives, the ship, and the cargoes.

Don't see any alternative. Have to resign again.

Going to make things tight financially. But if all goes well, should be able to bring this damn thing to a conclusion within a short time. If not? Will deal with whatever happens when it happens.

November 17—Hong Kong

The company surprised me by countering my resignation with an offer to put me on standby status. Gives me the discretion to take on or turn down assignments.

I accepted. Loyal to the core, that's me.

Came home to another surprise: Lai-ping said Raphael Tsao had been trying to get me all day. Finally left a message insisting I meet him tonight at Club Ferrari, anytime after ten. Just that, nothing else.

Do I want to get further involved with this man? Don't know squat about him, other than his sister died in that container with Sallee.

Is that enough of a bond to put my trust in him?

Will make that decision after I meet with him. Want to hear what he has to say first.

The fact that he called here makes me worry about Lai-ping's safety. Can't have her getting mixed up in this.

Think she knows what I've been up to. Doesn't say anything. She loved Sallee every bit as much as I did. More of a surrogate mother than nanny-housekeeper.

Have waited much too long to make arrangements for

her future. Something could happen to me at any moment. Must take care of that first thing in the morning.

November 18—Hong Kong

Tsao suspects I'm the Spice Pirate. Didn't expect that. Says he wants to throw in with me. Gutsy guy. Put on a real show of disappointment when I wouldn't confirm his suspicions. Tough shit! I don't owe this guy a thing. Did hear him out, though.

Claims he's learned the names of the men who were responsible for his sister's and Sallee's deaths. Thinks they'll be on the *Mariposa* when she makes her next voyage, supposedly the end of the month.

Held the information out like shark bait. Said there might never be a better opportunity to get the killers, along with more of Tan's cargo.

Tempting. Would like to believe him. Difficult decision.

May be just a ploy, an attempt by his triad to use me to further their goals against the Shan Triad.

Or, Tsao could be tied to Tan in some way.

Wish I could verify his story, his identity.

Can't get careless. Don't want to screw up things after coming this far.

Think I'll run with my gut and continue to let Tsao do his thing while I do mine.

Hope I'm not wrong. Damn!

November 19—Hong Kong

Told Lai-ping I put the apartment in her name and set up a trust fund for her. "Not necessary," she said. "You just kill filthy triad men who took Sallee from us."

Oh, yes, she knows!

November 20—Hong Kong

Can't leave the Tsao thing alone.

Agent at Papilio Coastal Line confirmed the *Mariposa's* next voyage is on or about the 30th, bound for Singapore. Told me she was booked to capacity before I could even say why I called, then hung up.

Strange. Hong Kong-Singapore is a very competitive route. Not one of the ships I raided was sailing with a full hold. Why suddenly is this one full?

November 21—Hong Kong

Decided it would be best to sell Tan's spices and use the proceeds to bolster my finances. Will also build up Laiping's trust account.

Only reliable person I could think of to help was Sang Choi. He didn't hesitate. Said he'd been waiting more than forty years to repay me for rescuing him after the Communist Chinese sank his junk off Shanghai.

What a character. Was running guns and ammo at the time for Chiang Kai-shek's Nationalists in Formosa. Continued that occupation long after Chiang died. Made a sizeable fortune. Became a kingpin in the black market. Later changed his name and retired. Now a highly respected financier and philanthropist. Never forgot his origins, though. Still knows who deals illicitly in what and where.

November 24—Hong Kong

The boathouse is empty of everything except the *Nolla*.

Choi handled all the money transactions, so nothing could be traced back to me. Told him we were now more than even. He says no, not until he's saved my life. Tried to convince him that's exactly what he's done. He went stone-faced on me.

Less than a week until the end of the month. Have to make a decision whether or not to go after the *Mariposa*, trap or no trap.

Tsao keeps leaving messages. Haven't returned any of his calls.

Lai-ping clucks her tongue at me. She doesn't trust him, either.

Chartered a beat-up old junk and anchored her near the Papilio dock. Using her as a cover to spy on their operations.

No sign of the *Mariposa*, but the *Schmetterling*'s tied up there for the first time and standing idle. She's larger than Tan's other two ships. Similar in size and configuration to the old "Victory" class freighters built in the States toward the end of WW II.

November 27—Hong Kong

Sudden flurry of activity on the Papilio dock.

Longshore crews working round the clock to load the *Schmetterling*. Saw Tan on-site, pacing back and forth.

About time.

Was beginning to go stir-crazy living aboard this leaky old scow.

Wish I could see what they're loading into the hold of the *Schmetterling*. Have the glasses on her, but the Chinese markings are only trade names. No cargo information.

Cargo's all plastic-wrapped, palletized, breakbulk. Heavy stuff, but no containers. She keeps settling lower and lower in the water. Will wallow like a clumsy barge when she finally sails.

November 28—Hong Kong

Just spotted the *Mariposa* standing off in the harbor,

riding high. Appears to be waiting for the *Schmetterling* to sail before docking.

Doesn't make sense. Plenty of room for her alongside the pier.

Waited until dark and took a water taxi back to shore. Managed to get a look inside the Papilio transit shed. Virtually empty.

So where are they going to get enough cargo to fill the *Mariposa* before her scheduled sailing on Monday?

November 29—Hong Kong

Good to be back aboard the *Nolla*.

Damn near didn't get to the warehouse and back out into the harbor in time. Assumed the *Schmetterling* wouldn't set sail until sometime after sunrise. Bad guess.

These guys are suddenly full of surprises. Mustn't lose track of her on the radar.

Almost dawn and there's still no sign of life on or about the *Mariposa*. Not even a deck watch. Hasn't been any activity at the Papilio truck gate, either. Don't think she intends to take on a single bale of cargo.

Okay, Mr. Raphael Tsao, fuck you *and* Mr. Tan Mong Kuan.

Chapter 34

"Sallee Boylan's death is a closed matter," Inspector Hsieh said after Paige and Max were seated in his small office. "The men responsible were convicted and are now serving long prison terms."

"You mean you were able to tie Tan Mong Kuan directly to the deaths?" Paige asked.

Hsieh removed his thick glasses with deliberate thoroughness. He cleaned the lenses with a freshly ironed handkerchief, and then examined his handiwork by the light of the window that overlooked the harbor. Satisfied, he refolded the handkerchief in the exact same creases and returned it to his jacket pocket.

"What do you know of Tan Mong Kuan?" he asked. He stared directly at Paige over the tops of his polished lenses.

"He's kingpin of the triad that ran the white slavery operation responsible for kidnapping Sallee, isn't he?"

The inspector leaned back in his chair until his head was resting against the stained wall behind his desk. After a moment he said, "Would you mind telling me where you obtained this unconfirmed information?"

"My uncle kept meticulous journals," she said.

Hsieh shook his head. "I never subscribed to your uncle's theory that Mr. Tan and the Shan Triad were responsible for his daughter's tragic death."

"Then just who did you arrest?" Max asked.

"A couple of undesirables named Johnny Ning and Raphael Tsao."

"Raphael Tsao?" Paige questioned. "Wasn't his sister one of the women who died in that container with Sallee?"

"Yes, that is true," the inspector said, tapping the file he held in one hand. "And he tried to use that fact as the basis for his defense. But the prosecutor was able to show that there was bad blood between him and the rest of his family."

Hsieh pulled two tissues from a box on his desk and blew his nose several times. "There is even evidence that Tsao once cleaned out his father's electronics warehouse and sold the goods on the black market."

"And there was no mention of the Shan Triad during the trial?"

"Mrs. Alper, I told you, this case is closed. There was never any evidence of a Shan Triad involvement. Further, it could be extremely dangerous for the two of you to attempt to pursue your uncle's unsupported suspicions."

The inspector stood and nodded toward a large map that covered one wall of his cramped office. "May I suggest instead that you spend your time taking in the many delights of Hong Kong? It is time to set aside the sad fate of Sallee Boylan, an event that can never be amended."

"But Jock specifically—"

"Mrs. Alper, please! During the short time I knew Captain Boylan, I grew fond of the man. Although, frankly, he was a constant thorn in my side." Hsieh shook his head. "He plagued me endlessly with useless leads. But that does not detract from the fact he was an excellent mariner and greatly respected in many quarters of Hong Kong. There are those who still talk sadly of his passing."

The short, slim, dark-haired inspector sat on the edge of

his desk and looked sympathetically down at Paige and Max. "Surely you can understand how distraught he must have been after he lost his daughter. But I would not put too much credence in what he wrote in his journals during that period."

"But he seemed so convinced that—"

Max sharply interrupted: "Inspector, you're probably right. There are indications in the journals that he was under great stress following Sallee's death; perhaps he was a little off-track."

Paige's sharp intake of breath was audible in the small room. Both Max and Hsieh glanced at her. Max pressed his knee against hers and continued: "Anyway, since we are in Hong Kong, your suggestion about sightseeing is an excellent one. I think that's exactly what we'll do."

Inspector Hsieh nodded agreeably. "It is a fascinating time to be in Hong Kong." He shrugged his shoulders. "For a long time, we thought our whole world would radically change once we became a part of the People's Republic of China. That has not happened."

"It must have been very frightening for you," Paige said.

"Frightening? No, I was more curious than anything." Hsieh stood, signaling the end of the interview. "You must understand, ninety-eight percent of our population *is* Chinese. Our cultural, political, and economic ties are intricately interwoven with mainland China, and its history."

"Yet the political differences must be . . ." Max searched for the right word, ". . . devastating?"

Hsieh gave a noncommittal shrug and looked toward the single window in the small office—frantic, loud traffic noise replaced the silence in the room. When the inspector's eyes returned to Max and Paige, his mouth curved into a soft smile.

"Do not let the metropolitan ways of Hong Kong deceive you, Mr. and Mrs. Alper. It is true we are a modern people ready to face the challenges of the twenty-first century, but we are also the bearer of an ancient lore." Hsieh's palms fanned out in front of him, then gently closed together, his fingers steepling in front of his chest. "Our teachings span vast stretches of time."

The inspector closed his eyes for a moment before continuing: " 'That which goes against the Tao comes to an early end.' "

Max nodded, took Paige's hand. "Perhaps 'yield and overcome' would be more fitting in this situation, Inspector."

Both men respectfully tilted their heads in acknowledgment.

The Alpers lingered at the office doorway as Max asked for specific directions to the address he had for Lai-ping.

"While we're here, we'd like to pay our respects to the woman who helped my uncle raise Sallee," Paige said.

Inspector Hsieh's gaze narrowed. "Please make no attempt to go beyond that simple goal, Mrs. Alper."

"Our only thought is to honor family obligations," she said.

The inspector frowned, nodded and then offered to arrange for a taxi.

Inspector Hsieh did not believe the young couple would suddenly turn into model tourists.

It was obvious that a family physical resemblance was not all Captain Boylan and his niece had in common. There was a stubbornness and sense of purpose that seemed to be basic to their personalities. Hsieh could still visualize her upturned chin, which emphasized an insistence that was at the same time brash and disciplined. Yes, the captain and his niece were cut from the same cloth.

He eased into his chair and again listened to the noise of the busy streets outside. For him, the hubbub was not the distraction others in the department claimed. Over the years he had become used to it, even found it difficult to concentrate when things were too quiet. When he closed his eyes and sought to lose himself in meditation, he often longed for the hum of urban dissonance.

He recalled the details of the Sallee Boylan case. It was not one that would ever fade from his mind. He could still see her and all the other twenty-six young women brought back and laid out on wooden pallets in a cold-storage warehouse near the morgue. They had never identified most of the victims, all of whom had suffered humiliation, indignities, and a horrible death.

After all this time, the excruciating expressions of panic and fear on their faces remained etched in his memory.

Now, as then, he thought about the well-being of his own young daughter, Mei-Ling. It preyed on his mind every day that the Shan Triad had threatened her life. Revenge was a two-edged sword he could not afford to wield.

Hsieh had allowed Jock Boylan a considerable amount of leeway because of the captain's despair. But Boylan was older and savvy in the ways of Hong Kong and Asia, attributes the Alpers did not possess. The couple would need to leave Hong Kong quickly, before they were discovered or before they uncovered something he might not be able to push behind a curtain of concealment.

"Let sleeping dogs lie" may be of English origin, but it is still a part of our culture.

Again, the image of his beautiful daughter's face flashed before his eyes.

The inspector pushed away from his desk and walked again to the window. Below, he could see the Alpers entering a taxi.

" 'Gravity is the root of lightness; stillness is the ruler of the moment,' " he said softly and nodded.

Yes, it is better for all concerned to let sleeping dogs lie.

"Why did you do that?" Paige asked once they were in the taxi.

"Do what?"

"Agree so readily that Uncle Jock may have slipped a cog or two. Do you really believe that?"

"Of course not!"

"Then why—"

"Inspector Hsieh was getting a lot more information out of us than we were getting from him. It was time to pull back, that's all."

"Point well taken." She nodded thoughtfully. "The inspector's certainly an interesting man, and he seemed genuinely fond of Uncle Jock." She laughed out loud. "But wouldn't he just flip if he knew Jock was behind all those hijackings."

"Do you think he has any idea why we came to Hong Kong?" Max said.

"Oh, yes! And I'll bet he knows a lot more than he's telling us."

They spent most of the fifteen-minute Hong Kong–Kowloon ferry ride in animated discussion about the soaring skyline and the harbor, the latter filled with traditional sampans and colorful junks that contrasted sharply with huge containerships and monstrous tankers from all over the world.

As their ferry entered the slip on the Kowloon side of Victoria Harbor, their conversation waned. Their frantic travels and the weather were beginning to catch up with them.

"This humidity is incredible," Paige said, resting her head on Max's shoulder. "I feel washed-out and listless. If you asked me to go for a run now, I'd fall flat on my face." She pulled a handkerchief from her purse and dabbed at her neck, front and back. "This must be how a greenhouse orchid feels. Drenched! And I thought New York was humid."

"Considering we're into the monsoon season, be thankful we're not being blown apart as well." Max threw an arm around her shoulders and nuzzled her damp neck. "You know, when this thing lands, we'll be pretty close to our hotel. I think both of us could use a little R-and-R before we see Lai-ping."

Paige nodded, then sat bolt upright. She clutched Max's arm.

"What's wrong?"

"Forget the R-and-R."

Chapter 35

The call from Kai Tak airport did not surprise Tan Mong Kuan. The Alpers were as irritatingly persistent as had been the woman's uncle, Captain Jock Ian Boylan.

First, the couple had ignored Martin Lester's ill-advised and crude attempt to intimidate them into returning to San Francisco. Then they eluded the Shan's agents in New York and San Jose. Tan had lost no time dealing with those incompetents—they would never again have the opportunity to fail him.

The critical issue now was to ensure that the information Captain Boylan had accumulated did not fall into the hands of the authorities.

"Chen!" he yelled into his intercom. "Here! Now!"

He watched the reflection of his manicured nails tic-ticking on the spotless, inch-thick glass of his desktop as he swore silently to himself in English. He repeated the curses in Cantonese, furious that after all these years his initial response was still to automatically speak English and not Chinese.

When Chen came through the door, Tan left the man standing uncomfortably in the middle of the room, shifting his weight from foot to foot on the plush, white carpet. Tan held the moment by taking several seconds to run a comb through his stylishly cut hair.

"I want this Alper couple followed around the clock,"

Tan said. "They are not to be out of our sight for one second." He brushed away an imaginary piece of lint from his coat sleeve. "Do you understand?"

"It will be done."

"I have heard that before, yet here they are in Hong Kong. Why is that?"

"I—"

"Don't bother me with useless explanations and excuses." He flicked the fingers of one hand at the Shan underling. "Go!"

Chen hesitated.

"I thought you understood my instructions."

"They have been persistent and elusive—"

"Idiot! You are close to earning the same fate as those bloody fools in America."

Chen silently backed out of the room.

Alone again, Tan kicked the chrome pedestal of his desk with a soft Gucci loafer, cursed loudly at the resulting pain, swore again because once more the expletives were in English. He did not like what was happening, did not like that once more there was a Boylan making him the prey instead of the hunter.

Tan wished he were someplace else. He closed his eyes, quickly envisioned himself living in London again, back where he had grown up and received a proper public school education.

His thoughts shifted to another of his favorite cities, San Francisco, where his father, a Hong Kong Economic and Trade Office attaché, had later been assigned. When his father's next posting came—to Brazil—Tan had remained behind to attend Stanford and earn an MBA. At the same time, he accumulated a small fortune by dealing recreational drugs within the academic community.

He now swiveled his chair to look out the window onto Victoria Harbor. He recalled his return to Hong Kong in the late 1960s, at the height of the Vietnamese War. He had known there would be huge profits to be made from that conflict, and he was right. Initially, he had brokered stolen relief goods, and later worked his way into becoming a link in the CIA's drug network.

Tan swung around and directed his attention to a pair of closed teak doors that displayed an intricate carving of floating butterflies. He squinted, and with an outstretched finger traced the graceful outline of the Shan, the butterfly.

The butterfly was his symbol: carefully conceived, nurtured, and feared. Beautiful but deadly.

After the war ended, it did not take long for him to accumulate sufficient power to take over one of the minor triads. He built it into the powerful Shan, which became the area's major secret crime society—*the* force to be reckoned with. At least until six years ago.

Tan flung his gold Cross pen across the room, arose, and paced randomly about the large office. He ignored the full-color paintings of grandiose butterflies—swallowtails, monarchs, morphos, and birdwings—that individually decorated each of the otherwise stark white walls.

He stopped, again looked at the teeming harbor, and shook a fist at the vista. The fury remained, the fury with those morons who had altered his destiny by kidnapping Boylan's daughter so long ago. That singular event had unleashed a series of misfortunes that continued to sap his energy.

He had been willing to accept the loss of the cargoes Boylan hijacked. He even wrote off the *Schmetterling*, tried to convince himself that any threat from the documents

Boylan stole had vanished with the captain's unplanned murder.

But there had been no serenity during these past five years. Boylan's ghost continued to haunt him—always ready to complete the captain's original mission to achieve Tan's destruction.

He was convinced Boylan's essence brought the niece to Hong Kong, and his spirit would never rest, never return to the infinite, without exacting complete revenge.

A chill rippled through him.

He leaned his head against the window frame for a moment, clenching and unclenching the fingers of both hands. With a deliberate, heavy exhalation, he walked slowly toward the teak double doors, selecting the proper key at the end of a gold chain draped across his vest.

He entered the private room. A single, rose-colored spotlight shined down on a large, circular bed. Spread-eagled in the center of pink satin sheets, a nude, pubescent girl—her wrists and ankles bound with silk cords—watched him with wary eyes.

He went to the child, cursorily examined her thin body from head to toe, and reached out to caress the freshly tattooed butterfly between her breasts. When she moaned and tried to twist away, he slapped her sharply across the cheek.

Tan watched her darting eyes and smiled at her growing fear. He slowly undressed, then examined the bedside array of leather whips and paddles.

Chapter 36

Journal—1997
Jock Ian Boylan

November 30—At Sea

More surprises.

The *Schmetterling* is headed north-by-northwest, hugging the Chinese coastline.

Thought they would sail into the South China Sea toward Singapore. That's been the course of all the other Tan ships.

This puts a different cant on things.

Maybe she's headed for Shantou.

Even if I knew that for certain, it wouldn't do me much good.

If she ducks into one of the uncharted mainland Chinese coastal ports, she'll be lost as a prize for certain.

Wish I knew what she's carrying in her holds. Will feel damn foolish if I board her and there's nothing I can transfer to the *Nolla*. Whatever it is, it's bloody heavy. She's yet to exceed eight knots, about one-half her designed speed. Damn ship is sloughing through the sea like a rudderless scow.

Think Tan expected me to go after the *Mariposa*. Good thing I didn't believe that nonsense from Tsao about the murderers being aboard.

Maybe I'm being suckered. Doubt it.

If I'm going to take the *Schmetterling*, I'll have to make my move within the next quarter hour. Wait any longer and there won't be enough fuel for the return trip to Hong Kong.

The risk factor multiplies with each passing minute.

Trying like all get-out to stay a safe league off their port stern.

Sooner or later someone in her wheelhouse is going to notice my speed-up, slow-down, circle-around antics.

Don't have much choice if I want to keep the *Nolla*'s high-performance engines from loading up. Can't risk a stall when I finally need to move out.

Will try one more throttle-clearing pattern, then either take the *Schmetterling* or reverse course for home.

What in hell am I going to do with a shipload of copper coils and titanium billets?

Everything happened quickly aboard the *Schmetterling*. No time to stop and think. Too late to worry about it now.

Was suspicious this wasn't going to be another run-of-the-mill spice caper. Damn if I wasn't right.

Oh, yes, the *Mariposa* was definitely set up as a trap.

Only two guards aboard the *Schmetterling*, plus a skeleton crew. They were genuinely shocked when I made my presence known. No heroics this time. A surly bunch, though. More afraid of Tan than me, I think.

The *Schmetterling*'s size made her more difficult to board. Almost didn't make it.

The bump-near-the-bow ploy didn't work this time. They might have been warned about my *modus operandi*. But none of the other hijacked crews ever gave any accurate details. All lied to protect their butts.

Had to use a grappling iron to get aboard.

Secured the line to the *Nolla*'s bow and hauled myself aboard hand-over-hand. Choppy water made it difficult. Almost gave up.

Getting too old to be dangling from a knotted line, bouncing off a ship's plates. Could have bathed in the puddle of sweat left under the lifeboat where I recuperated. Wouldn't have been a good time for the unexpected to happen. Damn idiot! Left my mask on the deck.

The *Schmetterling* is a big ship. Expected a crew of at least a dozen, even under Tan's close-fisted management style. Only half that number, plus the two security guards posted amidships.

Minimal crewing for a four-hundred-sixty-foot ship with a capacity of close to eight thousand tons is not good seamanship, although that may not be high on Tan's list of priorities.

Found all but the helmsman and the two guards watching a soccer game on television in the galley. Almost made me forget the pounding I'd taken hauling my ass aboard.

Locked everyone in the captain's cabin and inspected the cargo holds.

Why did Tan worry about the *Schmetterling* being hit by the "Spice Pirates?" Not one item of cargo aboard that could be transferred to the *Nolla* without breaking out the ship's on-deck cranes. Sorry I brought my sorry-ass out here.

Might have coerced the crew with my Uzi to help transfer a couple of pallets of copper coil or titanium billets to the *Nolla*, but to what end? Besides, no way to do that and keep everyone in sight at all times.

The solution seemed simple at the time.

Put the captain, crew, and guards into the only operable lifeboat. Sent them in the direction of the mainland China coast, about fifty miles east of Kowloon. They were none too happy about the choppy sea and its portent of a storm.

Same conditions made me secure the *Nolla* with something more substantial than the grappling iron line.

Took command of the *Schmetterling*, which definitely had not been part of my original plan.

Talk about insufficient crew.

Now I am a true pirate.

All I lack is a Jolly Roger flying from the mast.

Set a course for the southern edge of Hong Kong Territory. Don't know where I'm going to hide a ship this size. Have to keep her from being easily spotted, yet need to have her accessible.

Don't have the heart to scuttle her. Can't see doing that to any ship, no matter who owns her, how she's being used, or how old she might be.

Searched the captain's cabin, ship's safe, and the bridge before finding a manifest.

The *Schmetterling* was bound for Taiwan with a load of "Scrap Metal."

Some scrap metal. Rough calculation puts the cargo at about six thousand tons of mill-fresh copper coil and maybe two tons of titanium billets.

No idea of the total value. Obviously enough to attract Tan.

Some insurance company is going to hurt on this one.

Tan won't be satisfied with just offering a reward for my capture now. He's going to want his cargo back, along with a piece of my hide.

Will find anchorage at some unnamed island, then work

on a plan to lure Tan aboard. Force him to admit his connection to Sallee's death.

Make him squirm.

Maybe Inspector Hsieh will finally believe me when I turn over Tan, his taped confession, and the stolen cargo.

Chapter 37

"This is getting way out of hand, Max."

They waved down a taxi and jumped inside. Paige scootched down into the seat of the Mercedes after Max slammed the door closed.

"Have you noticed how little sightseeing we get to do in all these tourist meccas we've been visiting?" she said.

"Yeah, I have. We're either in cabs and airplanes, or running like hell from people trying to do us in. I'm beginning to have some doubts about this inheritance thing."

She looked out the rearview window at the scattering crowd that had been aboard the eight o'clock Star ferry. The majority boarded buses to take them to the Kowloon suburbs, others hailed cabs. Many were obviously tourists, milling around indecisively.

"You sure we're being followed?" Max asked.

"Trust me, sweetlump."

"How can I trust anyone who calls me sweetlump?" He tapped the cabby on the shoulder. "My wife and I are looking for some excitement," he said. "Any suggestions?"

"Sure, sure!" The cabby squealed the tires as he took off.

Paige whispered in Max's ear: "The son-of-a-bitch is right on our tail."

"I still haven't seen him." He started to look behind

227

them, then changed his mind. "How did they catch up with us so quickly?"

"The question is, did we ever lose them?"

The cab raced down Nathan Road. The day was growing short and the darkening sky accentuated the dazzling array of neon signs that blinked brightly back at them from either side of the busy street: cocktail lounge neon, in both English and Chinese, cried out for attention; garish signs announced the services of jade merchants, tailors, jewelers, and antique dealers.

"This isn't getting us anywhere," Max said. He tapped the driver's shoulder again. "I want to buy something special for my wife, something from the street vendors. Is there a market close by?"

"Sure, sure!" The driver hung a right and pulled up to the curb. "Temple Street!" he announced. "Very good shopping!"

Max and Paige jumped out. Hand-in-hand they merged with the crowd in the bustling night market.

"See him?" Paige whispered. "Over there on the corner. He's just paying off his cabby."

"Are you sure he's following us?"

"He's been on our tail since we left Inspector Hsieh's office." Paige pulled Max into a group of spectators who were applauding a trio of street musicians. Some of the onlookers pressed money into the performers' hands.

"At least that's where I first spotted him," she said. "He was trying too hard to act casual. Then seeing him on the ferry was too much of a coincidence. Besides, you can tell just by looking at him that he's up to no good."

"I'll take your word for it," Max said. "Let's get out of here."

They slipped through the crowds in the street market, ig-

noring the abundance of goods stacked on tables: jade of
every hue; delicate fans; piles of soft, rich-colored fabrics;
bright arrays of pewter and copper vessels jutting out between rolls of exotic carpets; cheap copies of name-brand
clothing and jewelry; dazzling earrings, necklaces, and rings
reflecting the light from large, naked bulbs strung between
the stalls.

"I think we've lost him," Paige said.

"Then let's make a dash for Lai-ping's."

"Do we have enough time to pick up something for her,
maybe some of that fresh fruit?" she said.

"Okay, but make it fast. That guy could be almost any-
place around here."

Lai-ping welcomed Max and Paige into her home
without showing the least bit of surprise at their sudden appearance.

"No apologies are necessary," she said when they started
to explain. "No call was required. My home is your home.
You are always welcome here."

Tiny and frail, she leaned heavily on a cane, which
didn't prevent her from rolling in a tray with a steaming pot
of tea and a plate of almond cookies. She ceremoniously
filled paper-thin porcelain cups with aromatic chrysan-
themum tea. The pleasurable essence permeated the room,
creating a welcome tranquility.

"It is a pleasure at long last to meet one of the captain's
nieces and her husband," Lai-ping said after Max and Paige
took their first sip of tea. "I recognized the two of you from
the wedding pictures you sent. I had them framed for your
uncle."

"Your home is very beautiful." Paige nodded at the ele-
gant furnishings surrounding them.

"You are very kind, Mrs. Alper."

"Please call me Paige."

Lai-ping nodded and smiled. She noticeably averted the left side of her face, which was disfigured by a jagged scar that arched from ear to eyelid before spiking down into the corner of her mouth. "Most of what you see here was left to me by Captain Boylan. He collected these furnishings from the many ports he visited during his long sea career."

Tears flooded her eyes as she picked up a delicate wood-carved pagoda. "Are you familiar with the captain's woodcarvings?" she asked. "This is one he made especially for me." She lowered her head. "Forgive me. It is still difficult to accept both his and Sallee's deaths."

"You must have been very fond of them," Paige said.

Lai-ping nodded.

"How did you meet Jock?" Max asked softly.

Lai-ping did not immediately respond.

"Forgive me, Lai-ping, I had no right to pry."

"Oh, no, your question is not an imposition." She smiled at him. "It merely made me think back. It was so many years ago. So much has come and gone since then."

Paige accepted one of the cookies Lai-ping offered from an ornate, lacquered tray.

"The captain had recently lost Miss Nolla and had just moved to Hong Kong from Sri Lanka. He ran an advertisement looking for a governess for little Sallee."

"I think he was very lucky to have found you," Paige said.

"He had many to choose from," she answered shyly. "It was I who was the lucky one."

"But he did choose you."

"He wanted, I think, someone with a varied background.

You see, most of my teaching experience was with shanty children."

"That certainly sounds like Uncle Jock. Wouldn't have wanted Sallee to grow up to be a snob," Paige said with a light laugh.

Lai-ping giggled. "Your uncle used other, cruder words, as I recall. But the sentiments are accurate." She nodded her head. "He was an exceptional man."

"But he had such a tragic life."

"Yes, there was much sadness in the captain's life, but he did have people who loved him. And he loved them. Fiercely. What more can any of us ask?" She paused. "He chose a profession that is known for its hardness, even cruelty. Yet, he was a kind and gentle man who tried to help those less fortunate than himself." She smiled sadly. "I know my life would have been empty without Sallee and the captain."

"You must have loved my uncle very much," Paige said.

Lai-ping hesitated, using the moment to pour more tea.

"I'm sorry, that was very rude of me," Paige said.

Lai-ping bowed her head again. "He never knew."

"You should have told him," Paige said.

"No, the captain could never have loved another woman after Miss Nolla." She eyed the pagoda on the coffee table. "You see, the fact that he referred to himself as an old sea wolf had more than one meaning. The wolf seeks a mate only once in its lifetime." She smiled, the scar on her cheek pulling and stretching her face unevenly.

"I was his friend," she continued, "and that was more than enough. Besides, there was Sallee. She was like a daughter . . . the child I never had."

Soon Lai-ping was telling humorous tales about Captain Jock Boylan. The three of them roared with laughter at some of his crazier antics.

Without warning, the front door shattered. The air filled with the strong odor of scorched wood and cordite. It happened so quickly that Lai-ping, Paige, and Max froze in their seats. Four men, armed with assault weapons, charged into the room.

Lai-ping launched into rapid-fire Chinese, directing her shouts at the man who was obviously in charge. As she raised her cane threateningly, he grabbed it from her and broke it across his knee. The other gunmen held their ground, guarding the fragmented doorway.

"Speak English, you cow!" the leader demanded of Lai-ping. "You mustn't be impolite to your foreign visitors."

Lai-ping spat on him.

He backhanded her across the face. She staggered backward. "How many times do we have to break your bones and rip your face before we get what we want?" He wiped slowly at the spittle on the side of his neck, then picked up the struggling Lai-ping and flung her against the wall.

"You son-of-a-bitch!" Max yelled, running toward her.

The leader grabbed Paige around the neck and jammed his gun up under her chin. "Sit down, Mr. Alper, or I will put a very large hole through your wife."

Max backed away from Lai-ping, looking from her to Paige and back again. Paige watched as Lai-ping pushed herself upright, leaning heavily on an ancient teak credenza.

"That's better." The man shoved Paige toward Max. "Mr. Tan was right: anyone associated with old Captain Boylan has to be either dangerous or crazy." He paced back and forth across the room. "That lunatic continues to reach out from the grave to cause us more trouble." He shivered slightly, then nodded a silent order. Two of his men grabbed Lai-ping and pinned her arms to her sides. "Where have you hidden the journals, you old pig?" asked the leader.

Lai-ping stared defiantly into his eyes.

"Tie her up." He snatched the embroidered silk scarf from her neck. "Stuff her mouth with this, and lock her in a closet where she can die in silence."

He turned quickly to Max and Paige. "You thought you were so clever, thought you were getting away from us." He laughed. "You have never been out of our sight since you left your cozy home in San Francisco. Never!"

When the other two men returned, he nodded again and watched as they battered the couple to the floor with their gun butts. The Alpers collapsed into limp heaps. Twin puddles of blood created ugly new patterns that flowed into the fibers of the hand-woven Chinese rug.

Chapter 38

Journal—1997
Jock Ian Boylan

December 1—At Sea

Sailing WSW toward Hong Kong, the *Nolla* under tow.

Monitoring Tan's Papilio Coastal Line radio channel. Nothing to indicate they are aware the *Schmetterling* isn't on her scheduled course.

According to the *Schmetterling* captain's orders, first port of call was to be Kaohsiung. Suppose Taiwan's as a good a place as any to get rid of a cargo of stolen copper and titanium.

Unless they catch on back in Hong Kong, I should have a good two- or three-day head start on them. Don't know if they expect regular radio check-ins. Makes no difference. No way I could imitate the captain's voice.

Best bet is to find an uninhabited island close to, but outside, Hong Kong waters.

Also, need to stay away from mainland Chinese territorial waters, if I want to salvage her later.

The least of my worries right now.

Would prefer sailing her on down past the Soko Islands in the South China Sea, but can't risk either the time or the distance.

Manning this damn ship single-handed is a bitch.

Thankfully she's well equipped with the latest electronic navigational gear, and an automatic pilot. Still a full-time, around-the-clock job.

Charts show no alternative but to seek shelter in the waters of Tai Pang Wan, bordering the mainland.

Maybe the Spice Pirate will get lucky and find an out-of-the-way island here in the area.

December 2—Offshore Island "X"
Good hideaway. A charted, but unnamed island.

Spotted a cove inside the rocky cliffs after sailing around the island twice. Very narrow inlet. Don't have any other choice.

Would prefer to reconnoiter ashore first, but afraid if I drop anchor offshore, I'll never get this monster under way again.

Hell, if I lose her going in, I lose her.

December 5—Island "X"
Third day of trying to camouflage the *Schmetterling*. Damn difficult. Not much to work with, other than tarps, shoring, and paint from ship's stores.

Aerial observation is the main concern. Would be obvious to almost anyone flying directly overhead that there's a large ship beached here. Best I can do is prevent her from being easily identified.

High rocky cliffs surrounding the cove will keep her well-hidden from any passing boats or ships.

Best part—charts indicate this is not a well-traveled route.

Ship is solidly beached. Tide hasn't shifted her position one way or the other since bringing her through the inlet.

Tidy piece of work, if I do say so myself.

Thought at one point she was going to broach in the narrows, wedge herself between the rock walls.

The inlet had less leeway than I'd anticipated. Dented a few plates amidships starboard, but nothing to threaten the integrity of the hull.

Taken the juice out of me. Damn near sucked me dry. Fall into the captain's bunk at nightfall, up again at the crack of dawn. So bloody stiff I can hardly move.

Glad I won't be the one who has to sail her out of here. I've had it with this lady.

December 6—Hong Kong

For better or worse, left the *Schmetterling* snug in her little cove.

Marked her location on two different charts. Will stow them in separate places for safekeeping.

Spent a long time trying to find identifying marks on the copper and titanium. Thought I might be able to trace their origins. Nothing. Like trying to trace coins.

Will check back issues of *Lloyd's List International* and *Lloyd's Weekly Casualty Report* for any reports of pirated cargo similar to what's in the *Schmetterling*'s holds.

Doubt if I'll find anything.

Brought the *Nolla* back to the boathouse after dark last night.

Sneaked into town and anonymously sent a photocopy of the *Schmetterling*'s bogus manifest to Tan Mong Kuan at Papillon Enterprises.

That should cause fireworks, sleepless nights on his part.

Before leaving the ship, gathered up every scrap of paper I could find in the captain's cabin and safe. Sent them off to Sang Choi for analysis. My Cantonese is good, but not that good.

Moved out of the apartment early this morning and set up camp in the boathouse. Will operate from here until I finish with Tan.

Or he finishes with me!

Sent Lai-ping off to visit relatives in Shanghai. She wailed like a banshee. Predicted my certain death, if she wasn't allowed to stay and help me do in Sallee's murderers.

Took forever to convince her I needed a confederate I could rely on outside Hong Kong. Don't know what I would have done if she'd refused. Couldn't allow her life to be put in danger.

Told her I would leave instructions for her, in the event anything happens to me. She cried, but made no more objections.

This whole business with the *Schmetterling* has taken its toll. More than I would have expected.

Need to take a short break.

Can't fall apart now.

Chapter 39

Maxwell. Maxwell!

It was a familiar voice. It vibrated, pounded in his head.

Maxwell!

He backed away, ran from a powerful presence bearing down on him. His legs pumped harder and harder. He moved only in agonizing inches. Turning, he tossed a backward glance, his face creased with pain and fear.

Maxwell!

It was gaining on him; he had to get away. He lifted, floated. Only his bare toes kept him in contact with the earth as he skimmed across a bleak landscape of skeletal trees. Bleached branches loomed, stretched toward a pitiless orange sky.

Maxwell! Do not hasten away. We are not finished.

Can't! Can't do it anymore, Master Lao. It's too much.

Lao Tsu materialized, a wavering shadow outlined in luminous white light. The ground ignited all around him, but Lao Tsu remained calm, untouched.

Max's arms started to blister; his hair burst into flame. He screamed.

Yield and overcome.

Help me!

Bend and be straight.

I'm burning—

Empty and be full.

—dying.

Wear out and be new.

Save me!

A flash of cold white light encircled Max. Lao Tsu's voice faded in the distance.

Yield and overcome.

A sense of wholeness washed over Max. His eyes slowly opened.

It took him a moment to realize he was on his back in Lai-ping's living room. Tongues of fire lashed out at him through a smoky haze that filled the room; above him, embroidered silk drapes burst into flames that raced to embrace the ceiling, leaving a spoor of thick soot.

He tried to sit, was stopped by a blinding spike of pain. Rolling onto his side, he bumped against a body. He pushed up enough to see that it was Paige. He reached out to her; his hand came away, the palm covered with blood.

"Paige!" he cried hoarsely. He lifted up on one arm to shake her shoulder, touch her hot cheek. "Wake up!" She remained silent, motionless, her face streaked with blood.

Her image faded out; the room did a slow turn. He squeezed his eyes shut, shook his head, winced as the pain pierced his skull again. Delicately, he fingered the back of his head and found a wet, spongy area. He tried not to think about the damage, the relentless pounding in his brain.

The smoke thickened, roiling down from the ceiling. Coughing, tears streaming down his cheeks, he grabbed Paige by the collar and dragged her through the shattered front door out onto the open balcony. Soft bay breezes quickly dispersed the smoke billowing out behind him.

He gently shook Paige's shoulders. She turned, grunted,

239

coughed, and murmured something indistinguishable. Her arms flew out, flailed at his chest, then stopped in mid-air when she finally recognized him.

"We've got to get out of here. Now!" He leaned over to examine her head wound, but all he could see in the dim light was matted hair and a constant trail of fresh blood dribbling down her neck.

"Here!" He handed her his handkerchief. "Press this against the top of your head."

"Are they gone?" She was hoarse; her eyes fluttered. "What happened to Lai-ping?"

"Oh, my God! She's still inside."

The distant sound of sirens drifted up to them as Max turned to go back into the apartment.

"No, Max!" Paige screamed. She tried to push herself upright. "Don't go back in there!"

He turned away and scurried into the living room, dropping to his knees to search for breathable air. The sofa, where they had comfortably lounged a short time earlier, was belching black plumes into the already smoke-filled room. He clutched at his throat, grabbed Lai-ping's porcelain teapot from the serving table, and held it with his knees. He yanked off his shirt and doused it with tea, then pressed the wet material against his nose and mouth.

"Lai-ping!" he called as he crawled toward the central hallway.

He veered off toward the nearest bedroom, then reversed course when he heard muffled groans coming from a hall closet.

He flung open the door. Lai-ping was crumpled on the floor, bound hand and foot, wheezing desperately through a cloth gag. He yanked the cloth from her mouth and untied her hands and feet. She took several ragged breaths and tried to stand, but he held her down.

"Stay low . . . easier to breathe."

They crawled toward the living room, Max half-dragging her behind him. As they passed a smoldering chair, it suddenly erupted into a pyre of shooting flames that lashed out to swallow them.

He heard Lai-ping scream as he merged and flowed with the flames in an undulating dance, then rolled onto the floor and rocked back and forth until the flames were smothered. He struggled to his feet, grabbed Lai-ping's hand, and dragged her to the front door.

Sirens screamed in the street below, almost drowning out Lai-ping's desperate shout: "I must go back." Her eyes were wild and pleading as she tried to wrench herself free from Max. "I promised!"

"You'll die in there, Lai-ping!" Max yelled.

"You don't understand. The key!" She escaped Max's grip and edged toward the flaming doorway. "I must get the key. Can't leave it behind. I promised the captain. Tan must not win."

"Please don't go back in there," Paige screamed.

It was too late. Lai-ping had already disappeared inside the apartment.

"Shit!" Max said. He ran after her, tried to stay clear of the blazing furniture and walls. He found her just a few feet inside the ravaged living room, trying to hold onto an ornate dragon lamp. The lampshade was in scorched tatters, the ceramic body too hot for her to hold for more than a second or two. Still, she persisted in trying to possess the ruined object.

"Leave it, Lai-ping!" he screamed. "It's only a lamp."

She gasped for air, grimaced, and cried out in pain as she raised the scorching ceramic base high over her head and smashed it down. Pieces flew helter-skelter across the smoldering teak table. She picked through the scattered shards to uncover a small key.

"Now we can leave!" she said. She scooped up the captain's hand-carved pagoda and pressed her key-clenched fist tightly against her chest.

Chapter 40

Journal—1997
Jock Ian Boylan

December 7—Hong Kong

Tan knows I'm the Spice Pirate.

He's on the warpath about the loss of the *Schmetterling.*

Sang Choi angrily chastised me for not having been more discreet. Bad mistake, forgetting the mask.

The *Schmetterling*'s captain recognized me and immediately called Tan once he reached the Chinese mainland.

With that cat out of the bag, my movements are going to be highly restricted.

Would have preferred a little more time before Tan found out. Can't change that.

What is, is.

Choi says the bounty on me has jumped to a hundred thousand dollars, delivered dead or alive to Tan's dock.

Every petty hoodlum in the Territory is looking for me.

Got to get out of here. Will hide out with Mattos in San Diego for a while.

On the plus side, the packet of papers I found aboard the *Schmetterling* includes a long list of Tan's contacts in Taiwan and on the mainland—people who help him dispose of contraband cargoes.

Choi said to make the list public would prove embarrassing, if not deadly, for Tan. Same thing for several highly placed government officials here, on the mainland, and in Taiwan.

Choi urged extreme caution. Suggested I burn everything connected with the *Schmetterling*.

I think not. This is exactly what I need to destroy Tan Mong Kuan.

The documents *must* be made public. Will turn them over to Peter Larkin, the Hong Kong correspondent for *Lloyd's List International*.

Shouldn't take long after that for Tan's world to come crashing down all around him. Wish I could take bets on which thieving bureaucrat will do him in first.

Not yet, though. Want him to see it coming. Want him to know why.

If there was some way to make him suffer as Sallee suffered, would do it without a second thought. No opportunity for that. The current plan will have to suffice.

Choi, bless his scarred old soul, fears for my life. Never before have I heard that tough old bird's voice break with emotion. Swears there is no way to get the head man of a triad. Thinks I don't fully understand that my life is in danger.

He's wrong.

Never before have I been so clear about what is happening, where I stand.

Tried to convince Choi that having the incriminating evidence in my possession will give me an edge, more leverage to bring Tan out into the open.

Choi will return the ship's papers to me tonight, along with printed English translations.

They will lure the spider from its web.

December 8—Hong Kong

Couldn't sleep last night. Plotted a dozen different schemes.

Decided to call Tan and just let it happen.

The following is a literal transcription of my conversation with Tan, in the event something should happen to the original tape:

Boylan—I understand you've placed a bounty on my head.

Tan—Let's say it would be in your best interests to return what you have so brazenly taken from me.

B—Surely, a man of your substance can afford the loss of a few spices.

T—If you are attempting to be humorous, Captain Boylan, it is not appreciated. (Pause) Where is my ship?

B—Safe.

T—No doubt. But that is not what I asked. (Pause) I don't understand why a man of your position and reputation has resorted to this type of misguided conduct. Is it possible that, like so many men of the sea, you didn't provide for your old age? Have you now decided to do so at my expense?

B—It isn't that simple.

T—I thought not. It seldom is. But it *is* about money, is it not?

B—Yes, it's given me great pleasure to know you have suffered financial losses. But personal gain isn't the issue here.

T—Then what is, Captain? To the best of my knowledge, we do not know one another, have never had any business dealings. It is therefore difficult for me to understand why you have decided to plunder, and steal my ships, if not for profit.

B—(Pause) A year and a half ago, a container was found in Bangkok. Inside were the bodies of twenty-seven young women. They died of suffocation while being transported from Hong Kong aboard the *Mariposa*. My kidnapped daughter died in that container.

T—I am familiar with that most unfortunate accident, Captain. I have daughters of my own. I can empathize with your grief. However, the authorities cleared Papilio Coastal Line of any responsibility in that dreadful event. If you had bothered to check, you would have learned that. Your acts of revenge are misdirected, and dangerous.

B—Papilio was not cleared. It was a matter of not being able to prove there was a connection between the white slavery ring, the death container, your ship, and the Shan Triad.

T—We are quibbling over words, Captain.

B—No, you and your triad are guilty as sin.

T—I think that if you had come upon any hard evidence to implicate my company, or me, you would have turned it over to the police long before now.

B—This has never been a matter for the police. It is strictly personal.

T—In other words, you have no evidence.

B—That remains to be seen. What I do have is good enough for me, good enough to see you turned into fish bait.

T— (Pause) You are a dangerous man, Captain Boylan. Paranoid, I think. Perhaps it is the result of your daughter's death. But you leave me no alternative but take measures to defend myself, measures that can be rescinded should you see fit to return both my ship and the documents you found aboard her. As for the money you made from selling my spices, there are, shall we say, occasional losses in any business. I realize that is small compensation for the loss of a child, but I offer it as one father to another. Not, however, because Papilio bears any responsibility for what happened.

B—I'm touched by your generosity, Tan. But even if I were willing to accept your offer, I doubt I would ever get the chance to spend the money once you have what you want.

T—I have gone as far as I intend to go with this, Captain Boylan. Further reprisals on your part will be dealt with harshly. (Pause) Goodbye, Captain.

December 9—Hong Kong

Tan will certainly kill me.

So tired. Can't think straight.

Can't afford to mess this up.

Very clear on one point. The Shan will not take me alive.

Need to get out. See Mattos. Might be our last time.

Choi has agreed to put the manifest, documents, and their translations, along with this journal, in a safe deposit box under Lai-ping's name. He is to mail the key to her in Shanghai.

Have sent her instructions to hold onto the key until she hears further from me.

Will go to Macao aboard the *Nolla* tonight, fly to San Diego from there.

Chapter 41

Inspector Hsieh lectured Paige and Max as they left Lai-ping's hospital room: "You are just like Captain Boylan, Mrs. Alper." He turned to Max. "And you, sir, are no better. Neither of you is able to leave well enough alone. You could have been killed."

Paige and Max remained silent as they held hands and followed Hsieh through the maze of hospital corridors.

The burns on Max's legs were minor and caused him little discomfort, but when he touched his temple, his head throbbed a painful rhythm in tempo with the inspector's every word.

Paige fingered her stitched scalp wound, but the collodion dressing and a numbness made it feel alien.

"A lacerated scalp and a few minor burns," Hsieh continued, "are inconsequential in the face of the enormous danger you exposed yourselves to."

"Easy for you to say," Paige snapped. "You're not the one with a blinding headache."

"Forget about us, what about Lai-ping?" Max asked. "She's lying in that hospital bed with blistered hands and smoke-damaged lungs, not to mention the destruction of her home, her belongings."

Hsieh nodded benignly. "The doctors say she will mend. As for her possessions, unnecessary luggage always seems to find its way back into our lives."

Max and Paige glared at him, but he ignored them. At the emergency entrance, he gave them a simple directing nod toward a curb-parked black sedan. They walked silently in that direction.

"You seem quite perturbed with me, Mrs. Alper."

"She's not the only one," Max said.

"I do not understand," Hsieh said. He unlocked the passenger side of his unmarked car so Paige could enter. "I warned you to stay out of this matter . . ."

"Wait a minute," Paige interrupted. "I can't see how going to Lai-ping's apartment could possibly be misconstrued as anything but what it was: a visit to a family friend."

"If it was that simple, why did you deliberately avoid the detective I assigned to you?"

"That was *your* man?" Paige asked. "Why? You had no reason to have us followed."

"We thought some thief was scoping us," Max said.

"A *thief*? Please, Mr. Alper! At least give me the courtesy of the truth." His normally soft-spoken voice took on a slicing edge as he unlocked the driver's door. "You came to my office with unsubstantiated accusations against Tan Mong Kuan, who, although not the pillar of our community, nonetheless must be given the protection of the law."

Hsieh turned towards Paige. "You even claim that he murdered your uncle. Where is the proof? Everything is based on journals . . . nothing but the rambling notations of a bereaved father." His gaze softened for an instant as his eyes met Paige's. "Forgive me, Mrs. Alper, but considering the circumstances . . ." His voice trailed off.

Max, tight-lipped, climbed into the back of the car after Hsieh and Paige were seated. "You won't accept that murder's even a possibility," he snapped, slamming the door.

"You yourself said the coroner declared Captain Boylan's death was the result of a hit-and-run accident," Hsieh said.

"Now just a minute, Inspector," Paige said. "No one saw my uncle die. No one, except, of course, the driver of that car. We have reason to believe it was deliberate. In fact, we were told by one of Tan's thugs in New York that it *was* deliberate."

"Hearsay, Mrs. Alper. Can you produce that man?"

"Then what about tonight?" Max said. "Assault! Arson! What more do you need? You're treating us as though we're the criminals, instead of Tan and his triad."

The rest of the drive was in silence. When they pulled up in front of the hotel, Hsieh turned off the ignition and turned in his seat. The lights from the lobby illuminated his face. His eyes were hard and flat as they stared first at Paige and then at Max.

"Our investigators have found no physical evidence to indicate that Tan had any part in this evening's unfortunate incident. Your attackers could have used his name merely for effect."

"Lai-ping recognized them! They even admitted they'd attacked her previously. For God's sake, she's disfigured and crippled because of those animals!"

Hsieh sighed. "I fully intend to question Lai-ping when she has sufficiently recuperated. Until then, she will be under my protection." He reached across and opened Paige's door. "In the meantime, the two of you will behave yourselves, or I will confiscate your passports and have you placed on the first available flight to San Francisco."

Paige and Max were silent as they exited the car. They slammed the doors and walked slowly toward the hotel entrance with locked arms to support one another. They did not look back as Hsieh drove away.

Hot and sweaty, they entered their hotel room and shed their torn clothes like last year's wasted snakeskin. Neither had spoken since leaving Hsieh, and they remained silent as they dragged themselves toward the spacious bathroom.

They showered for a long time, scrubbing at the filth that seemed to clog every pore. The bathroom fogged with moist air, mirrors flashed a blurry pink as Paige moved across the plush, white carpet.

While Max finished washing, Paige filled the large Jacuzzi with cool water and poured a mixture of sweet-smelling essence under the faucet's full flow. When they finally eased into the tub, they leaned back among huge mounds of opalescent bubbles and allowed the burbling water to surge around them.

"I feel like I've been squeezed though a garlic press," Paige said, breaking the silence. Her eyes fluttered open and she stared into the eyes of a gaudy, gold-plated swan faucet. She pushed at a winged handle with a big toe and more cool water poured out. Sliding deeper into the water, her face became a mixture of pain and pleasure.

"Chain on the door?" Max asked drowsily, his leg rubbing against hers.

"Yeah," she whispered. "But I ache so much, if one of those goons found me, I think I'd beg him to put me out of my misery."

Max scooped up two cupped hands of suds and tossed them at her. She retaliated by halfheartedly throwing a sponge at him.

"You know, love," he said, "this is really ludicrous: people are trying to kill us and I'm lying here with bubbles all around me, wondering what I'm going to do to earn a living when this is all over."

"We're going to enjoy our little windfall, remember?"

"Jock's money won't last forever. But even if it did, we're not going to want to just sit around doing nothing."

"Are you sure about that?" she laughed.

"Okay, so what would you do if money wasn't a problem?"

"What would *I* do?" She stretched and drew lazy circles through the bubbles. "What would I do? What would I do? Well, one thing is certain: I'd still want to be a journalist. Uncover all the nasty things people do to other people."

"You mean keep working for the *Bay Sentinel*?"

"No way! I want us to be able to work together, as a team . . . Paige and Max Alper."

"You mean, Max and Paige Alper, don't you?" He gave her a mock scowl. "I'm very sensitive about bylines, you know."

"Okay, so we could alternate." She caressed his face; a handful of soapsuds peaked on his cheek. "What I mean is, wouldn't you get a kick out of going after the bad guys on a full-time basis? For instance, people who are screwing up the environment?"

"Become muckrakers?"

She smiled, but her face was pale and drawn with exhaustion. "Right now, I don't care what we do with our tomorrows or what you call us. I just want to soak in this cool water with you next to me. Enjoy being alive."

Max reached through the bubbles and caught her hand. "Maybe we should just leave, get out of town while we still can."

The Jacuzzi hummed, the water swirled and splashed. Paige spoke dreamily. "Maybe so. I've dealt with a lot of unsavory people. We both have. But I never once thought I was going to be killed . . . not until today."

"It's an eye-opener."

"Covering crime stories, writing about the sleaze, is not the same as being actually caught up in the middle of something like this. You don't realize how vulnerable you are, until some vicious bastard like Tan splits your noggin open."

"But you're talking about becoming a slayer of dragons, dropping our computers on their fire-breathing heads," Max said.

Paige splashed at the suds around her. "Someone has to stand up to wicked, disgusting, awful people."

"After what's happened, doesn't that frighten you?"

"Baby, it scares me shitless." She studied her mid-section, gently pushed at the myriad of bruises. "But in some perverse way, it also excites the hell out of me."

"If it gets any more exciting than this . . ." He retraced the pattern her fingers had taken across her battered skin. "Who are we kidding, love? We both know we're not going to walk away from this until it's over, one way or another."

"I guess you're right," she said. "That nightmare at Lai-ping's? Do you think they were really trying to kill us, or just frighten us away?"

"Neither," Max said. "I think it was an elaborate ruse. Those guys would never accidentally bungle a simple job like that. If they wanted us dead, we'd be dead. And if they'd wanted Lai-ping dead, she wouldn't have been at her apartment when we arrived."

"It all falls back to my uncle's journals. Until they have those, we're not as expendable as they'd like to scare us into believing."

"They want us to think we've miraculously escaped their

death plot. That way we might get careless and lead them to whatever Jock had on Tan."

"Must be damning." She sat up taller, her face animated, hands waving at Max. "It was sheer idiocy to kill Uncle Jock before they got what they wanted from him."

"Like I said before, I think it was a huge error. Some incompetent boob screwed up, and Tan has been playing cover-your-ass catch-up ever since."

"Right," she said, slapping the water. "That's why they continued to harass Captain Mattos and Lai-ping after Jock died. It was just another opportunity for them to get the journals when we surfaced at Ocean Shores."

Max scooted down until the water lapped at his chin. "So why did they try to scare us off in San Diego, when they really wanted us to keep searching?"

"Something tells me those guys in the red monster pickup weren't Tan's boys," Paige said. "They were too sleazy and they didn't have that killer instinct."

"Could only have been Martin Lester, covering Ocean Shores' and his rear end. Besides, he's more the money-yes, murder-no type."

"And when we didn't turn tail and go home but went to Mattos," Paige said, "the triad picked up on us and saw it as the best chance they'd had in five years to find those journals. My uncle's journals must be so incriminating, they *have* to kill us."

"Come on, love, they haven't done us in yet," Max said scooting closer.

They soaked in silence until Max switched off the Jacuzzi and stood, reaching out for one of the hotel's plush bath sheets. He dabbed at the burn marks splotched across his legs and wrapped the terrycloth around his waist before reaching down to pull Paige up out of the water. The few remaining bubbles floated on the surface—sad gray blobs of foam.

"Wish we weren't so far from home, so out of our element," he said, wrapping Paige in another huge bath sheet. "Hard to know who all the players are."

"And what kind of player is Hsieh?"

"Certainly one who's working from a different script," Max said.

She flipped off her towel and crawled into the waiting bed. "Oh!" she sighed. "Wait until your body hits this heavenly cloud."

Max turned out the light, nuzzled in next to her. "Here I am in the largest bed I've ever seen . . . wrapped in your beautiful arms . . . in a romantic, faraway port . . . and all I can do is say, goodnight, darling."

"Goodnight, Max. Welcome to Hong Kong."

Chapter 42

The next day, Paige and Max left the hotel through the back exit. They caught a taxi to go see Lai-ping at the hospital. It was a relief to find a uniformed policeman guarding her room. Inspector Hsieh had kept his promise, but the officer refused them entrance until he checked their IDs and radioed the inspector for confirmation.

"You must think my hospitality very strange," Lai-ping said, lowering her eyes when they approached her bed. She was fumbling to feed herself with heavily bandaged hands, adamantly refusing assistance from a hovering aide. "Hoodlums, beatings, fires . . ."

"We thought maybe it was a Hong Kong custom to offer such a *warm* welcome," Max said with a smile. Before she could respond, a nurse came in to change her dressings. The nurse informed Lai-ping that things were going so well that she probably would be discharged the following day.

"Lai-ping, we feel so terrible," Paige said. "As if we've done this to you. If we hadn't come to see you, none of this would have happened."

"Those animals have violated me and my home repeatedly, looking for the trail to Captain Boylan's journals," she said. "It is unfortunate that you had to be there during one of their brutal visits."

Lai-ping leaned over a straw to sip from a glass of water offered by the nurse.

"Have you gone to the bank yet to see what Captain Boylan left behind?" Lai-ping asked when they were alone again.

"No," Paige said. "We knew they wouldn't allow us access without you there to sign the log."

"Unnecessary inconvenience!" Lai-ping snorted and waved her freshly bandaged hands in the air. "I can't use these useless appendages. You must call for me. I will talk to my cousin, a very influential man at that bank."

Paige dialed the number and held the receiver to Lai-ping's ear. After a lengthy conversation in Cantonese, she gave them a look of satisfaction.

"When you arrive at the bank, ask for Chester Ng," Lai-ping said. "He will take care of everything."

On the way to the Kowloon National Bank, Paige and Max picked up a pair of cheap briefcases to carry whatever they found in Jock's safe deposit box. As promised, Lai-ping's telephone call worked miracles. Presentation of the key and their passports to Chester Ng gained them immediate access to Jock's secreted papers.

They sat ensconced in a small, glass-enclosed cubicle at the rear of the bank, leafing through the contents of one of the bank's largest safe deposit boxes. The booth was contained, muffled, as if they'd been sealed in a soundproof room, yet they remained in full view of the gaping safe deposit box vault, with its constant swirl of activity.

They sorted through the material in silence, passing back and forth journals, sailing charts, and sheaves of documents, half of which were in Chinese, the other half in English. There was also a tape cassette, which they would listen to later. After they finished reading everything, they sat silently side-by-side at the ornate, inlaid wood table.

The safe deposit box was centered between them, its lid flipped back against the cream-colored wall, the contents displayed on either side of the gray metal box.

"God, what a wildcat," Paige whispered, gently closing a journal.

"Battled them right up until the end," Max said. He took her hand and pressed it to his lips, then absently ran a finger back and forth across a purple discoloration on her arm. "He just kept going. Most people would have given up in the face of such overwhelming odds."

"At least he found what he was looking for," she said, "and he had that cretin Tan nailed." She fingered through the English translation of the documents her uncle had pilfered from the *Schmetterling*.

"Easy to see why Tan wants these trashed," she said, pointing to some of the more incriminating paragraphs.

"And easy to see why Tan is so desperate to deep-six anyone or anything that's even remotely connected to your uncle."

"My God!" Paige said. "There's no way we can leave Lai-ping alone in that hospital." She turned nervously toward the door of the cubicle. "They only *hurt* her before, hoping she would lead them to this. Now that they don't need her, they'll certainly kill her."

"They won't try anything while she's under police guard," Max said. He gathered up the papers and stuffed them into one of the two identical briefcases.

"I hope you're right."

"The sooner this stuff gets plastered across the front page of the local newspapers . . . like Jock originally intended . . . the sooner we'll all be off the hook."

"Mr. Tan Mong Kuan's future should be worth zilch," Paige said. "He was obviously in bed with a lot of big guns in the Chinese and Taiwanese governments. A lot of heads will roll . . . the ones who turned their backs and raked in the money, while Tan disposed of all that contraband over the years."

"And they'll be working their asses off to have Tan's throat cut, in or out of jail," Max said. "They can't risk being incriminated by him."

"Wonder which Tan wants the most . . . the ship's papers, the journals, or this?" Paige said. She held up the chart that pinpointed the location of the beached cargo ship.

"No contest," Max said. "He wants the cargo ship's papers. Those are what's going to put his neck in the noose."

Paige smiled for the first time since they'd entered the bank. "And the tape's probably Jock's conversation with the great Tan." She picked it up and held it in the palm of her hand. "All of this will have been worthwhile if I can just hear Uncle Jock's voice again."

"Captain Jock Ian Boylan finally caught the prize butterfly specimen." Max picked up the empty briefcase. "Let's fill this one with a bunch of scrap paper or newspapers before we leave here. Might come in handy as a decoy if we need one."

"You know what really bugs me?" Paige said. "Why didn't Uncle Jock just finish it, take the whole damn bundle of evidence to his newspaper friend right away? He would have been safe enough when the story hit the streets." She lightly tapped the pile of journals. "It all sort of ended in a stalemate when he decided to take off for San Diego."

"Everyone was trying to kill the poor guy . . . and he was beat."

"My poor, Uncle Jock . . . he did sound exhausted. Even his handwriting began to change."

"Remember, even though the Spice Pirate thing has a

swashbuckling appeal to us, Jock pissed off a lot of people
. . . a lot of the wrong kind of people." Max placed his
hands gently on her cheeks and looked into her eyes. "And
even if the triad hadn't killed him, he would have ended up
in jail."

"I suppose you're right."

"Don't judge him too harshly, Paige. He was tired,
alone, and running out of time. He wanted to say goodbye
to his best friend."

"You think he knew he was going to die? That's why he
went to see Mattos?"

"He never accepted Nolla's death, and all his personal
aspirations . . . his goals . . . his future ended the day Sallee
died." Max thought for a moment. "What do you think?"

"Yes, his journals made that very clear," Paige said.

"And when Sallee was abducted and killed, he became
obsessed with only one thing . . . destroying Tan. In some
perverse way, that goal kept Sallee alive; he still didn't have
to give her up."

"When he turned in the evidence, it would *truly* be
over," Paige said. "No matter what he did to Tan, it would
never bring back his daughter."

"Sallee was gone forever."

"A bitter pill." She leaned forward. "Why do we do it?"

"Do what, Paige?"

"Risk loving, when it's all doomed sooner or later?"

"Because, my love, it's the only thing worth having.
Even the worst among us knows that."

Paige smiled. "What a wild, crazy man he was." She
lifted the last journal from the briefcase and flipped through
the pages. "And a tough old bird."

Max laughed. "Definitely a family trait."

Paige leaned over and kissed him.

Chapter 43

Max held the briefcase containing all the journals and documents from Jock's safe deposit box. Paige clutched the one they'd filled with magazines, newspapers, bank brochures, and anything else they could grab as they dashed through the bank. A guard frowned and reluctantly directed them to the rear exit.

"Remember," Max, said, peering out the glass door, "we only have to make it to the newspaper office. Then we're home free."

"Baby, I'm scared." She hesitated at the door. "You know they're going to come for us."

"No choice, love. Do this now, or spend the rest of our lives fighting a losing battle with Tan Mong Kuan. Sooner or later, they're bound to corner us."

They held hands as they stepped out into a narrow alley that emptied into Nathan Road. Their eyes darted from face to face, studying each person scurrying along the passageway. No one seemed interested in them other than to shove by to get to where they were going.

As they turned onto Nathan Road, the low-hanging sun blinded them. They paused, blinking away the harsh light.

Out of the din of street sounds they heard a distinct, discordant rasp of un-muffled exhausts. The rat-a-tat-tat sounds grew louder and louder.

Paige squinted through the glare, was the first to spot a

pair of motor scooters heading in their direction, rapidly darting in and out of the dense, stalled traffic. The two riders swerved back and forth from street to sidewalk, forcing pedestrians to scatter.

Paige grabbed Max's sleeve. She pulled him back against the wall.

Less than half a block away now, she saw the lead rider flip back the face of his helmet. He blew through a loud police whistle to scatter the remaining stragglers in their path.

"They're after *us!*" Paige shouted.

"Don't move," Max, said, mashing her tight against the building. "I'll try to draw them off." He charged across the street, holding his briefcase away from his body for them to see.

The riders separated. One headed for Max, extending an arm, ready to snatch Jock's papers. Max feinted and the rider reached out too far and lost control. The scooter sideswiped the brick wall, sending the man sprawling onto the pavement.

The other scooter bore down on Paige. She gave the rider a head shot with her briefcase. He blocked the blow and grabbed her around the waist, tossing her face-down across his lap as he kept moving. Zigzagging, legs extended, he tried to maintain control as he accelerated in short bursts of speed down the street.

"Max!" she screamed.

He ran toward the fallen rider, who was starting to push himself up from the pavement. A field goal kick slammed the man down again. Max righted the scooter, straddled it, and pressed the starter, grunting his satisfaction as the engine caught. Paige and the other rider were still in sight as he took off after them.

Riding solo, Max quickly caught up. The two scooters

raced south on Nathan Road. The other rider, like a circus juggler, tried to manipulate his scooter through the heavy traffic while dealing with the squirming, kicking Paige. He barely managed to slip between the cars, buses, and pedestrians to stay just beyond Max's reach.

At the Waterloo Road intersection, a taxi shot out in front of the triad rider, forcing him into the lane alongside Max.

"Grab my hand!" Max yelled, reaching out to Paige. He felt the satisfying double slap of her grasping hand and wrist. He tugged. Nothing happened.

"Let go of me, you ape!" Paige screamed as the rider yanked at her other arm, trying to break the death-grip she had on the briefcase.

"Let go of the case!" Max shouted.

"No way!" she yelled back, shaking her head.

"Let him have it! That stuff's not worth dying over." A blaring horn from an angry bus driver drowned out her response. Max yanked hard at her wrist, bringing them closer together. "Let it go!"

Paige allowed the case to slip from her fingers and drop between the two scooters. As the man realized what had happened, Paige dug the nails of her free hand into his genitals. He jerked backward, letting go of both her and the handlebars.

Max braked hard, swung to the right, and pulled Paige from the driver's lap. The other scooter T-boned a Rolls Royce limousine as Paige thumped onto the street and rolled.

"Behind me!" Max screamed above the clamor of squealing brakes, blasting horns, and foreign curses. Paige scrambled to her feet. "Get on!" Before she was fully settled, Max was accelerating down Nathan Road again.

"Where are we going?" she asked.

"Don't know. But we've *got* to get off this main drag." He slowed, turned right onto Public Square Street, and came to a stop at a motorcycle parking area.

"We'll hoof it from here," he said, hiding their vehicle between two similar scooters. As they started across the street, a sleek Jaguar sedan careened around the corner, tires squealing in protest.

"Let's get out of here," Max said. He grabbed her hand and tucked the remaining briefcase under his arm.

"There!" Paige cried, pointing as they ran toward a temple. They raced through the doors into the sudden quiet of the sanctuary.

"Did they see us?" Paige said panting.

"I hope not."

The temple shut out the dissonance of the city. The only sound was the rasp of their ragged breathing.

The serene face of an all-knowing goddess greeted them from an altar filled with other statuary, brass vessels, tapestries, ornamental lights, and a basket of fresh oranges.

"This is eerie," Max said.

No one was around, yet they could hear the faint tinkle of bells. The remains of a joss stick sent a thin ghostly spiral of smoke into the air.

"Which god have we called upon, coming into this place?" Max whispered. They squeezed behind the altar.

"I don't know, but I feel safe here." She took a deep breath of the heavily scented air.

They crouched together in the narrow space. Soaked with perspiration, they waited and listened, and both were startled by the sudden sound of heavy shoes.

"Mr. and Mrs. Alper, please show yourselves!" boomed an amplified voice.

"Is that Hsieh?" Paige gasped.

"Where in hell did he come from?"

"Do you hear me?" the voice demanded. "Please do not make me waste valuable time searching the temple."

"I think we're trapped," Paige said. They squeezed hands and walked out from behind the altar.

Inspector Hsieh stood with a small bullhorn clutched in one hand. Several uniformed police officers were on either side of him.

"The two of you are really rather tiresome," Hsieh said. He turned his back on them and indicated with a wave of the bullhorn to follow him.

The entire group exited into the garden surrounding the temple of Tin Hau, patroness of seafarers.

Chapter 44

"What exactly were those men on the motor scooters after?" Inspector Hsieh demanded, leaning against the front fender of his black sedan.

"What they've always wanted." Paige's fists were clenched, her body shook with tension. "The evidence Uncle Jock had on Tan Mong Kuan."

"Magazines and bank brochures?" Hsieh responded with the edge of a smile. He nodded to one of his assistants, who took the discarded, battered briefcase, held it out in front of him, and pulled out some of what was inside.

"Just a ruse," Max said with a flip of his hand.

"I see. Then what *did* you find in Captain Boylan's safe deposit box at the bank?"

Paige planted her hands on her hips and glared at him. "You've never been interested before."

"It is my job to be interested."

"The Shan Triad runs roughshod throughout this part of the world," Paige said, "and you just *happened* to show up here."

"Suspicious of us?" Max asked.

"Not suspicious, Mr. Alper, concerned."

"So that's why you've had someone following us, ever since we arrived in Hong Kong?"

Hsieh sighed. "It has been my experience that unfortunate circumstances seem to befall anyone with the Boylan name." He paused and stared abstractly at the temple. "Bad karma, perhaps."

"Or poor police work," Max said.

Hsieh's head snapped around. He fixed them both with dark, angry eyes. "Must I remind you that if Captain Boylan had ever offered me any hard evidence, something more than his suspicions, I would have acted on it immediately?" He looked directly at the briefcase dangling from Max's hand.

"That sounds like a cop-out," Paige said, "no pun intended."

The inspector pushed himself away from the car fender and took a moment to straighten his tie and button his suit jacket. "Perhaps you are right. Maybe I should have been more cooperative with both you and Captain Boylan. But these notorious criminal societies are not only extremely dangerous, Mrs. Boylan, they have been the source of considerable embarrassment to us."

Paige nodded, studied the inspector for a moment. "Perhaps our goals have been the same all along," she said. "And neither we nor Uncle Jock ever wanted to hinder your investigation."

Hsieh looked past them to the Tin Hau Temple before responding. "If you have *anything* that might help us prosecute Tan and the Shan Triad," he said finally, "we would be most appreciative if you would allow us to examine it. And if it is productive, it would give great honor to your uncle's memory."

Paige looked at Max, then at the briefcase, then back at Hsieh. "A little reciprocity might well serve us both."

Two uniformed policemen flanked Tan Mong Kuan, his hands handcuffed behind him, as he exited the offices of

Papillon Enterprises. Inspector Hsieh followed closely behind.

Max and Paige had waited as agreed in Hsieh's car, but jumped out to intercept the approaching entourage before Tan could be placed in one of the waiting police cars.

Max could feel Paige tremble as she stood glaring at the head of the Shan Triad.

"Who are these people?" Tan demanded of Hsieh.

"They want to question you," the inspector said placidly.

"I have nothing to say to them, or anyone else."

Paige stepped forward, stared at the Shan leader, then backhanded him hard across the nose. A trickle of blood ran down onto his upper lip.

"You really *don't* know who we are, do you, Tan?" she demanded.

He glared at her with contempt.

"My, God, you are a despicable creature. How could you order my entire family murdered, without knowing what any of us look like?" She moved even closer. "*I* had to know what *you* looked like before I destroyed *you.*"

Tan turned to Hsieh. "Are you going to just stand there and allow this crazy woman to attack me? Your job won't be worth a penny when my lawyers are finished with you." When the inspector remained silent, Tan turned back to Paige. "I have no idea what you are talking about, madam."

"You damn well *do* know who the Boylans are," Paige said. "You've been after one or all of us for the past several years."

Tan's eyes narrowed into slits. "Are you referring to that miserable pirate who died before he could be punished for his crimes? The one who ranted and raved that I was responsible for his daughter's death?"

268

"That one," Paige said. "Captain Jock Ian Boylan, the man who collected enough evidence to expose you and all your criminal associates."

Max took her arm and gently pulled her back. "Well done," he whispered in her ear.

Paige nodded her thanks to Hsieh and turned once more to Tan. "Nothing would give me greater pleasure than to think of you in some rat-infested cell."

Max held out an arm; Paige threw her head back and laughed as she looped her arm through his.

"But you know," she said, "I don't think your business associates are going to allow you to enjoy that kind of luxury."

Chapter 45

TRIAD LEADER JAILED
M. K. Tan Charged with Murder,
High Seas Piracy, Prostitution

"How about that!" Paige yelled, holding the newspaper up in front of Max's face. "Look at that banner headline!"

"What does the story say about Tan's contacts on the mainland and in Taiwan?" He pushed the newspaper aside so he could see his wife's face.

"Heads are rolling."

"Good! I knew Jock's friend would write a great exposé. Almost as good as we would have done ourselves," Max said with a laugh.

"The main thing is that what Uncle Jock started is now finished," Paige said. "You have no idea how it pleases me to know we got the bastards who killed him and Sallee."

"Guess we can go home now," Max said. "Actually, I'm getting sort of bored with this place. Nothing interesting or exciting has happened around here for hours."

Paige yanked a pillow from the bed and began beating him over the head. "You want action? I'll give you action."

They were interrupted by the telephone. It was Inspector Hsieh, offering to give them a ride to the airport.

270

★ ★ ★ ★ ★

"It continues to trouble me," the inspector said, "that you believed I was derelict in my duties with respect to Captain Boylan's suspicions about Tan Mong Kuan." He had parked in a NO PARKING ZONE at Kai Tak International and had turned to talk to them over the back of the front seat. "But a policeman, like a journalist, cannot go public on mere suspicion."

"Not exactly derelict, Inspector," Paige said. "But it's still hard to believe that you had *nothing* on the Shan Triad prior to our opening Uncle Jock's safe deposit box."

"Are all of the known members of your so-called Mafia in jail, Mrs. Alper?"

She scooted across the seat to exit the car. "Touché. I confess that sometimes it's difficult to be objective, especially when events get so personal."

Hsieh, carrying a small package, came around the car, obviously ready to accompany them into the terminal. Suddenly he stepped back, and leaned heavily against his car.

Paige and Max looked at each other with puzzled expressions.

"I must confess that I have not been entirely forthright with the two of you," Hsieh said. "The fact is, you and Captain Boylan had good reason to question the diligence of my investigation into the death of Sallee Boylan."

"How so?" Max asked.

Hsieh slumped, his normally serene face reflecting some painful inner conflict. "Sallee Boylan's death, and that of the other women found with her, was a horrible thing. And while we were suspicious that it was an operation-gone-bad by one of the area's criminal societies, we were unable to find any physical evidence to support our theory."

"We understand, Inspector," Paige said. "Not every

crime gets solved, despite what we see on television and in the movies."

Hsieh shook his head. "You are too kind, Mrs. Alper. But regardless, I must humbly ask your forgiveness for being unable to uphold my obligations to the Boylan family."

"I'm not following you, Inspector," Paige said.

"You see, I did start an undercover investigation into the activities of Tan Mong Kuan after we found the bodies of those twenty-seven women in the container."

"You never said anything about that," Max said. "Did you ever find anything that made a connection?"

"No, but that does not mean there was actually nothing to find. I suspended the investigation a few days after it was started." He paused, took a deep breath, and said, "The Shan threatened to kill Mei-ling."

"Mei-ling?" Paige said.

Tears glistened in the inspector's eyes. "Mei-ling is my daughter, my only child."

"How horrible," Paige said.

"I have told my superiors about the incident," he said. "There is to be an internal investigation."

"But the crime has been solved, Tan Mong Kuan is in jail awaiting trial, and the Shan is being dismembered," Max said. "That should count for something."

"But not because of any evidence that I gathered," Hsieh said. "Captain Boylan and the two of you were the persistent ones, the brave ones. I contributed nothing but fear, the fear of losing my only child."

"If you want us to speak on your behalf, we would be happy to do that," Paige said. "Your superiors need to understand that, like my uncle, you, too, could see only a bleak future if you lost your child."

"Thank you, that is very kind of you. But I do not think it will be necessary for you to delay your departure. There is great satisfaction among my superiors as a result of Tan's arrest. They may not deal too harshly with me."

Paige reached out and placed a hand on the inspector's. "I think you are a fine, dedicated policeman, Inspector Hsieh. I have no doubt that you did your best under very trying circumstances."

Hsieh bowed his head. "Perhaps if I had been more vigilant, Captain Boylan might still be alive today."

"I'm sure my uncle would never have wanted you to risk the life of your daughter, for him or anyone else. That would have been too much to ask."

"Still, if I had been more vigilant, Captain Boylan . . ."

Max put his palms together and bowed. " 'Great understanding comes with great love.' "

Hsieh bowed in response, then clasped hands with both Paige and Max.

"Thank you for telling us this, it answers many questions," Paige said.

They moved towards the airport entrance. "If there is ever anything I can do for you . . . I owe you both a great debt of gratitude. I almost forgot," he said. "As part of our follow-up, I called the San Diego police to tell them of the connection between the Shan and Mr. Martin Lester at Ocean Shores."

"At least they'll toss him in jail . . . that's where he belongs," Paige said.

"I'm afraid it's too late for that, Mrs. Alper. Justice and cosmic destiny have taken the same path in this instance. Mr. Lester was murdered. He was found in his establishment with a dragon knife lodged in his throat."

"Ugh," Paige said.

"It seems 'the seeds of the past are the fruits of the future,' " Max said.

"Ah, yes! Mr. Lester must not have lived up to Tan's expectations. That weapon is favored by the Shan Triad." He handed the package he'd been carrying to Paige.

"A present?" she said.

"It is something I would like you to have. We found it while going through Tan's Papillon offices."

"What is it?"

"It appears to be your uncle's final journal."

Chapter 46

Journal—1998
Jock Ian Boylan

January 4—Sunair
 Enough of this bare skin and sun.
 Plan to leave Sunair for Hong Kong next Monday.
 Time to go beard the lion in his den.

January 12—Sunair
 Damn Mattos. Canceled my flight. Insisted I take a few days to get over whatever the hell it is that's put me under the weather.
 Probably just a cold from making a fool of myself at the nudist dance on New Year's Eve.
 Cold or no cold, I'm leaving on next Monday's flight.

February 2—San Diego
 First day I've had the strength to pick up a pen.
 Goddamn Lassa.
 Burning up with fever. Been that way now for almost three weeks. Lost the rest of what hair I had left. Shit.
 Kept trying to convince myself it was something else. Hung on too long before giving in to the inevitable.
 Got away from me again.
 Just reread my January 12 entry. Apparently haven't

learned much over the years. Still making flat-ass pronouncements.

Nolla's out there somewhere, laughing her head off at me. She always said my arrogance would be my undoing.

Everything's still fuzzy.

What happened after the fever hit?

Have only vague memories of Mattos toting me off to Ocean Shores. Must have scared the bejesus out of him. He's never seen me on the downside of this stinking disease.

Better call and let him know I'm back among the living, if not exactly up and about.

Will tell him I'll be back at Sunair to stay until I'm seaworthy enough to travel.

February 3—San Diego

That prick Lester.

Rich says he made him come up with the admission fees out of his own pocket. I hadn't expected this and didn't have enough transferred funds.

Really pisses me off. After all the money I've poured into this place over the years.

Goddamn bean counters are taking over the world.

No sense getting a burr up my ass. Need to get out of here. Will give me great pleasure to tell Lester this is the last he'll see of me.

Is that a threat or a prophecy?

Better make arrangements with The Seamen's Bank to transfer funds. Need to cover whatever charges I've rung up or they'll keep bleeding Mattos. Old money-grubbing Lester might have me arrested for failing to pay for one of his overpriced aspirins.

Should give Rich power of attorney.

No, been enough of a burden to him.

February 14—San Diego

Still at Ocean Shores.

Still in isolation. No improvement. Worse, if anything.

Barely able to move.

They must be doing something wrong. Maybe they're poisoning me. Why else is it taking so long to get back on my feet?

No one will tell me anything.

Lester's gone to ground. Haven't seen that bilge rat for days.

February 20—San Diego

One of the aides says a specialist was being called in. Supposed to be here again this afternoon.

What the hell does that mean?

Can't get a straight answer from anyone.

Where's Mattos?

Can't get through to him on the telephone. Switchboard says he doesn't answer.

Must be lying.

Know damn well he would have told me if he was planning to go away.

Where is everybody? Anybody?

February 21—San Diego

Coughing, headaches, vomiting. Starting all over again. No fever, though. Strange.

Trouble concentrating. Barely able to hold onto the pen. Keep drifting off.

If this new gal's a medical specialist, I'm Captain of the *Enterprise*. Wasn't even able to operate an IV by herself.

What's she giving me? Feeling worse.

She won't discuss it. Another goddamn inscrutable

Asian. Is that prejudice? Don't care anymore.

Sallee was here. Took my hand. Danced me around the bed. Told me not to worry. Wrapped her arms around my neck. Hugged me. Thought my heart would burst.

Hard to write. Damn tears smudge the paper.

February 28—San Diego

Can get out of bed now on my own, at least until that damn woman shows up.

Injections every other morning.

She comes in at the stroke of ten. Squirts something into an IV. Never speaks. Just stands there and stares.

Try to stay awake. It's no good. Float off among the stars. Start to merge, plummet down.

When I wake up, she's gone. Everything's the same.

Know she's been asking questions. About what? Can't remember. Can't focus.

Sick as a dog. But out of isolation. Now have my run of the place.

Everyone stares at me. All of them Tan's people, all against me.

March 1—San Diego

Keep talking to myself. Hard to make connections.

Why am I here? Why are any of us here?

Peeling away memories, layer by layer. What's at the core? Got to find the core.

Got to what? Got to find a way to keep them from stealing my soul.

March 2—San Diego

That bitch works for Tan. I knew it.

Goddamn Lester sold me out. Will kill the bastard, if I

ever get my hands on him.

Specialist, my ass. She's here to find out what I have on the Shan. Giving me something to make me talk.

Not this time. After she hooked me up, punctured the IV tubing with a paperclip. Hid my hand under the sheet. Most of the solution ran down under my ass.

Some of the stuff got to me. Not enough to put me under.

This morning she tried for the location of the *Schmetterling*. Fed her phony coordinates. She went out looking like she'd just won the lottery.

Don't know how long it will take them to check the information. A few days? A few hours?

Can't be here when she comes back.

Got to get the hell out of here.

March 3—San Diego

Only an hour before their dinner break. Must stay calm. Can't arouse suspicion.

Will go to the rec room and keep an eye on them.

Difficult to wait.

Keep wondering what it might have been like if Nolla and Sallee hadn't died.

Can't handle that now. Can't get lost in the in-between.

The in-between. That's what Sallee called it.

A place among the stars where all is knowable, all is understandable.

Sallee. My little Sallee.

What a silly kid you were.

Epilogue

Paige had her usual death grip on Max's arm as they took off from Kai Tak International Airport. She remained incommunicado until the plane finally leveled off.

Max broke the silence: "You know," he said, "those journals Jock left behind are such a gift . . . gave so much insight into the kind of man he was. You're very fortunate to have them."

"I feel that way."

"What struck me the most throughout the pages was his love for his wife and daughter. That's the way I love you, Paige Boylan Alper."

She held his face in her hands and leaned across to kiss him. "We are so lucky to have each other."

She closed her eyes for a moment, but soon she was smiling. "At least we finished what Uncle Jock started. Maybe we couldn't bring him or Sallee back, but their murderers will pay dearly for messing with any Boylan . . . or Alper."

"Where in the hell are you?" Sheryl demanded. Her voice screeched over the kitchen speakerphone. "We've been cooped up in this cabin at Angel Fire for ten stinking days, waiting to hear from you."

"We're home in San Francisco," Paige said nonchalantly, and gave Max a big grin.

"What took you so long? What's happening?"

"Well, first we had to make a little side trip to Hong Kong."

"Hong Kong? Hong Kong? I thought after New York you were going back to San Francisco to straighten out this mess so we could get our money."

"There were a few problems," Paige said.

"You didn't get the money, did you?"

Paige raised her eyes to the ceiling and mimicked pain. "The money's secure, Sheryl. You should get your share any day now."

"How much?"

"Well, we got the whole thing and didn't have to split with Heirs Apparent, who, by the way, may soon be out of business, if they aren't already."

"How much?"

"Almost a hundred and sixty thousand dollars."

"What?" Sheryl yelled. "You mean it's going to be more? What happened?"

Paige shook a fist in the air and grinned at Max.

"You're really enjoying this, aren't you?" he whispered.

She nodded enthusiastically.

"Well?" Sheryl demanded.

"The Atlantic-Pacific Trust is sending you a check for your share. The hundred and sixty thousand dollars, which includes your half of the original two hundred and fifty thousand dollars, *plus* accrued interest."

"Don't screw around with me, Paige. I'm in no mood for one of your games."

"It's not a game, Sheryl. That's the amount, which, by the way, is only the first installment."

"What do you mean 'first installment'?"

Paige patiently told her sister why she and Max had gone

to Hong Kong in the first place, then explained about the beached ship and its cargo of copper and titanium.

"I don't understand how that translates into more money for us," her sister said.

"It's all very complicated, Sheryl. Some bad guys in Hong Kong stole the metals; Uncle Jock sort of liberated them, along with the ship they were on."

"So what does that mean in dollars?"

Paige winked at Max. "That's our old Sheryl," she said *sotto voce.*

"Frankly, we don't know, Sheryl. We've hired a maritime attorney who specializes in salvage and finds. George can fill you in on what it means. Anyway, we could own all of it, part of it, or none of it."

"Look, Paige, that's a very nice story, but give me some kind of real figure—ten, twenty-five, fifty thousand, what?"

"More," Paige said. She covered the receiver and said to Max, "This is fun!"

"Damn it, Paige, how much more?"

"You never change, do you, Sheryl?"

"How *much?*"

Paige mimed a primal scream. "Let's just say your fourth should solve all your money problems for a long time."

"My *fourth?* You mean *half,* don't you?"

"No, Sheryl, I mean one-fourth. Max and I did all the work, took all the risks, and got beat up pretty badly. So, it's one-fourth for each of us. We're also giving one-fourth to Lai-ping, Sallee's nanny and Uncle Jock's long-time housekeeper."

"You're giving a fourth of our fortune to some servant? I don't think so."

Paige slipped her hand over the mouthpiece again. "I

may kill her, even if she is my twin sister."

Max grinned.

"Paige?"

"First off, Sheryl," she said evenly, "it's not legally *your* fortune. It belongs to Max and me because, under the law, we found it. So, basically, it has nothing to do with Uncle Jock's estate. How we divide it is entirely up to us. Actually, we didn't even have to *tell* you about it. We're offering you a one-fourth share out of the goodness of our hearts. But if you're going to argue about it, forget it!"

It took a long beat for Sheryl to respond. "I'm . . . I'm sorry, Paige. It's just been so miserable here the past week or so. And we had no idea what had happened to you and Max . . ."

"We're both okay. And it's now safe for you and your family to return home. I'll tell you more when I know more."

"Okay, but, uh, couldn't you just give me a tiny hint about how much that cargo might be worth?"

Paige laughed and pounded a fist on the table "We're told the market value for metals fluctuates. But we figure you can expect a good bit more than the hundred and sixty thousand from Jock's account. Maybe something in the neighborhood of another two hundred thousand to three hundred thousand dollars. Minimum."

"My God!"

Paige could hear her whispering to George, who must have been standing right next to the phone.

"And the maximum?" Sheryl finally asked.

"Don't even think about it."

"Tell me, Paige. Please! Please tell me! I can't stand it."

Paige scribbled on a notepad the ten million total estimate they'd been given and held it up for Max to see. "Should I tell her?"

Max nodded

"We're millionaires!" Sheryl shouted so loudly the speakerphone vibrated.

"Look, Sheryl, don't go doing anything foolish. I mean, the minimum looks like a certainty, but anything beyond that is not much more than wishful thinking at this stage of the game."

"Paige, I love you."

Paige closed her eyes and sighed. "I know you do, Sheryl." She looked up to give Max a wink. "We'll talk more later, okay?"

Max grabbed both of Paige's shoulders after she hung up. "Something just occurred to me," he said. He took the notepad from her and tossed it away.

"What?"

"I'm not only married to a rich woman, you're married to a rich man."

"Works out nicely, doesn't it?"

About the Authors

Bette Golden Lamb and J. J. Lamb, authors of *Bone Dry*, live in Northern California and when not writing collaboratively and individually, Bette is a practicing RN and a professional artist and J.J. is a freelance writer.

Bette is a published short story writer, while J.J. is the author of three private-eye novels featuring Las Vegas–based Zachariah Tobias Rolfe III.

Heir Today . . . is their second co-authored novel.